Still Life

AND OTHER STORIES

Still Life

AND OTHER STORIES

JUNZO SHONO

translated from the Japanese and with an introduction by
Wayne P. Lammers

STONE BRIDGE PRESS
Berkeley, California

Macrons (long signs) on Japanese words are not used in this edition.

Except on the cover and title page, Japanese names are given in customary Japanese order, with the family name followed by the given name.

The stories in this book were originally published in Japanese as follows: *Buto* ("A Dance," 1950), *Purusaido shokei* ("Evenings at the Pool," 1954; awarded the Akutagawa Prize, 1955), *Seibutsu* ("Still Life," 1960; awarded the Shinchosha Prize for Literature, 1960), *Kani* ("Crabs," 1959), *Tori* ("Birds," 1963), *Makigoya* ("Woodshed," 1962), *Soten* ("Azure Sky," 1964), *Akikaze to futari no otoko* ("Two Men and the Autumn Wind," 1965), *Shigotoba* ("The Workshop," 1971), *Eawase* ("Picture Cards," 1970; awarded the Noma Prize for Literature, 1971), *Ondori* ("The Rooster," 1973), *Nezumi* ("The Mouse," 1973), *Okujo* ("On the Roof," 1975).

Published by STONE BRIDGE PRESS
P.O. Box 8208, Berkeley, CA 94707

Library of Congress Cataloging-in-Publication Data

Shono, Junzo.
    Still life and other stories / Junzo Shono : translated from the Japanese by Wayne P. Lammers.—1st ed.
    p.   cm.
    ISBN 1-880656-02-7.
    1. Shono, Junzo, 1921– —Translations, English.   I. Title.
PL861.H6L36   1992
895.6'35–dc20
            92-28639
            CIP

CONTENTS

PART THREE
still together

INTRODUCTION

So little in these stories by Shono Junzo is overtly "Japanese" that readers of the translations may at times even forget that the stories are set in Japan. This gives them a universal appeal and familiarity, allowing them to become stories about any family of any modern society, not merely exotic stories of a country far away. The stories gently illumine the essence of human existence in a manner not unlike Thornton Wilder's *Our Town*.

But at the same time, there is much in these stories that will strike the reader familiar with Japan and its literature as being, indeed, very "Japanese." The family appearing here is, after all, a Japanese family: Even when most of the day-to-day activities described could belong to any modern society, the patterns of relating between family members, and the whole family's experience of life's major milestones, clearly bear the imprint of Japanese traditions and values. Not only for this steady focus on the family but for their intimate, "snapshot" style—a progression of brief episodes capturing moments in the life of a family almost like an album of photographs—the stories bring to mind the films of Ozu Yasujiro, with their low, stationary camera. The constant attention to nature, the autobiographical method, and the inclination toward reflective musing rather than analysis, all have deep roots in Japanese literature, both classical and modern—though Shono combines them in a refreshing new way. The stories are quite unlike those that have been associated with the haiku aesthetic before this, but there is nevertheless a quiet and spareness about them that make one think of haiku poetry—especially the way haiku describe scenes or momentary events as if to say "Look!" but then leave it to the reader to ponder the significance of those scenes or moments. The simplicity, both in haiku and in Shono's stories, is deceptive: if we heed the command and turn our attention in the direction pointed, we see more than we had ever noticed before, even among the most commonplace of things.

And this is true of every reading. As translator, I have now read these stories a great many times, but continue to be moved by them anew. Sometimes I marvel at the simple beauty of the stories and their wonderful, unstinting, trueness to life. Sometimes I am warmed by their normalness and happiness—by the light Shono casts upon successes and joys and satisfying connections between people instead of dwelling on failure, dysfunction, and alienation as so many of his contemporaries have done. Other times I am put on edge by the fragility, the subtle tensions, the dark and chilling shadows that I find lurking behind the apparent calm in places I had never noticed before. Even more than most, these stories call for several readings.

A few words about the stories selected: All but the first two belong to a series of stories about a family closely modeled on Shono's own, written over a period of more than three decades and together forming, in effect, a single, continuing narrative—a work still in progress at this writing. If the stories create the illusion of being chapters in a novel, that is the reason. It is an illusion I have deliberately fostered in my selection and arrangement of the stories because I believe they gain by being read together in this way. But I must give one caution: the stories were all originally published as short stories, self-contained and intended to stand alone; they should be viewed first as short stories, and only then as parts of a larger whole. This caution is especially important for the first two stories, "A Dance" and "Evenings at the Pool," which were written before Shono established the method of his later stories and therefore show substantial differences from the rest of the collection in subject, psychological detail, descriptive style, point of view, and mood. The discontinuities are quite obvious for "Evenings," which is about an entirely different family; less so for "Dance," in which the family is virtually a younger version of the family in the later stories even if its experiences do not jibe. On certain levels, though, both of these stories belong to the longer narrative, are even essential to it, and that is why I have included them here in spite of the discontinuities. Some of the power of the later stories comes from knowing what went before.

In the years I have worked on these stories, it has been a continual struggle to find the right words for describing them to those who cannot read Japanese. It is both a pleasure and a relief that I can now let Shono's stories speak for themselves. Shono's voice is a quiet one, easily drowned out by the clamor of other voices in our frenetic lives. Yet, for those who will pause and lend an ear, it is truly a voice worth listening to.

Acknowledgments

Please see the copyright page for the original Japanese titles of the stories. All of the translations in this volume are complete.

A slightly different version of my translation of "Still Life" has previously been published in *The Showa Anthology*, edited by Van C. Gessel and Tomone Matsumoto (Kodansha International, 1985). I am grateful to the publisher for agreeing to allow re-publication here. The translations of the other stories are all entirely new.

I am deeply indebted to Robert Lyons Danly, who first introduced me to the writings of Shono Junzo and gave generously of his time to guide me through my initial translation of "Still Life." He, more than anyone else, must be credited with teaching me the art of literary translation (though I hasten to add that the responsibility for any inadequacies in the present translations remains entirely my own). Thanks go to him as well for helping me obtain a small block grant to defray expenses as I embarked on the earliest stages of this collection. The grant was from the Horace H. Rackham School of Graduate Studies at the University of Michigan, to which I am also grateful.

I would like to thank Judy Weiss for her expert editorial advice in smoothing the "rough edges" of the manuscript, and Peter Goodman, my publisher, for the enthusiasm and sensitivity with which he took on this manuscript and turned it into such an attractive volume.

Finally, I would like to thank my wife Cheryl for reading the manuscript and offering invaluable suggestions, in some cases through several drafts. And I wish to thank both her and my son, Michael, for their interest, patience, and encouragement over the many years it has taken to bring this project to fruition. I dedicate these translations to them.

—WAYNE P. LAMMERS

PART ONE
marriage

A DANCE

a crisis in the home is like the gecko you find clinging to the overhead vent in the kitchen.

You never noticed it creeping up on you, but there it sits, looking ominous and putting you on edge. And it settles there as if it belongs, like any other fixture in the house, until pretty soon you get used to it and stop paying attention. Besides, we all prefer to avert our eyes from unpleasantness.

Take this home, for example.

The husband and wife have been married for five years, and they have one three-year-old daughter. The family of three lives meagerly on what the husband brings home from his job at city hall.

The husband loves his wife, and the wife loves her husband, yet the husband dreams of a carefree life all by himself, while the wife suffers from a nagging but inexplicable sense of loneliness.

For reasons we need not go into, the husband is estranged from his family. As for the wife, she lost her parents when still a child, and the grandmother who raised her in their stead passed away soon after her marriage, leaving her all alone in the world. The husband sometimes wondered what his wife would do if he were to get run over by a streetcar and die. How would she manage without him?

But nothing could be gained from worrying about it, so his dire imaginings never went very far.

One night in early summer, the husband came home from work to find on his desk a single sheet of white stationery. The hand was his wife's.

> In the darkness of night, you fly off into a sky filled with twinkling stars. I gaze after you as your cape grows smaller and smaller, until it disappears. "Take me with you!" I want to shout, but my voice will not come.
>
> Hiroko

The husband read the note, crumpled it into a little ball, and dropped it gently into the wastebasket. When he emerged from his room he gave no hint that he had encountered anything out of the ordinary. But the first line of the note had sent an icy chill up and down his spine. His conscience, he had to admit, was not entirely clear.

The wife had a way with her premonitions: they proved correct with uncanny frequency. It had happened again not long ago, when her best friend from girls' school showed up unannounced at their front door one afternoon. She had lived in faraway San'in since getting married.

The two women did not correspond regularly, writing only when something chanced to make one of them think of the other, and no word had come of an impending visit. But for some reason that morning the wife had decided to do the laundry and clean the house and take care of an errand at the post office before noon. And all the while she busied herself with these tasks, she repeated in her mind like a refrain:

"This way, if T comes to visit, we can sit down and talk to our hearts' content without having to worry about anything else."

When shortly after noon a voice called at the door, she practically flew to the front hall.

"It's T, right?" she cried out from her side of the door even before she could see who it was. "I'm so glad you came!"

She slid the door open, and there stood her friend, smiling cheerfully.

T, for her part, assumed they had gotten the letter she sent before leaving home. But in fact the letter hadn't arrived until the next day. Since the husband had seen his wife's premonitions work this way before, it was no wonder that the note on his desk made his blood run cold.

The husband had a secret: he was in love with a girl of nineteen who worked in his department at city hall. They went to movies together after work, or strolled about town in the evening twilight.

Now his wife had apparently guessed his secret. But how was he to respond? To say the wrong thing would be to stir up a nest of snakes. And besides, what did she expect him to do? He had fallen in love, and he could hardly change how he felt about the girl just because he'd found out that his wife wasn't happy.

It was a hard thing to fall in love, and harder still to actually win the heart of the one you loved. It happened once in a lifetime. Maybe. If you were lucky. Now a nineteen-year-old girl, so beautiful, so innocent, had given him her heart—even knowing that he had a wife and child. How could he simply abandon a love that brought him such intoxicating joy? And besides, this was only what any wife in any home ought to expect—that sometime in her long married life, perhaps even several times, she would experience the loneliness of realizing that her husband's heart had wandered away from her. Recognizing this and accepting it as inevitable was what life was all about. He now turned his inward voice directly toward his wife: Look, I know you love me, and you devote your whole life to me. And I love you, too. Just because I've fallen in love with another woman doesn't mean I'm dissatisfied with you or I've grown tired of you. It's simply one of those things that happens. It doesn't make me never want to see your face again. You are still my good wife, and I still love you as before.

Having delivered this self-serving tirade in his mind, the husband came out to the dining room for his supper, determined to ignore his wife's desperate plea.

The wife, too, said nothing about her note. She merely chattered on in her usual way about the sundry trifling things that had occurred while he was away. Much relieved, the husband responded with similar benign talk, playing with his daughter on his lap to avoid meeting his wife's eyes. Supper concluded without incident.

After the husband had fallen asleep that night, the wife wept in silence over the letter that had failed to reach her husband's heart. Beside her lay her daughter, her face soft with the unguarded innocence of a sleeping child, but the wife felt no different than if she were utterly alone.

She had written the letter like a prayer. After much agonizing and crossing out, after several times nearly giving up, she had finally come up with those few lines. But now, before her eyes, the letter had become a tiny bird shorn of its wings, wavering, then tumbling toward the black surface of the sea.

As she watched her husband coming home each day like a man who'd lost his very soul, the wife's feelings of affliction advanced from loneliness to painful despair. She'd never seen her husband behave this way before.

True, it was not unusual for him to come home in a state of distraction, lost in some deep and impenetrable contemplation. But you could say that was a longstanding habit with him. Once, in grade school, he got so wrapped up in thinking about fish on his way to the streetcar that he held out his money and said "Fish" when the ticket lady asked him where he was going. And he'd done similar things as an adult, any number of times. In fact, this occasional absentmindedness was one of the things the wife liked about her husband. People who were always on their guard and never missed a beat made her feel creepy.

Her husband's recent behavior was quite a different matter, though, going well beyond what could be called occasional absentmindedness. He had come to seem as weightless and unreliable as an empty cicada shell, and this was what had sent the wife plunging into the deepest kind of anxiety. Her husband acted like a man who had learned a terrible secret, and whose entire life had been taken over by that secret because he could not tell it to anyone.

She was reminded of an old children's story called "The King's Ears." A young barber is summoned to the palace and commanded to cut the king's hair. When he enters the king's chambers and the king removes his crown, he is astonished to find donkey's ears protruding from among the royal locks. Having learned the king's shocking secret, the barber must now keep it tightly hidden within his heart for the rest of his life, for he is under the threat of death if he should ever reveal it. In time, the anguish of not being able to tell anyone grows too great for him to bear, and he falls ill. His condition worsens day by day, and it seems certain he will die. His grieving family does everything they can to determine the cause of the illness, but the barber never says a word. Then one day he staggers out of his house and into the nearby woods, where he finds a tree with a small hollow at the base of the trunk. He puts his mouth to the hole and shouts three times, "The king has donkey's ears!" as loud as he can. From that very day, his health takes a turn for the better, and in no time at all he has recovered his former strength....

The wife repeated the phrase to herself: "The king has donkey's ears. The king has donkey's ears." If only my husband would open his heart to me, she thought, how much happier I would be! Even if his words meant my devastation, even if they thrust on me the full burden of his secret and made me waste away day by day until finally I died—still I would be content. How much easier that would be than the pain of watching helplessly as my husband agonizes over a secret he cannot tell!

I can pretty well guess what he's trying so hard to keep from me. So why won't he just come out and tell me? Any woman who can make him change as much as I've seen him change must surely be a very special woman. I can't think of any other explanation. So why won't he share with me the joy of having met such a remarkable person? Why does he go on trying to hide it. Can he really believe I haven't noticed? Of course, it hurts to think that he loves another woman. But it hurts even more to see him struggling so painfully all by himself like that, day in and day out, never saying a word. It makes me feel like I'm nothing but a burden to him, and that I'm the one responsible for all his torments. That's what really hurts.

Every night after dinner, he goes straight to his room, and I never hear another peep out of him all evening. I used to take him some tea after a while, but now I feel like there's a tight web of invisible threads stretched across his doorway, and I'm afraid to touch the door. I don't know how many times I've carried the tea tray halfway up the stairs only to turn back. Once when I slid the door open after saying "May I come in?" I saw him hastily pushing the stationery he had spread on his desk under a book. I pretended I hadn't noticed and forced a cheerful voice:

"Hey! Stop working so hard, you rascal."

But actually it was all I could do to keep my face from showing my wretchedness.

Now I'm scared to go into his room. Even in the daytime, when I go in there to dust, I get this eerie feeling that he's still there, sitting at his desk like the night before, and I'm scared to look that way. What if I were to see something I shouldn't? When I play with our daughter alone in the evening, the silence from my husband's room upstairs weighs heavier and heavier on my mind until I begin to wonder how much more I can take.

My wife has the child, was the husband's attitude. She may have no other comfort, and she may feel my heart drifting away from her, but she at least has the child. Even when her happiness as a wife is incomplete, a woman can still find a measure of meaning to her life in nurturing and protecting her child. The husband sought excuses for his behavior in convenient clichés.

Though intoxicated with love, he had not failed to notice the new look of desolation on his wife's face. Especially after finding the letter on his desk, he made a point of trying to say nice things to her as often as possible. It pained even him to see his wife looking so unutterably forlorn.

Sometimes, when he was in his room, he would hear his wife open the front door and step outside. Holding the fussy child in her arms, she would walk back and forth in the street, singing gently, for as much as an hour. Or if the child was already in bed, he might hear the slap-slap of a jump-rope against the pavement. Ahh, she's skipping rope again, he'd think. This image of his wife, skipping on and on in the dark, deserted street, pressed in on him like some desperate appeal. The staccato slap of the rope as it whipped through the air and the tap of her feet springing from the pavement seemed to fly at him like a million invisible needles piercing his entire body. He tried to hide from the needles.

The husband's thinking went something like this: I've never considered abandoning my wife and child to run off with the girl. The last thing I want is to destroy my home for the sake of this love, and I really don't feel I'm in danger of making that happen. All I'm saying is that I want to be left alone for a while. Let me follow my heart, wherever it may lead. It's not as if a paltry wage earner like me could do anything all that outrageous.

If I invited the girl to go on a trip with me, I doubt she'd refuse. In fact, I can already see her eyes lighting up with excitement. She's always dreaming about traveling to unknown places. But could I actually take such a trip? My wife and I can't even go somewhere for a single night without risking the total collapse of our household finances; how could I possibly afford a major trip? I've never even bought the girl a present. She doesn't go around dropping hints like most girls these days, but I know she'd be as happy as any to get a new purse. Her family's no better off than mine. But some of the purses in the window come close to my entire salary for a month, and even the small ones that look more like toys than anything else would take all my spending money for the month and then some.

Love on empty pockets is like trying to light a cheap match: it takes forever to burst into flames. I could never simply forget about my family and abandon myself to whim. There's nothing quite so pathetic as being poor. I've felt that to the quick. But please, just let me be for a while. Don't ask me any questions, and just let me be.

One evening, the husband took the girl to a movie, and afterward they strolled around talking for another hour. It was past nine by the time he got home. His wife did not come rushing out to greet him as she normally did.

He went on inside and heard her muffled voice upstairs. It sounded like her usual greeting, but her voice had an odd note to it, like the pleading of a spoiled child or like someone on the verge of falling asleep. Following this for a time came the sounds of trying to get the child to go down for the night, and then everything became silent.

Only a few minutes before, he had been with his girlfriend, holding her hand in his as they said goodbye, so he was hardly in a position to scold his wife for failing to greet him at the door. He sat down to the dinner laid out for him on the table and began eating by himself. His wife's dinner was there, too, untouched. She had probably been waiting to eat until he got home but went to put the child to bed when she got fussy.

"You're like a boarder," his wife had joked a few days before, and a sour smile came to his lips as he recalled it. Indeed, more often than not he skipped breakfast. Either he didn't feel very hungry when he got up, or there wasn't enough time before he had to leave for work, so he just grabbed his lunch box and headed for the office. When he got home in the evening it was straight to dinner. If his daughter was still awake, he'd spend a little time with her, and then he went right to his room upstairs. He could easily be accused of coming home only to eat and sleep.

"Let's play some *shogi*," he had suggested one evening upon seeing his wife's long face. With immediate cheer she went to get the dust-covered game board from the closet and began setting it up. Two pieces were missing, so she cut some replacements out of paper and wrote "pawn" on them with a pen.

"Here goes. You just watch. You're going to wonder what hit you," she said spiritedly as she made her first move. If truth be told, the wife had no interest in *shogi*, and the husband knew it. The husband didn't like it much either. He never played games like *go* or *shogi* or mah-jongg. Their *shogi* board was one they'd inherited from his brother when he died, and, in fact, the husband barely even knew the moves well enough to keep from making a mistake. His wife's skill was about the same.

Twice the husband won after a protracted battle. They started a third game, but when he looked up from the board he found his wife starting to nod off. He threw in his pieces in exasperation and stood up. His wife was too tired. After that he never wanted to play *shogi* again.

"I wish we had a Ping-Pong table," his wife sometimes said, and *he* thought it might be nice, too. He wasn't especially fond of this game either, because it always seemed like such a game of cunning, but having a Ping-Pong table might cast a different hue on their inert and desolate home. For something like badminton you had to have more open space. When it came down to it, what amusements were possible in the contemporary Japanese home?

Waiting to begin her own dinner until her husband's return, the wife had fallen asleep beside the child. This hadn't prevented the husband from starting in on dinner, yet he didn't feel like he should just leave her sleeping indefinitely, so he went upstairs to wake her. But what could be the matter? She would not wake up. Normally, no matter how tired she was when she dozed off, she'd spring right up as if hit by a jolt of electricity. He never had to call her more than two or three times.

"Hey, wake up," he said again, this time poking her on the shoulder. She went on sleeping. If he raised his voice, he might disturb the child, so he called the same way again but tried grabbing her shoulder and shaking it as well. Still no response. His irritation mounting, he got rougher. "Wake up I said! Hey!" he shouted, shaking her shoulder hard enough to make the flesh on her face jiggle limply. Her eyes remained closed.

The thought that flashed through his mind at that moment made the blood drain from his face.

"Hiroko!" he cried, his voice now at high pitch. He brought his face close to hers. She was breathing. He put his hand to her fore

head. It felt normal. She had not changed out of the dress she'd
worn that day. He leaned over her and shook her again.

"Hey, Hiroko, what's wrong?"

Finally she stirred. She opened her eyes a crack and looked at
him. Her lips moved as if she were trying to say something, but he
couldn't tell what.

"What's wrong? Tell me what's wrong."

Twisting her head back and forth as though in pain, she groped
for his hand. When she found it, she said, "I drank . . . some . . ."

"Some what?" he demanded sharply, and this time his voice woke
his daughter. Sitting up, she stared at her father for a few seconds
before starting to crawl up onto her mother lying next to her.

"Ohhh. I feel like I'm gonna die," his wife groaned, writhing
back and forth in pain and sending the child tumbling. The child
wailed. That moment, for the first time, the husband noticed the
smell of alcohol.

"Was it whiskey?" he demanded.

She nodded.

"And nothing else but whiskey?"

She nodded again. A surge of relief spread through his body. The
child wailed louder and louder.

He went to check the closet downstairs. The bottle of the cheap-
est whiskey was missing. He'd had doubts about that whiskey when
he first bought it and tasted it, so he'd always been careful to drink
only small amounts at a time. Even then, it gave him headaches, and
his worried wife had finally gone to buy him a better brand. The last
third of the cheap brand had remained untouched since he'd gotten
the second bottle.

When he found the bottle in the kitchen, completely empty, it
sent a shudder through his body. Is she out of her mind? he
thought. Even I played it safe and never drank more than three
shots at a time. I don't suppose it'll kill her, but it sure wouldn't be
funny if it did. What could she have been thinking?

When she first failed to respond, he'd turned blue in the face
with the thought that she might have taken a massive dose of sleeping pills. Back in college the wife of a friend in his apartment house
had tried to kill herself with Calmotin, and the things his friend had
told him then had suddenly flashed through his mind. It hit him at
once that his own wife was acting just like his friend's wife had

acted. His friend's wife had finally come back to life after being in a coma for two full days and nights. The dose had been barely short of fatal.

No! he'd screamed inwardly as the worst fear burst upon his mind. Not suicide!

Panic ripped through his body like the lash of a savage whip. A moment later, when he discovered it was not suicide at all, his alarm and dismay quickly changed to indignation.

"Mrs. So-and-so, age twenty-something, died at approximately such-and-such o'clock on such-and-such a day, of methyl alcohol poisoning from the whiskey she drank while waiting for her husband to return home from work. She and her husband were the parents of a three-year-old daughter. Their home had always been a peaceful one, with nothing to suggest a possible suicide."

Some such article would appear off in the corner of the newspaper, drawing the final curtain. The headline: "Methyl Alcohol Kills Housewife." Could anything be more absurd than this? His neighbors and colleagues at work would see him and not know what to say. Some would express their sympathies; others would stare at him suspiciously, as if wanting to know what he had to hide.

He would learn to endure such stares from the world at large, no doubt, but he couldn't bear to think what a blow his wife's death would be to his girlfriend. It would instantly and cruelly shatter all the sweet memories he and the girl shared, and then the wounded girl, irreparably scarred, would leave him. Deprived of both wife and girlfriend in a single stroke, he'd find himself standing alone, in an utter daze, with a child in arms. How was he to build a life for himself after that? The rest of his life would proceed under a curse. A brand would be burnt upon his forehead, and all he could do would be to contritely endure his punishment. But what about the child? Why should *she* have to suffer?

Such were the husband's visions of the unhappiness that would follow his wife's suicide. They were quite predictable, for the most part, but they lacked one crucial element: reverence for the individual human life. And in place of this reverence stood nothing but a fearsome personal egotism. The husband was oblivious to this truth.

In a fit of temper, the husband took the more expensive bottle of whiskey from the closet, knocked back ten shots one after the other, wildly shoveled down the rest of his dinner, and went to bed.

The wife woke up in the middle of the night and pulled herself precariously to her feet, propping herself against the wall. She almost fell several times on her way down the stairs, but made it safely to the kitchen, where she gulped down a glass of water. When she started to fill her glass a second time, she suddenly felt sick, and she barely managed to stagger into the bathroom before vomiting. A dark, tea-colored liquid came up, over and over and over, and her nausea did not subside even after there was nothing more left to come.

When she raised her head, a face as ashen as a corpse stared back at her from the mirror. With her head spinning, she stumbled back into the kitchen, where she fell to her knees, then collapsed full length onto the floor. Was she going to die? she wondered, as she felt her consciousness slipping away. She did not awaken again until morning.

When she could no longer suppress her desire to paint, the wife would leave the child with the lady next door and set out with her box of watercolors and drawing board.

Attending art exhibits had always been her greatest pleasure, and even after the birth of her child she had done her best to make time for them. Though she had no favorite artist, she usually found one painting she really liked at every exhibit she visited. Finding that single painting always brought her an indescribable joy. When she was especially fond of the painting, she would go back for another look. The second time, she would go straight to that painting, and then go straight home again without looking at any others.

Of all the paintings she had admired, a seascape by Dufy remained most vividly imprinted on her memory: sky and water, the same deep blue; smoke rising from the stacks of a steamship in the distance; sailboats like white butterflies; red-parasoled figures standing on the beach and gazing out to sea; a large starfish on the sand. No doubt the actual picture was somewhat different, but these were the images that came back to her. Two or three people were looking at the sea, she thought.

She had been strangely moved by that painting, and the emotional currents it had stirred within her still flowed. What had moved her so? she wondered. Was it perhaps a recognition of human loneliness?

People who stand looking at the sea are people deep in thought.

They gaze as though without concern, and before them stretches the vast expanse of deep, blue water. The wife liked the idea of standing on the beach and gazing at the sea with no thought for anything else. She could feel the loneliness of the sea. Or should she call it the loneliness of the starfish? . . . It seemed a frightening picture, but then again it seemed to evoke such gentleness and nostalgia that it made her want to cry. What could have been going through Dufy's mind as he painted that picture?

She entered the gate of the nearby high school. The hush of evening had settled over the schoolyard. As she passed through the quadrangle, three young boys appeared from the opposite direction, chasing dragonflies. The large, grass-covered playground stood empty. Clear on the other side, by the clump of oleanders framing the back gate, she saw a tall man in a white summer kimono with two little girls in tow. He had a birdlime pole and was looking up into the trees.

She cut across the playground toward the swimming pool. Beside the pool stood three tall poplars. These three poplars were what she had come to paint. She had come to paint them once before, during summer vacation last year, but she'd found the swim team using the pool and watched their practice instead. Today no voices came from the pool. She broke into a run and dashed up the embankment.

"Oh no!" she exclaimed.

The pool was dry. She stood there gaping in surprise and disappointment.

"I can't believe it! There's no water."

Suddenly it all seemed funny, and she started to laugh. Eggplant and sesame grew in a tiny little garden someone had planted on top of the embankment. Who would be tending a garden in a place like this?

She decided to draw the three poplars from a position diagonally across the pool and sat down at one corner. The pool without water would make an interesting effect, actually. The far end was shallow, to about half way, and then there was a steep drop that made this end much deeper. Tiles in dotted white lines marked the lanes on the bottom, and a few stray pebbles lay here and there. She would have expected the empty pool to be encrusted with dried moss, but it looked as though someone had polished it clean. Perhaps they really did that.

A popular song blared from the coffee shop behind the school:

We'll meet again tomorrow
Under the apple tree.

A steady breeze blew through the early evening light. The branches of the poplars swayed and rustled without pause, their leaves in rapid motion like the vibrating of a stringed instrument. How she loved to watch the poplars swaying tall in the wind! They seemed to blow the murky gloom in her heart completely away. No, that wasn't true. They didn't blow it completely away, but somehow they softened it. As she watched the leaves fluttering in the wind, she had the feeling that they were all speaking some fervent message—though she could not tell what that message might be.

Do thoughts like these come to me because I'm depressed? she wondered. I can't understand my own behavior anymore. I mean, look at the other night, when I made myself so sick guzzling all that whiskey, one glass after another. Looking back on it now, I can't think why I would have done such a thing. And I wonder that I didn't die of alcohol poisoning. No matter how desperately alone I might have felt, how could I have been so reckless and vulgar as to swill down the whole rest of that bottle by the glassful?—especially when I knew it might not be safe. I really can't understand myself anymore. It frightens me that I could do such a thing.

My husband really lit into me the next morning. Why had I gone and done such a fool thing? he demanded over and over, and the more I didn't answer, the angrier he got, until finally he stormed out of the room and slammed the door behind him. But I just couldn't answer. "You could think about Michiko a little, too, you know," he said. I guess I really was being a bad mother.

But I simply had no room for Michiko in my mind. It was all I could do to think about my own problems. What might affect my child ten or twenty years in the future is hardly my first concern when I can barely sustain myself from one day to the next right now. So even if people say I'm a bad mother, there's really nothing I can do about it. Of course, I love Michiko. She's such a good-natured child, and she's been learning so much so fast recently that watching her grow isn't just a pleasure, it's endless amazement. If I were to lose her now, I'd be so devastated, I can't begin to imagine what it would mean. But I've come to doubt even my ability to go on living, and stumbling through each day as it comes is the best I can do. Maybe I went terribly astray somewhere along the way. Maybe I got spoiled growing up in my grandmother's care and turned into an incurable egotist. Maybe all my suffering comes simply from loving myself too much.

It was thoughts like these that had made her life seem an impossible burden to bear. She had come to the school ground with her watercolors precisely to forget such thoughts, but here she was caught up in them again, her palette and brushes abandoned at her side. Four or five damselflies had appeared in the sky above the poplars, circling round and round.

She heard voices and turned to see three boys walking from the dormitory toward the tennis courts, swinging their rackets as they went. One of them wore no shirt. Were they going to play tennis with three? Oh, if only I could play, too, she thought. To run back and forth across the court, chasing the ball, laughing without restraint, soaking myself in perspiration—just think how refreshing that would feel! Oh, how I wish I could be a student again! When I was young I had a world of my own, and everything in the larger world matched up perfectly with my own world. I was the ruler of that world. There, in complete abandon, I could bask in the sunshine and breathe the air and fly on the wind like a bird. Surrounded constantly by benevolence and love, I never knew a moment's despair. If only I could go back to that world! If only I could be like the monkey magician Songoku and fly back instantaneously to that wonderful, lost world!

No, no, forget all that. It's not true. Wanting to go back to my school days is nothing but sour grapes. But I'll tell you, oh dear God, what I truly do want. One thing, and one thing alone: I want my husband to love me. When I say all that stuff about doubting myself and barely being able to go on living—those are just ways of avoiding the real issue. I want my husband to love me, and to love me alone. That's the real issue. Let me say it now without hiding the truth. I want my husband to love me. That's my whole life.

The husband was writing in his diary when he became aware of muffled sobs coming from the kitchen downstairs. He felt a sharp stabbing in his heart but decided to wait and see what might happen.

At that moment he had been writing about going to the symphony with his girlfriend last night, so he had good cause to be startled when the house suddenly filled with his wife's late-night sobs. Indeed, it was a concert his wife had wanted to attend. She hadn't said so directly, but her hints had been clear enough. And, in fact, he could have taken her; at one point he had even thought he might. But one day as he and the girl were leaving the office together, he found himself making a date with her instead. She had mentioned the concert first—speaking very much as though she wished she could go, needless to say. Thinking of his wife, he hesitated. If he had already made a definite date with his wife by then, he would no doubt have let the girl's remarks pass unanswered. In retrospect, though, he had to admit that he'd probably delayed saying anything to his wife precisely because he thought he might want to ask the girl, and he wanted to keep that possibility open.

The husband himself was not that much of a music lover. Without someone else to nudge him into action, he wasn't one to go and buy expensive tickets to a concert on his own. Even if he had decided to go with his wife, it would have been essentially as a favor to her. So you could say his decision to go with his girlfriend rather than his wife simply reflected the natural inclinations of his heart. At any rate, silencing his guilty conscience as best he could, he had lied to his wife and invited the girl to the concert. He discovered that the mixture of thrill and anxiety he experienced from going out in public with the girl—just the two of them, where anybody could see them—easily eclipsed the pain of lying to his wife. His earlier qualms remained almost entirely forgotten until the concert was over and he returned home.

As he listened, the sobs came faster and at a higher pitch—like a child cutting loose after some catastrophic disappointment. His twenty-four-year-old wife was crying with her whole body, a body that had not yet lost all its girlishness. He had never heard her cry like this before.

Now she's really getting hysterical, he thought with a grim frown. This is serious; it's going to be troublesome. But he could not immediately decide whether he should go down and tell her to stop it, or just ignore her and let her cry herself out.

He turned the situation over in his mind: Had she perhaps managed somehow to find out about last night's concert? Maybe one of her friends had seen him there, and came by today especially to tell her. It wasn't impossible. If so, what a fool thing he'd done. Or maybe something about the way he'd acted yesterday had tipped off that uncanny intuition of hers. There had been that time the other day when the girl had taught him a new song as they took an evening stroll along the river. "On fields and hills of tender grass, a thousand flowers bloom; their radiant colors of every hue, alive with sweet perfume." It was an old folk song from England, as he recalled. He and the girl had sung it together in two-part harmony. Then, later that evening, when he was playing with his daughter after dinner, his wife had started singing the exact same song, as she did the dishes. Talk about spooky. It could have been pure coincidence, but it had given him quite a turn.

Even if it were true that she'd found out about last night, though, he'd be better off not to say anything. He couldn't undo what he'd already done. Yes, he had lied to his wife, but it had all happened in the natural course of things, kind of like water seeking it's own level, and there really wasn't anything he could have done to stop it. Besides, what could he possibly say to his distraught wife that would actually make her feel better? At times like this, the thing to do was to act as though nothing were amiss, rather than to risk saying the wrong thing by trying to comfort her or cheer her up. If he responded to this outburst, she might start making a habit of such behavior, and he'd never see the end of it. Now *there* was a depressing thought. He'd never survive. She might be hurting, but his best bet at this point was to turn a cold shoulder. Surely she wouldn't ever actually try to kill herself.

Rationalizing first one way, then another, the husband held his ground, but his wife's sobbing showed no sign of abating. Though the sobs were far too deeply colored with the tones of despair to be regarded as a momentary fit, they were persistently deflected by the tough surface of the husband's heart and failed to touch its inner core. Yet, could the husband really have been unaware of how deep his wife's anguish had become? Was it not rather that he deliberately closed his eyes to her pain, to the blood spurting from her wounds, so as to save his own self from injury?

As the wife's sobbing continued endlessly, on and on, the husband's annoyance grew. What if Michiko should wake up and start crying? he scolded her in his mind. How could you respond to her needs when you're in such a state yourself? Enough is enough already. What's the idea, anyway — bursting out like this for no reason at all? It's practically an act of violence, if you think about it.

He got to his feet and stomped loudly down the stairs, where he found his wife with both hands pressed to her face, leaning against the sliding doors that divided the kitchen from the dining room.

Her shoulders shook out of control with each sob, and she did not let up even when she knew he had come down.

An icy chill swept over the husband's heart. He watched her in silence for a few moments, and then spat out venomously:

"You're acting like some homesick housemaid just come down from the mountains—crying in the kitchen like this. Stop it! It's stupid!"

Without waiting for a response, he turned on his heels and stomped back upstairs. The sobbing below changed to sniffles, but the sniffles still went on for quite some time before finally fading away.

By the next morning the husband was feeling sorry about how he'd treated his wife. He spoke to her at breakfast, this time in gentle tones.

"I'm sorry for the way I yelled at you last night. Please forgive me. I apologize. I think you've been under a lot of stress lately, and you're tired. Isn't that right? When you're tired, it's easy to let little things bother you more than they should—things that don't mean anything at all. You have to realize, there isn't a person on this earth who's not unhappy. Everyone bears his own particular burden of unhappiness. That burden may not be obvious to others, but it's always there, and even if it *were* obvious, no one else could really feel the unhappiness the way the person does himself. So what can you do? Basically, whatever may happen, you have to stop thinking that you're the only one who's unhappy. Everyone's alone in this world, and everyone goes through life enduring his own unhappiness. That's the way it is. You can't be looking only at yourself. If you do that, then your own unhappiness starts to seem a lot bigger than it really is. You have to realize that there are lots of other people who are much, much more unhappy than you ever were. In fact, that's the only way you can endure your own unhappiness. You have to go on living. No matter what happens, you have to go on living. Do you understand? I don't want you to cry like you did last night anymore. It's too depressing. It's through things like this that you learn what life's all about, little by little. You can't let it get you down. You have to live on, strong and unflinching. You have to become invulnerable, and live a long, long life. Okay? Do you hear?"

Stringing together the kinds of phrases he'd read in books, the husband spoke as if with the wisdom of generations. They were selfish words, spoken very much for his own advantage. But they were also words that expressed his genuine feeling for his wife. His wife listened silently, nodding her head over and over, looking as meek and complaisant as a child after an outburst of tears. Seeing his wife this way brought the husband a small measure of relief. But as her husband's words flowed over her, the wife could do nothing to stop the feeling that she was plunging deeper and deeper into a bottomless void.

"We're eating upstairs today," the wife said when the husband arrived home wiping perspiration from his brow. Making no response except an unimpressed snort, he ducked into the washroom to strip down to his undershorts and splash cold water over his head. Then he climbed the stairs.

"What in . . . ?" When he entered the room, he stopped short and turned around. His wife, following close behind, looked at him with a radiant sparkle in her eyes and let out a tiny giggle. She had brought up the small round table and folding chairs from the front hall and got everything ready for dinner. From the ceiling hung three cute little lanterns, red and yellow and light blue.

"Do you get it? Today's the—"

"Oh, that's right, it's Bastille Day."

This was the fourteenth of July.

Spread colorfully on the table was the kind of feast normally seen in this house only on one of their birthdays or on their wedding anniversary. A moment later the wife returned from downstairs with a bottle of ice-cold beer.

"Wow! This is great!" the husband exclaimed. But then he thought of their household finances, and his face turned sour.

"Now hold on just a minute," he said. "If we start celebrating every time there's a Bastille Day or an Independence Day we'll go broke before we know it. There's no sense in getting so carried away about foreign holidays. You should be thinking more about the long term."

The wife smiled gently. "The long term?" she said, her tone a question.

But the first glass of cold beer quickly revived the husband's initial cheer. He could hardly go on sulking in the face of so much fine food. With a special place set just for her, his daughter, too, had started eating amidst repeated squeals of delight. The husband felt the effects of the beer beginning to spread through his body and looked up at the evening sky beyond the sycamore tree outside the wide-open window. What a beautiful shade of blue it was!

"I'll bet Paris is really hopping tonight," he said. "Fireworks shooting up one after the other. Dancing everywhere."

"I wish I could be there!"

"Nah, forget it. If you actually went, you'd be disappointed. Paris isn't like it used to be."

"As if you would know," she mocked.

"The Paris of old in all its splendor doesn't exist any more. Sure, it may look the same on the outside. But the people's hearts have changed. The citizens of Paris are mostly no different from us, scraping along, trying to make ends meet. They limp from one day to the next thinking what a hard life it is. And that's exactly why on a night like tonight they really whoop it up. They dance all night long. They kick up their heels and dance. People like us can know just how they feel."

The husband tended to turn commiserative when he got drunk.

"I've made up my mind," the wife declared. "I'm going there to live—among those people."

"They'd say you've got to be kidding. You'd only be an added drain on the city's food supply."

"I don't care what they say. I'll live in the old part of town and work as a seamstress."

The husband shrugged his shoulders at the absurdity of it. The wife went down to the kitchen and came back with a second bottle of beer. Grabbing it away from her, the husband opened it with an exaggerated flourish.

"I'll let you have just one glass," he said.

"*Merci, monsieur.*"

"Ooh! I'm impressed! Cheers!"

When he finished his beer, his daughter was chewing on a wedge of tomato. Carrying her to the window rail, he began to sing:

> *Gin-gin gira-gira*, the burning sun goes down.
> *Gin-gin gira-gira*, the sun goes down.
> Red as red as red can be, the clouds in the sky;
> And all the people's faces, too, red as red can be.
> *Gin-gin gira-gira*, the sun goes down.

The child begged him to sing the song again so he started in a second time. A dragonfly flew by overhead, skimmed past the leaves of the paulownia tree next door, and disappeared, but not before the sharp-eyed girl had caught sight of it.

"Butterfly! Catch it!" she cried in a rising voice, looking up at her father's face.

"Not a butterfly. A dragonfly."

"Dramfly? Catch butterfly!"

"All gone."

The wife, who had been listening to the exchange between her husband and daughter, now went downstairs and came back with the portable record player.

"Shall we dance?"

"*Oui, Madame.*"

The lovely glow of the lingering light slowly melted away into the summer night. A waltz began to play. The husband, still wearing only his shorts, turned to his wife in her white dress.

"*Pardon,*" he said, and took her in his arms.

"What?"

Ignoring her question, he drew her close and started to dance. The fragrance of a fine perfume tickled his nose. In his wife's hair was a small white ribbon. He thought how nice his girlfriend would look if she wore a brown ribbon in her hair. As they turned, their cheeks touched.

The child tried to approach but bumped into the wife's leg and fell down. She had been taught not to cry when she fell.

They danced to five or six tunes, and the husband's face dripped with sweat.

"Are we stopping already?" the wife asked.

"It's just too hot," the husband said.

"In Paris they go all night long."

The husband went downstairs, and the wife could hear him pouring water over himself in the washroom. She stood by the window and gazed up at the stars beginning to twinkle in the sky. The child lay on her stomach on the tatami, fast asleep. The wife continued to gaze at the sky in silence, but the sound of her husband coming back up the stairs brought her out of her reverie with a start, and she quickly moved away from the railing.

EVENINGS
AT THE POOL

*a*t the pool, a series of spirited final sprints were in progress.

Chestnut-tanned swimmers hit the water in rapid succession, chased by the shouts of their coach.

One girl pulled herself up beside the starting block and collapsed on her stomach, her back pumping up and down as she struggled to catch her breath.

At that moment a commuter train came around the gentle curve of the tracks skirting the school grounds beyond the pool. Salary-men returning from work crowded every car, hanging onto the straps. When their view opened up as the train emerged from behind the school building, the blue of the water stretching across the face of the new pool and the swimsuited figures of the girls resting on the concrete deck leaped into their eyes. We may imagine this scene cast a measure of comfort upon the hearts of the sorry, wilted workers besieged by the heat of the day and a thousand private woes.

A single tall man stood watching the animated practice from the far end of the pool. He had the air and features of a gentle, easy-going man. He wore swimming trunks, and a cape hung from his shoulders.

The man's name was Aoki Hiroo. He was an old alumnus of this school, and his two sons were now enrolled in its elementary division. He had long worked for a certain textile company, most recently as acting section head.

In the open lane at one side of the pool, Mr. Aoki's boys frolicked like two happy puppies. The older boy was a fifth grader, the other a year younger.

The Aokis had first appeared at the pool four days ago, and they had returned each evening since. Mr. Aoki and the coach knew each other by sight, and the coach had agreed to let the boys practice their swimming so long as they didn't get in the way of the swim team.

Every so often, Mr. Aoki would dive smoothly into the water and do a slow crawl to the other end of the 25-meter pool. He was quite an accomplished swimmer. Lest he distract the swim team, though, he mostly just stood at the side of the pool while his boys played in the water by themselves. Now and then the boys would ask him something, and he would give them a pointer or two about their form, but the rest of the time he gazed at the intense training of the girls with a look of quiet admiration.

After a while, Mrs. Aoki appeared at the pool gate leading a large, white, bushy-haired dog. When he finally noticed her several minutes later, Mr. Aoki immediately called to the boys, now engaged in a contest of who could send a bigger splash into the other's face. The boys did not dawdle. They leaped from the pool and raced for the showers.

After changing into his shorts, Mr. Aoki went to thank the coach, ensconced as usual in his chair at the center of the starting blocks, and then followed the boys out of the enclosure. Mrs. Aoki smiled and bowed to the coach from where she stood at the gate. She handed the dog's chain to the older boy and started off down the street, walking side by side with her husband. The family lived only two blocks away.

As he gazed after the Aokis disappearing into the shade of the Chinese tallow trees, the coach felt a wonderful warmth fill his heart.

Now that's living, he thought. That's really living the way we all should live. Going home together for a family dinner after an evening dip at the pool . . .

In the deepening shadows, the Aoki family walked homeward

down the paved street with their large, white, bushy-haired dog leading the way. Awaiting them at home was a bright and joyous table, and a summer's evening full of family fun.

But, in fact, it was not so. What really awaited this couple was something quite different—something neither the children nor the neighbors nor anyone else could be told.

It was hard to know just what to call it—this thing that lurked at home.

A week ago, Mr. Aoki had been let go from his job. The cause: embezzling company funds.

Now each evening, after the children went to bed, husband and wife were left to face each other alone. Stretched out on deck chairs on the patio beneath the wisteria arbor, neither said a word. Their only motions were to wave their fans in pursuit of an occasional mosquito hovering near their legs.

Mrs. Aoki was a smallish woman of trim build. When she came down the street in her red sandals with her hempen shopping bag over her arm, she was the picture of youthful buoyancy. Sometimes she could be seen with her dog in tow, eating ice cream at the coffee shop near the station; sometimes she could be seen running races with her boys and laughing gleefully when she won.

But her husband's firing had come as no small blow to her. It was like the punch that sends a boxer down on one knee in the ring.

"What in the world for?" she had asked with rounded eyes when her dazed husband came home and told her he'd been fired.

Before this, he had seldom returned home until near midnight. Sometimes he was out even later and had to come all the way home by cab. But she'd gotten used to that and thought nothing of it anymore.

His explanation had always been the same: he was entertaining clients. That could hardly be *every* night, though, so a lot of those times he must have been entertaining just his own sweet self. As a matter of fact, she had no way of knowing where he went, or what he might be doing.

But what good would it do to make an issue of it? Since all those late nights didn't seem to bother him, and since they didn't seem to have any ill effects on his health, she figured she should count her blessings.

As far as his work itself was concerned, he had never had much to say, nor had she ever bothered to ask. So when he told her he'd been fired, all she could do was wonder what on earth could have happened.

"I borrowed some money," he explained (the amount was equivalent to about six months of his salary), "and they found out about it. I was planning to pay it back, but, before I did, they found out."

Common sense said he should have had to pay the money back even if it meant selling his house, but in this case the company had decided to forgive the debt in exchange for his immediate resignation.

How could this happen? Mrs. Aoki wondered. After working for a company for eighteen years, to suddenly get fired just like that. If only it could be a joke—a practical joke her husband was playing on her because nothing ever seemed to faze her. How happy she would be if that were all it was!

But, in fact, she had known from the instant her husband walked in the door that it could be no mere joke. The ominous cloud hovering over him had told her instantly that something serious had happened.

"There's nothing you can do?"

"Nothing."

"Didn't you ask Mr. Komori to help?"

"He was the angriest."

On the board of directors, Mr. Aoki had been closer to Komori than anyone else. Mrs. Aoki had visited his house several times and enjoyed long talks with his wife.

"Maybe I could go and apologize," she said.

"It's no use. Everything's already been decided."

She fell silent, and, after a few moments, began to weep.

Soon the initial shock passed, and she was able to regain a certain calm. But then something akin to terror came to her all over again when she thought of how easily their secure, worry-free lives had crumbled to nothing.

It could almost be called spectacular.

This is what life is like, she thought.

When she looked rationally at what had happened, she had to admit it was not at all beyond imagining. Her husband had never been a particularly conscientious worker. Nor could you call him a man of strong character. Indeed, she had seen him make time, against all obstacles, for the sake of entertainment and drink. Who could ever have guaranteed that he would not make a mistake?

Even if some of the time he had gone out on company business other than entertaining clients, there had to be limits. And on his salary, he could hardly afford to go out much at his own expense. She had been a fool to take it so casually, and to never once question what was going on.

It had probably never occurred to her husband that things could get out of hand and lead to a crisis. He had a tendency not to take things very seriously to begin with, which, no doubt, was exactly what had led him to his ruin. If he had truly intended to pay the money back, it wasn't such a large sum that he couldn't somehow have done it. Her husband must never really have felt in his bones what a serious business his work was.

On the other hand, in fifteen years of marriage, it had never once occurred to her that she should be worried about her husband's ways. She could not recall ever having reminded him how important his work was, and that he must never take it lightly.

When she reflected on her marriage like this, she realized for the first time just how foolishly and carelessly they had spent the time they shared as husband and wife. And suddenly the successful man who had risen all the way to acting section head only to be fired began to look like an absentminded half-wit. Her husband might be fun-loving and a bit of a heavy drinker, but these qualities were counterbalanced by his good work—wasn't that how she'd reassured herself? Hadn't she described her husband to her school friends exactly that way? Now she was furious with herself for it.

How in the world could a man thrown out of a job at the age of forty rehabilitate the family name? How in the world would he balance his accounts in this life?

Her head filled with questions that made despair raise its head with every turn of her thoughts. But they were not questions she could simply push from her mind and ignore.

An amazingly large, yellow moon emerged from among the leaves of the sycamore tree in the yard. As she gazed at it, an almost inaudible sigh escaped her lips.

The children were delighted by their father's unexpected vacation. The older boy begged to go hiking in the mountains, while the younger wanted to go on an insect-hunting excursion.

"No, your father is tired and needs to rest at home," their mother headed them off.

Her husband smiled weakly. "That's right. Daddy just wants to rest right now," he said, "so please don't ask me to take you anywhere far away this time."

The boys reluctantly withdrew their requests. In exchange, beginning on the third evening, they dragged their father out to the new pool that had been built at the school. The high school girls' swim team was in training camp for an upcoming meet, so normally the Aokis could not have used the pool.

To tell the truth, Mr. Aoki had no energy for stripping down to his trunks and diving into a pool. He really didn't feel up to anything but lolling about on the tatami with his long legs and arms thrown out every which way. It was Mrs. Aoki who'd insisted he take his swimsuit and cape and get out of the house for a while.

"If all you do is lie around like that, the next thing you know you'll get sick as well. Go swimming. It'll help get you out of your doldrums."

Mr. Aoki had always been fond of athletics. In his student days he had played on the volleyball team, and on Sunday mornings and such he often played catch with the boys in the street out front. During the college rugby season, he liked to take his wife and boys to see the games. And he'd started going to the beach with the boys when they were barely toddlers so he could teach them how to swim.

The first evening, when her husband and the boys had not returned by the time dinner was ready, Mrs. Aoki went to fetch them, and she found her husband quite changed from when she had watched him leave the house tagging along after the boys. Standing with folded arms, he gazed intently after the swimmers as they slowly pushed their kickboards across the pool, beating the water into foam behind them. He didn't even notice her arrival.

Can you believe this man? she muttered inwardly, not knowing whether to feel shame or pity.

On the second evening she bought a box of chocolates as a thank-you to the coach and a treat for the swimmers. She called her husband to the fence and asked him to take it to the coach.

Her husband took the chocolates to where the coach sat at the center of the starting blocks and gave them to him with an amiable smile. The coach beamed back.

"Okay!" he boomed. "Whoever betters their record gets one of these chocolates from the Aokis. Come on! Let's see what you can do!"

All around him swimmers sprang to life, and several shouted back:

"That's mean!"

"Give us a chocolate first, and then we'll beat our records!"

Mr. Aoki looked on contentedly, still smiling.

The coach opened the box to pass out the chocolates, and the swimmers quickly pressed in on all sides. Clamoring noisily, they took their pieces, called "Thank you" to Mr. Aoki, and tossed them into their mouths.

Why doesn't he hurry up and come on back? Mrs. Aoki thought, but her husband continued to stand among the swimmers. Eventually, the coach held the box out to him and asked, "Would you like one?" Even her husband had sense enough then to say "No thanks" and excuse himself, and he finally returned to the far corner of the pool where his boys were playing.

Was he a big kid, or a fool, or what? Mrs. Aoki wondered as she watched him come.

When the Aokis started home in the gathering dusk, the swimmers by the pool turned toward them and called out in a chorus of charming voices:

"Goodbye! Thanks again!"

Looking rather embarrassed, Mr. Aoki returned an awkward wave.

The leaves of the Chinese tallow trees glowed an eerie green in the lingering light of the evening sky. As the family walked along beneath those leaves, Mrs. Aoki sensed the gloom slowly returning to her husband's face. Even as she pretended not to notice, she could feel her own face sagging into much the same expression.

The two boys walked ahead, pulling the dog behind them. Now and then they would call out the dog's name. The energy in their voices grated on Mrs. Aoki's nerves.

"Talk to me," she said. "All this silence only makes it more depressing."

"Yeah, I guess you're right," he said, as though noticing for the first time. "But what shall I talk about?"

"The bars," she said.

He stared at her in bewilderment.

"Tell me about the bars you go to a lot."

"There's not much to tell, really."

"Never mind that, just tell me about them. You know, now that I think of it, you've never said a word about the places you go—your favorite bars and whatnot. So come on," she said, putting more cheer in her voice, hoping to raise both of their spirits. "Tell me about the places with the pretty girls where you spent all that stupid money."

She was being deliberately flippant, but her husband grimaced. It brought her a twinge of pleasure.

"There were lots of places," her husband said, recovering himself.

"Start in wherever you like, then, and take them in order."

So, in the light of the moon filtering through the wisteria over the patio, Mr. Aoki began with a place he frequented when he didn't have much money.

Two sisters ran the bar—the older one beautiful but brusque, the younger not at all pretty and very slow mannered. The place always looked as though it had gone out of business two or three days before, but if he went on inside and perched himself tentatively on one of the bar stools, the younger sister would soon emerge from the room in back. The way she came out invariably had a "Who cares?" sort of air about it.

He would half expect her to tell him they were closed, but she would sluggishly duck under the counter. After tidying up a bit, she would finally turn around to face him. At first he had thought she must be in a bad mood, or maybe she wasn't feeling well, but he soon learned this was just her normal way.

For example, if a patron were to say, "No matter when I come, this place has about as much life as an empty depot in a cowboy movie," she would break into a broad, happy smile.

The older sister was much the same—except that she seemed to care even less than the younger and wouldn't come downstairs at all unless she had gotten herself into a really good mood.

As a bar, it made for a very odd atmosphere. If someone came charging in the door ready to party, he'd likely be thrown so completely off balance by the dull and indifferent reception, he'd be stopped dead in his tracks, unable either to forge ahead or to back out.

The bar's drawing card was its cheap prices. Of course, for the patrons to be willing to put up with such indifferent service, the prices would quite naturally *have* to be low.

But Aoki did not frequent the bar solely for its prices. For him, the real attraction of the bar was the older sister. The very first time he went there with a friend, he'd been struck by the older sister's resemblance to the French movie star M, with her worldly looks and otherworldly air. In her beautiful features he found something a tiny bit scary, but he also found something supremely romantic. What would it be like to go for a stroll down deserted nighttime streets with a woman like this? he wondered, and from that moment forth a vague desire arose in his heart. Before long, his wish was fulfilled.

He bought tickets to an international swimming competition in which a famous American swimmer was scheduled to appear, and he gave one of the tickets to this sister to see what she might do. He hadn't really expected her to come, but when he arrived, she was already there.

Afterward they went from one bar to another, then hailed a cab and drove aimlessly around the late-night city streets. It wasn't a "stroll," but he could say that he had gotten his wish.

As they drove, the girl told him in a somber voice about living with her father in Harbin as a child. In the summer he would take her to the Isle of the Sun, where they mingled with Russian families for a day of fun on the banks of the muddy Songhua River. On the way home they stopped at a restaurant facing the promenade along the river, and at a table right in front of the orchestra her father would drink mug after mug of beer while she chewed on black bread. Together they gazed at the river in the twilight.

The girl spoke with her cheek pressed against Aoki's shoulder. Now's the time to kiss her, he thought, only half listening to her story. But what if he tried to kiss her and she got angry? That would ruin everything. Too worried about what terrible thing might happen if she got angry with him, he could not bring himself to do it.

Never again had another such opportunity presented itself. Several times he had wasted expensive tickets to the ballet or the symphony, hoping for a second chance. But as Aoki continued to observe the girl over the next few months, he came to understand that she had not been her usual self on the night of the swimming competition. If he were ever to have a chance, that night had been it.

In the days and months since, she had become like a castle with mirror-slick walls offering no holds to grasp. Each time he saw that miraculous smile of hers, he'd be filled anew with a longing to somehow make her his own. But he could not gain the faintest hint of what she might be thinking. Were her sights set on marriage, or did she not care? Had someone else already won her heart, or was she available?

Especially frustrating were the days when she knew perfectly well that Aoki was waiting but still chose not to come downstairs. Times like that, he was left sipping drearily at his beer as he carried on an awkward, slow-moving conversation with the younger sister.

Even worse was when neither of the sisters appeared, and a prune-faced old lady took their place. If the disgruntled Aoki asked the sisters' whereabouts, old Prune-face would tell him the older one had a visitor upstairs and the younger was in bed with a bad toothache, or something of the sort. In a fit of irritation Aoki would sometimes settle in on his stool for an even longer stay than usual, drinking to the old woman's pouring. The old woman must have felt sorry for him at times like this: she would only charge him for one beer even when he had had three.

By probing Prune-face for information, Aoki managed to verify the sisters' claim that the older sister had no patron or lover, and that they'd opened the bar on money from their father. He got her assurance, too, on the occasion when she said there was a visitor upstairs, that the man was merely a friend of their father's and not anyone of questionable repute. Still, it irked Aoki to no end to think that the girl was alone in her room with another man, talking hour after hour about whatever it might be.

Actually, all the men who frequented this bar were, like Aoki, in thrall to the beauty of this older sister. The others, like Aoki, had all felt the same cold shoulder turned against their yearnings; and yet none felt able to make a clean break and give the girl up, either, so they kept drifting back for one more visit. Whenever Aoki happened to find himself with another of these men at the bar, they both could tell immediately by the other's behavior. From this, too, Aoki knew it was nothing but foolishness to keep coming back, but he still couldn't bring himself to turn his steps away once and for all.

One thing never ceased to puzzle him, though. How was it that a bar with so rare a beauty in the house could remain in such a fear-somely depressed state no matter when he went? Why had he never once seen the bar draw a large, boisterous crowd?

What Mr. Aoki told his wife was not exactly as written here, but it covered roughly the same ground.

"That's it?"

"Uh-huh."

Mrs. Aoki let out a little laugh. "You never told me anything like that before."

"Well, if I'm always getting jilted . . ."

"But I don't suppose you always were, were you?" she shot back.

His throat tightened.

"Never mind," she went on. "You don't have to tell me. I know you won't tell me the truth anyway, so forget it."

How could she have been so dense? she wondered. The news that her husband had been fired for embezzling money had put her in such a state of shock that she'd been going around as if in a trance.

There's another woman! My husband spent all that money on another woman!

It had hit her like a thunderbolt as she listened to her husband's story. A violent quaking seized her heart, but she took care to hide it, and when her husband was through, she moved swiftly to head off any further confessions of a similar kind.

The story her husband had told her meant nothing to him. The secret he had to guard was something else entirely, and the story of the girl who grew up in Harbin and looked like the French movie star was nothing more than a smokescreen. She knew this instinctively.

If she were to press him, her husband would no doubt entertain her with other stories about women—stories to make her think he was being open, while in fact steering clear of any real danger. But she would not fall for that.

The things that didn't really matter he could speak of with abandon. But behind them all there was something this man would not touch with the tiniest tip of a needle.

A Medusa's head.

She must not attempt to see it. She must not pursue. She must quietly pretend to suspect nothing at all.

"Talk to me," she had said, but not in her remotest dreams had she anticipated this result. When she'd suggested he tell her about the bars he went to, she really *had* thought it might help raise their

spirits. But look what had happened instead! Quite without intending, she'd built herself a trap, and she hadn't even realized it until
after she'd thrown herself into it.

The next evening, Mr. Aoki once again went off to the pool with
the boys, and as she prepared dinner at home Mrs. Aoki wondered
how long these curious days would go on. Their household kitty
would be exhausted in two weeks. Their savings account had long
been empty—they were both the kind who spent whatever money
they had. So once they used up what was on hand, they would have
to start pawning their possessions. Would that get them through
another six months, perhaps?

Her own family had prospered in the foreign trade before the
war, but they'd fallen on hard times since. As for her husband's side,
his three brothers all subsisted on the meager wages of civil servants
and salarymen. She'd never given it the slightest thought before,
but this crisis had awakened her to the fact that she and her husband
were like orphans, without any family they could turn to for help in
times of need.

Were it not for the children, they might somehow manage. If
Mrs. Aoki went out and got a job, she no doubt could fill at least
her own stomach—though, lacking any skills, she'd have to be prepared for the worst. But with two grade-school-age boys at home,
any such plan was out of the question.

That meant that unless her husband succeeded in finding a new
job, their family of four could no longer stay together. But where on
earth was he likely to find an employer willing to take in and provide
for a married man of forty who'd been fired from his job and
thrown out onto the streets?

Mrs. Aoki tried to recall what kinds of things had gone through
her mind while preparing dinner just one week before, but she
could not remember a single thing.

Somewhere along the line, for some unfathomable reason, her
whole world had been transformed. How could a single bolt from
the blue have twisted the course of their lives so completely awry,
leaving them to suffer such undue pain and fear? What sort of god
had permitted this catastrophe to occur?

The motions she was going through now, lighting the stove or
taking the frying pan off the heat: what meaning did any of this
have? Why did her hands go on working so busily as though nothing were amiss? Why did she still find herself going through the

same routine motions she had gone through day in and day out for
as long as she could remember? Was the whole thing just some
bizarre mistake?

All of a sudden she felt like everything was collapsing into an ever
more incomprehensible jumble.

That night, after the boys were in bed, Mr. Aoki sipped at some
whiskey and told his wife this story.

In the building where I work, there's a mail chute next to the elevator on each floor. It's essentially a long square tube running all the
way from the ninth floor down to the first. The side facing the hallway is clear, so you can watch from the outside as your letter begins
to fall. Sometimes when you're walking by, you see a white envelope
drop soundlessly through the chute from ceiling to floor; or you see
several, one after the other.

The hallway happens to be very dim, and it can give you quite a
start to see one of these flashes of white go by when there's no one
else around. I'm not quite sure what to say it's like. It's like a ghost,
maybe—like some strange, lonely spirit.

One step away, in all the offices along the hallway, is a world
where you don't dare let down your guard for a single moment.
That's why you get such a start when you emerge into the hallway,
to go to the bathroom or something, and you see one of those
white flashes.

Some mornings, when I have something I need to get done early,
I arrive at work before the normal starting time. I glance around the
office, looking at all the empty chairs waiting for the people who
usually work there to arrive. Each chair, in the absence of its occupant, seems to assume the shape of its occupant's head, or the way
he moves his eyes, or the turn of his lips when he speaks, or the
curve of his back as he hunches over his desk.

The patent leather seat where the occupant will soon plant his
bottom shines like it was polished with oils that oozed from his
body. It's as if, through the years, each man's indignations and fret-
tings and gripes and laments, or his incessant fears and anxieties,
have been slowly secreted from his body in the form of an oil. At
least that's how it always seems to me.

Each chairback, too, uniquely bent by the press of its occupant's
own back, seems to express that man's feelings about his workplace.
Willy-nilly, day after day, he's had to come into this office and set

himself down on that same desk chair. Is it any wonder that something of his heart might transfer itself to the chair?

I look quietly down at my own chair as well, thinking, Ahh,
what a pitiable chair. What a poor, wretched, acting section head's
chair . . .

And I wonder: When have I ever sat here without feeling afraid?
If someone behind me suddenly clears his throat, it practically star-
tles me right out of my seat.

I know I'm not the only one who trembles in such constant fear.
I can see it in the others' faces as they arrive for work. The few who
come in looking cheerful and contented must really be happy.
They're the fortunate ones—the ones who've been blessed. But the
vast majority aren't like that, and they show it in the expressions
they have on their faces the moment they push open the door and
step into the office. What is it they're so frightened of? Is it some
particular person? Is it the company executives—their section head
or department head, or the president himself, perhaps? That may be
part of it, certainly, but it can't be all. It can only be one of several
elements, for those very section heads and department heads come
in the door with the exact same look on their faces.

But again, what is it that so frightens all these men? It is neither
a particular group of individuals, nor anything else you can really
put your finger on. It haunts them even at home, in their time for
resting and relaxing with their wives and children. It enters even
into their dreams and threatens them in their sleep. It's what brings
them the nightmares that terrorize them in the middle of the night.

Sometimes when I gaze around at the vacant chairs and desks,
and at the hat stands with their empty hangers here and there, I find
myself getting all choked up. Everything I see takes on the image of
someone who works there, and seems to have so much to tell me.

"My old lady came on to me again last night with tears in her
eyes, begging me, please, please, it's okay if my pay is low and we're
always on the verge of going broke, just watch my temper and don't
do anything rash and never forget how important my work is. She
cried and pleaded with me on and on like that, you know, and hey,
it really made me stop and think."

Pressed up against one desk is the chair of the man who spoke
these words to me. Every time I look at that chair, I remember how
he started in with a simple remark about making ends meet at home
and wound up with this doleful lament. I remember it as clear as

day—the tone of his voice and his embarrassed smile and everything. . . .

There Mr. Aoki's story came to an end.

His story about the bar had been an eye-opener as well, but Mrs. Aoki now asked herself whether her husband had ever said anything like this about his anxieties at work before. Little had she imagined that he was going off to work feeling like this every day. How could she have missed it all those years? What in the world had they talked about in a decade and a half of living together in the same house as husband and wife?

Even if her husband never got home until midnight and then had to hurry off to work as soon as he got up the next morning, how could they have spent that many years together and never spoken about a single important thing? Even with his long hours, they'd always made a point of going somewhere as a family on Sundays. But what had her husband spoken of, and what had she asked him about, in the time they actually spent together? Never once had it entered her mind that her husband might hold such feelings about his work at the office. She'd always simply assumed that he stayed out late every night because he enjoyed a good time, and she'd thought nothing more of it than that.

He had tended to be out late every night from the time they first got married, so apparently that image of him had become etched in her mind at the very beginning. Their regular Sunday outings compensated for the lack of any kind of family life from Monday through Saturday, and she had always thought it more satisfying that way than if he came home earlier during the week but then had to go in on Sunday as well, leaving her to while away another dull day at home.

Having listened to her husband's story tonight, she now understood why he never came straight home after work even when he had no clients to entertain. It was the deep anguish he felt about his life as a working man. And she understood, too, that he hadn't felt he could find comfort for that anguish at home. Facing his wife and children apparently only increased his pain, while the women at the bars and cabarets let him forget it.

In that case, what had she been to her husband all this time? she suddenly wondered. If their marriage had not been one of fulfillment and trust and mutual support, then what had she been doing all this time?

But she also wondered: if her husband had never told her about the anxiety and pain he experienced in his job, didn't that just go to prove that he had been unburdening his heart to someone else all along? And wasn't it that very someone who was really to blame for their present troubles?

When her husband had told her about the sisters at the bar, the image of a woman had come before her like a flash of revelation. She shuddered at the terrifying reality of that image and tried hastily to push it from her mind, but it would not leave her.

At first she had found it a little bewildering to have her husband get up in the morning only to stay home all day, but by the time a week had gone by she began to think she preferred it this way.

If only their family could always live like this, she thought, without her husband having to go off somewhere to work every day! If only they'd been born in ancient times when this was how everyone lived! Having nothing to do, the man grabs his club to go on a hunt. He tracks down his prey, leaps upon it, and battles it to its death. He carries his trophy home on his shoulders and hangs it over the fire as his woman and the children gather about to watch it cook. If only their lives could be like this—how much happier they would be!

Instead, every morning the man dons his suit and rides the commuter train to a distant workplace, and every night he returns home sullen and spent. Wasn't this the very prescription for an unhappy life? To Mrs. Aoki, it had certainly begun to seem so.

In the darkness, her husband seemed lost in thought.

"You can't get to sleep?" she asked.

"No, no," he said in haste, "I was just starting to drift off." After a pause he added, "I guess it's because of that long nap I took."

"Shall I do some magic that'll help you sleep?"

She brought her face directly before his and edged slowly closer until their eyelids almost touched. It was not magic; it was a special caress she'd invented. With their eyelashes touching, she began blinking her eyes, stroking his eyelashes with the up and down of her own. It brought an odd sensation—like the rapid-fire chatter of two tiny birds absorbed in conversation, or like the last stage of a Japanese sparkler when the tiny ball of fire on the tip starts shooting snowflake sparks in every direction.

In the darkness, she went on blinking her eyes. The motion of her eyelids comforted and soothed, but she could not keep them from also questioning, reproaching.

Mr. Aoki decided to start going to work again.

His vacation of ten days was over. He'd had to call an end to it when the boys began to ask, "How long do you get to take off?"

He also had to consider the suspicious glances some of the neighbors had begun to cast his way. One of the ladies had even asked Mrs. Aoki some rather prying questions at the grocery.

Secrets like this had a way of spreading with astonishing speed. Though none of his former colleagues lived nearby, you could never tell where one of the neighbors might hear something through the grapevine.

But his more immediate concern was the boys. Since he had told them that he was on vacation, he could not simply go on lolling about the house forever; and in any case, he needed to start looking for a new job. Thus, Mr. Aoki decided to resume leaving the house every morning at the same time as he used to leave for work.

The first day, after her husband had gone, Mrs. Aoki suddenly felt limp with exhaustion. In her mind she saw the figure of her husband walking aimlessly through the city streets beneath the late summer sun. The pangs of her husband's anguish as he trudged uneasily along the bustling street, ever fearful that he might meet someone he knew, seemed to pierce her own heart.

She imagined him gazing up at the screen in the darkness of a movie theater where he'd gone to escape being seen. Or she imagined him sitting on a bench at a department store, watching the mothers who had brought their children to play on the rooftop playground.

But then these images abruptly broke up, to be replaced by a vision of her husband quietly climbing the stairs to an unfamiliar apartment building. Her blood turned to ice.

"No! Don't go there. Don't, don't, don't!" she screamed, but her husband continued his slow ascent. "Stop!" she cried. "If you go there, it's all over. It's all over."

The vision returned again and again no matter how many times she tried to drive it away.

Evening came, and Mrs. Aoki found herself in the kitchen once again. Like a person who has come down with a fever, a feeling of listless fatigue weighed heavy on every corner of her body.

In the street out front the boys jabbered back and forth as they played catch.

"They're incredibly fast!"

"Mexican Indians."

"They can chase antelopes all day and not even get winded."

"The tribe's name is Tarahumara. Ta-ra-hu-ma-ra."

"I sure wish they'd come to Japan sometime."

Disjointed snatches of the boys' conversation came to her between pops of the ball.

Will he come home? she wondered miserably. I just want him to come home safe and sound—that's all. I don't care if he doesn't have a job, I don't care about anything else, just so long as he doesn't abandon this family.

She took a match and lit the gas burner, then reached up to get a pan from the shelf.

"Just so long as he comes home . . ."

A quiet hush hung over the pool.

The ropes separating the lanes had been removed, and in the middle of the pool bobbed a lone man, only his head showing above water. The interscholastic swim meet would begin tomorrow, so today's practice had been cut two hours short and the swimmers sent home early. Now the coach was picking up debris from the bottom of the pool with his toes.

The evening breeze sent a rush of tiny waves rippling across the surface of the water from time to time.

Soon a train slid into view along the tracks beyond the pool, and the eyes of the passengers returning from work took in the quiet scene. The usual girl's swim team was gone, and a man's head bobbed all alone on the surface of the water.

PART TWO

family album

STILL LIFE

"Can we go to the fishing pond?" the boy pleaded.

It was a beautiful, windless day in early March, and spring seemed just around the corner.

"You don't want to go fishing," his father said. "You know you'd never catch anything."

"I do too want to. All the kids go. Masuko caught five the other day."

"What were they?"

"Goldfish."

"Oh. Goldfish." Father's voice showed his disappointment. "It's not much fun if all you get is goldfish."

"It is too fun. Some of the kids even catch big ones."

"Oh?"

"You'll catch something too, Dad. You will." The boy would be entering the second grade in another month.

"I don't know," Father said. "It'd be my first time. The only fishing I've ever done was in the ocean. I've never been to one of those artificial ponds." Even to him the excuse sounded rather feeble.

"You should try it," chimed in his daughter, soon to be a sixth grader. "Who knows? You just might catch something. And so what if you don't? It'll be fun anyway."

"I suppose you're right," he said. "I'll never know if I don't give it a try."

"If all three of us go, maybe at least one of us'll catch something," the girl said, seeing that her father had abandoned his reluctance. She often spoke to him like this, in an encouraging tone, when he seemed hesitant or worried about something. It was a remarkable way she had with him.

On that morning so many years before, this girl had lain in the corner of the room with her stuffed puppy, alone like an orphan, oblivious to the possibility that anything could be wrong. She had been just over one year old then.

"Have a good time!" Mother called after them. "Bring home your appetites now, all of you." The three-year-old boy had to stay behind. He was too small to go fishing.

As they left the house, Father had a pleasant feeling inside. It felt good to set out on something he had never done before. And the children's enthusiasm was contagious.

The boy had brought along the tin bucket he used for his water projects in the yard. As they walked, Father watched it swing back and forth at his son's side. He should get out and do these things more often, he told himself. It was better to go along, to stop making excuses. It didn't really matter whether or not they caught anything. They had set out, bucket in hand—that was the important part. It seemed a little thing, but perhaps it was these little things that did the trick.

To begin with, anything was better than just sitting around doing nothing. All he ever did on his days off was loaf about the house. He never made plans for a Sunday outing, much less went anywhere when Sunday finally rolled around. Sometimes he felt sorry for his family. But he had been this way for a long time now, and the children had grown used to it. So far as they were concerned, holidays were for staying at home and playing by themselves. They had fun enough.

Still, it wasn't good for him to be so lazy. After all, the fishing pond was hardly ten minutes away.

Down the road, the pond came into view, surrounded by rice paddies. Beyond it rose the slope of a wooded hill. There were two ponds, actually—one stocked with small fish, for beginners, and the other with larger fish, for more experienced fishermen. As might be expected on a Sunday, both were crowded.

"One adult and one child," Father said, as if he were buying tickets for the train. He didn't know any differently, since this was the first time he had come. He paid for an hour and got two fishing poles and some bait. But the last person to use one of the poles had returned it with the line badly tangled. No doubt he had gone home in a huff after failing to catch anything. Father couldn't tell where to start, so he asked the lady at the gate to unravel it for him.

"There you go." She handed the pole back to him with a smile.

"It's fixed?"

"Yes, it should be okay now."

Too eager to wait, the boy had run on ahead, but now he was back. "C'mon, Dad, hurry up," he shouted. "I found a good spot. Over there." The place he pointed to, however, was at the pond for experienced fishermen. Not one of the people there was using the sort of flimsy pole the three newcomers had rented. It was also more expensive to fish there.

"We can't go over there," the girl said.

"But you should see. There's lots of big ones."

"No," the girl said softly. "That pond's too hard for us. Beginners have to fish here."

"Oh."

After the lady had shown him how to bait the hooks, Father joined the children at the beginners' pond. There were quite a few adults fishing there, too—men fishing alone, young married couples fishing together.

The three of them shared the two poles, but they failed to get so much as a nibble. Whenever someone else caught something, the boy ran off to have a look, and each time he would call back in a loud voice, "It's better over here, Dad."

"Listen," Father admonished. "Whether you catch anything or not, you're better off staying in one place. When somebody over there catches something, you might think it's a better spot, but it isn't really. It just seems that way. Some people are good at it and some people aren't, but even the good ones have to wait and be patient and not change places all the time if they want to catch anything. You'll never have any luck if you don't sit still."

His own words reminded him of a story he had read in English class in junior high school. It was called "Stick to Your Own Bush." As he remembered it, several children go off into the woods to pick wild raspberries. They spread out among the raspberry bushes scattered here and there, and before long shouts of "I found some! I found some!" ring out, first from one direction, then another. One of the boys, who has yet to find a single berry, races about from place to place pursuing each new shout. When all the others have filled their baskets, he has only a few berries. "You'll never get very many that way," he is told. "Stick to your own bush." And that was the moral of the story—that it's the same with everything we do.

As a boy he had found it a dull and uninspiring story. But now he was a father, and here he was, telling his own son the same thing.

The scolding put an end to the boy's shouting, but, with no change in their own luck, he still darted off periodically to examine the fish that other people caught.

From where Father was sitting he could not actually see the fish in the water. He had to admit there might not be any there. Nonetheless he stuck to his own bush.

"I guess this isn't our day," he said to his daughter beside him. "It's not so easy after all." She went on gazing at her float.

Every now and then women with shopping baskets passed along the road in front of the pond. Some of them stopped briefly to watch the fishermen. Father had been observing these movements on the road when he turned around to find his float bobbing up and down. He raised his pole with a jerk. On the end of the line was a tiny orange glimmer.

"We got one!" cried the girl.

The boy, who had been watching an older boy fish, heard her voice and came running.

"We got one! We got one!" he clamored.

"Simmer down. Don't make such a racket," Father scolded. But his face beamed. It was indeed a tiny goldfish that had come up on the end of his line, hardly any bigger than a guppy.

Now for the first time they had a use for the bucket the boy had brought along. The little fish swam about in the pail as if to belie the fact that a moment ago it had been caught on the tip of a hook.

2

"W-w-when they've tried it once," the elderly doctor said, "they get so they try it again and again."

"That's what I was afraid of," the young husband sighed. Never had he imagined that only three years after his marriage he would feel so beaten and discouraged.

"At least that's frequently the case."

Would it happen again? he had asked disconsolately. Was she likely to try it again?

"T-t-t-taking it hard, are you?" the doctor burst into a boisterous, stuttering laugh. But there was a measure of sympathy in his voice. This distinctive laugh of the doctor's had long been familiar to the young man.

"Once is enough, I suppose?"

"It certainly is."

The doctor reached for the bottle and poured some more whiskey for his guest. The young man watched as the dark liquid rose inside the glass.

"These things can happen. You just never know," the doctor said. He picked up the pitcher and mixed a little water with the whiskey.

"As they say, we all walk in darkness."

The old doctor's sitting room was an annex of sorts, built on a level slightly higher than the main section of the house. He spent most of his time alone here, apart from the rest of his family. When he needed something, he simply clapped his hands. He never left the room except to see a patient.

The two sat facing each other, the bottle of whiskey on the table between them. Somehow, the young man always felt reassured when he talked with the old doctor like this.

The young man had been born and raised in this town, and his earliest memory of the doctor's clinic went back to when he was in the third grade. One day he was playing in a field near his house with a friend, running about barefoot on the grass, when all of a sudden he stepped on a piece of wood with a large nail sticking through it. His friend rushed off to get his mother, while he sat there crying. It had seemed an eternity before she appeared at the edge of the field.

The next thing he remembered was lying on an examination table in a dimly lit room while the doctor removed the nail. Tense faces peered down at him from above.

That had been his first visit to this place.

"H-h-how's her foot coming along?" the doctor asked. "Where she burned it."

"I think it still hurts her to walk on it."

"Yes, I'm sure it does. The burn's right on the bottom of her foot."

"She claims it doesn't bother her anymore, though."

The doctor gave him a sympathetic smile, then lowered his eyes.

"I was practically in a state of shock myself," the young man said after another sip of his drink. "I didn't realize the cloth had come loose."

"Of course not, of course not," the doctor laughed with his usual stutter. "It was hardly the time you would notice something like that. Not even your wife noticed, and it was her own foot."

The young man remembered the chill he had felt when he touched his wife's arms and legs. At first he had still been able to detect a slight warmth, but gradually her body had turned colder and colder. Frantically, he had filled three hot water bottles with piping hot water and put them in her bed: one on either side of her chest, the third at her feet.

Later he had held her—first one way, then another—for the doctor to examine her. Beads of sweat had dripped from his forehead. He couldn't tell exactly when she had gotten burned; the cloth he had wrapped around the hot water bottle must have come loose when her legs moved.

The doctor reached for the whiskey and poured himself another glass. "This kind of burn takes a long time to heal. I've had cases before: people go to bed with a hot water bottle and don't realize they've burned themselves until the next morning."

"So it happens often?"

"I guess if you're sleeping soundly it doesn't hurt enough to wake you up. That's the big problem. The damage goes a lot deeper than other burns."

In his mind the young man pictured his wife still limping a little from the accident as she made her way about the quiet house.

3

"Eight-year-old Susie died three days after coming down with the flu," Father read from the paper. He had found an article among the news from America that he thought the others might like to hear. They were all sitting around the breakfast table, eating.

"Susie is a little black girl," he explained before reading on.

"Many friends and neighbors came to express their sympathy to the grief-stricken parents. The funeral service took place without event. But then, when it came time to lower the casket into the grave—"

"Did something go wrong?" the girl broke in.

Father answered her interruption with a sharp look that said "Let me finish," then continued the story. "When the parents raised the lid of the casket for a final look at their daughter, Susie opened her eyes and said, 'Mommy, can I have some milk?' The incident has put the entire town in an uproar."

"She came back to life?" the girl asked. She seemed anxious to have her father say it in so many words.

"That's right, she came back to life."

"Weird," the older boy said and flopped backward onto the tatami. The three-year-old promptly followed suit.

"Imagine what a shock it would have been!" Father said. He tried to form a mental picture of the small southern town where Susie and her parents lived, though, of course, he could not really tell how the houses or streets would have looked. The cemetery would be on the outskirts of town, no doubt, but what was the surrounding area like?

"What an awful story!" his wife said.

"Why? What do you mean?"

"Oh, I don't know," she said, looking very ill at ease. "I mean, my goodness, the child was supposed to be dead when all of a sudden she wakes up and starts talking. If I were the mother, I'd have been terrified." Her husband stared back at her but said nothing. "Wouldn't *you* be scared?"

Suddenly a strange voice filled the room: "Mommy, can I have some milk?"

It was the girl. She had leaned back against the wall and was gazing blankly into space, pretending to be Susie at the moment she came back to life.

What would it sound like? Father wondered: the voice of someone who had all but entered the realm of the dead and then returned suddenly to the brightness of this world.

"Ohhh, don't do that," Mother scolded the girl. "It gives me the shivers."

4

The goldfish from the Sunday excursion was given a place in the children's study. It swam about happily in its glass bowl on the sill of the bay window.

"What a healthy goldfish!" Mother often exclaimed. She was the one who looked after the new family pet most of the time—changing its water, feeding it little scraps of bread, and giving it a pinch of salt every now and then.

When Father and the children had come home with their tiny catch in the toy bucket, she had remarked on what a nice shape it had. It was true, Father had had to agree: It might be only so big, but it did have a nice, sleek body.

An almost invisible tinge of red showed here and there on its stomach and fins as well as on its head.

"I caught it when I was looking the other way," he had said. "We'd better take good care of it."

The study held quite a few things besides desks and bookshelves for the two children who were in school. Their mother's dresser was kept here, together with her sewing machine. In one corner was a basket containing some wooden blocks, the base of a ring-toss game, a baseball glove, and several other items—the few toys the children hadn't managed to break. In another corner stood two large suitcases, one on top of the other. They had seldom been used; most of the time they merely took up space.

To call it the children's study, then, was something of a misnomer. It was the room where they put everything that didn't fit anywhere else.

On the wall were two pictures. The one entitled "Star Children" had been made by the girl as a summer vacation project several years before. Two little girls were holding hands and floating in a light-blue sky, a star made of silver paper atop each of their heads. Their clothes had been cut from scraps of leftover fabric, and bits of yellow and gray yarn had been pasted on for hair. The second picture, entitled "Cowboys on the Plain," was a crayon drawing done by the older of the boys. One of the cowboys, a rifle at his shoulder, had just shot a large bird in a tree; the other was about to lasso a runaway horse. A bull came charging toward them and a rabbit was scampering by.

Two rattan chairs had also found their way into the room. Since they would block the doorway if set side by side, they were usually stacked on top of each other. The children liked to hitch these together with their desk chairs to make a stagecoach. One of them sat on the coachman's seat and the other two would get inside. Then, with many a shout and crack of the whip and clatter of the wheels, they would be off, racing full tilt along some old highway.

Such was the room into which the goldfish had come. It hardly seemed a safe place for a fragile glass bowl filled with water. There was no telling when a ball or some other toy might land in it, or when one of the children would get pushed against it and knock it over.

But incredibly enough, nothing happened. The children were no better behaved than they had ever been, yet somehow the bowl survived. As the days went by it blended in with the other things in the room, and no one worried about it anymore.

Still, Father could never quite get over the feeling that someone would break it yet, someday.

5

"Good night, Dad!"
"Good night, Mom!"
"Good night, everyone!"

The echo of the children's voices seemed to linger in the air. Only a short while ago they had been racing to see who could put on his pajamas and make it into bed first. Now, with the hush of night settling over the house, only Father remained awake.

He contemplated the figure of his wife sleeping beside him. This woman, lying on her side, facing him—this was the woman he had married. For fifteen years he had slept with her, in the same bed, every night.

As a child he had slept alone, and in the navy he had slept alone. But from the day he was married, he had started sharing a bed with another person. Two people who scarcely knew each other had begun to sleep together, just like that.

There had in fact been a short time when they did not share the same bed. How long had it been? Three months? Not even that, probably. They had slept in separate rooms, his wife with their baby daughter, who had just turned one. But the arrangement had come to a quick end. After the incident, they had gone back to sleeping together. And they had done so ever since.

Awake alone in the stillness, Father thought back to their wedding night. He remembered the bright moonlight shining through the window, illumining his wife's face as she slept quietly beside him. She had hardly seemed to breathe. There was a small ribbon in her hair.

That was our first night together, he thought to himself.

The book he had been reading slipped from his hand. He picked it up again and started looking for his place.

"Here it is," he mumbled. "No, wait, I've read this already." He turned several more pages. Was this it? No, he remembered this part too. Where could it have been?

Choosing a page at random, he forced open his heavy eyelids and began to read. Within moments they drooped shut, and the book fell from his hand.

6

"I forget if it was England or America, but I read a story about a boy who found a duck's egg and made it hatch," the boy told his father in their evening bath.

"He *hatched* a duck's egg?"

"Uh-huh."

"Where did he find it?"

"I don't know."

"Somewhere in the country?"

"Uh-huh, in the country."

"Near a stream or pond, I suppose."

"Maybe. Anyway, he wanted to make it hatch, so he tied it to his stomach with a piece of cloth."

"Where?"

"Right here." The boy cupped his hands at his side. Father could tell that he had picked the spot arbitrarily.

"He kept it warm like that all the time for twenty days or so. Even at school, and even when he went to bed."

"For twenty days?"

"Uh-huh, something like that, I don't remember exactly. Anyway, the egg finally hatched right in the middle of class, and the teacher and everyone was really surprised."

"That's amazing," Father said. "It actually hatched during class?"

"Uh-huh."

"And everyone was surprised?"

"Uh-huh."

"Is this something you read at school?"

"Uh-huh. On the bulletin board in the hall. There's a big paper with stories from all over the world."

"Was there a picture?"

"Some of the stories have pictures, but this one didn't."

"When did you read this story?"

"A long time ago."

"Back in first grade?"

"Uh-huh."

"And you happened to think of it now?"

"Uh-huh."

Father wondered what had made him remember the story. "You'd think he would've broken it," he said. "I wonder how he had it tied."

"I bet the egg wouldn't last a day if I did it," the boy said. "I'd forget about it when I was playing. Do you think you could do it, Dad?"

"No, I doubt it. Probably not," he said. "All right, ready to get out?"

"Yep." The boy jumped out of the tub.

"Just a minute," Father stopped him. "Did you wash your face?"

"My face?"

"If you have to think about it, you obviously didn't."

"Yes I did."

"Ohhh no, you can't fool me. Your face isn't even wet. Since when do you take a bath without washing your face? Come on. Stop stalling."

"Okay." The boy took the lid off the soap dish and filled it with hot water.

"Hey, no playing around now. Just wash your face."

"I will, I will." He laid his washcloth over the soap dish.

"Come on."

"Just a second." With a slow and deliberate motion he rubbed soap into the washcloth. Then, bringing the cloth to his lips, he blew on it gently. A soft bank of suds began to form.

"See."

"So that's what you wanted to do."

"Watch. They'll get bigger and bigger."

"Fine, fine. They're plenty big already."

"Isn't it neat?"

"Sure."

"You wanna try it?"

"No. You've shown me your little trick now, so hurry up with your face."

"Just a little more."

The heap of suds quivered gently as it swelled. Before long the boy's face was completely hidden.

7

"I wonder if you remember that movie we saw," Father said to his daughter. She was sewing a blouse for her doll.

"What movie?"

"When you were in the first grade. Or was it kindergarten? No, it wasn't the year we moved; it was the year after. So you would've been in first grade."

The family had moved here from another city when the girl was in kindergarten. The older boy had just started putting a few words together; the second had not yet been born. Father could still remember the long train ride and his first glimpse of their new house standing by itself in the middle of some open farmland.

The following year, in the winter, he had taken his daughter to see a movie.

"The foreman at a construction site falls into a pit being filled with concrete."

"Oh yeah, I remember," the girl said.

"How much do you remember?"

She stopped stitching. "The man was a carpenter, wasn't he?"

"Well, yes, he built houses. He laid bricks, though, so I suppose you'd call him a mason. He was in Italy at first, but then he got on a ship and came to New York."

"He was really poor."

"That's right. That was why he came to America. He couldn't make a living in Italy."

They had seen the movie in a theater at the back of a short alleyway, just off the main thoroughfare in front of the station. Even with their overcoats on, it had been chilly inside.

"He was sick or something and couldn't go to work."

"I think he had hurt himself," Father said, still trying to retrieve the details from his own hazy memory. "That's right. He becomes foreman of a demolition crew tearing down an old building, but then something goes wrong between him and his men and they don't get along very well anymore. First the men stop speaking to him, then they walk out on him. So he has to work all by himself. Pretty soon a wall falls over on him and his leg gets crushed."

"That's why he couldn't work?"

"Something like that."

"Oh, I remember now. It's when his leg finally gets better and he goes back to work that he falls into the hole they're filling with concrete. He screams for help but there's too much noise and no one hears him. So the concrete keeps getting higher and higher."

"And in the end only his head shows."

"I covered my eyes, it was so scary. But I couldn't help hearing his screams."

"What happened next?"

"His wife comes out with kind of a blank look on her face, and someone's talking to her."

"Right. Since her husband was killed on the job, she's supposed to get paid a lot of money. Someone asks her what she plans to do with it, but she only shakes her head, to say she doesn't know. Or maybe she means she hasn't even thought about it. Do you remember anything else?"

"Unh-unh."

"No? How about the book I bought you before we went into the movie?"

"Unh-unh." She picked up her sewing and began stitching again. Father watched the way her hands moved.

As he remembered, it was a picture book, but he couldn't recall the title. He had bought her the book to try to make up for dragging her along, on their one day off, to a movie that *he* wanted to see. Not only was it a foreign film, but the things he had heard about it suggested that it might be a bit heavy going for a six-year-old.

The first few scenes were mild enough. One of the mason's friends at work tells him he ought to get married and suggests a girl he knows. The mason starts seeing the girl and falls in love with her. And she falls in love with him.

"But what about a house?" she asks. "I can't marry you if you don't have a house." Her family, too, had emigrated from Italy. She knows what it's like to be poor. She knows how miserable life can be for a couple who marry without a house of their own.

The mason tells her that he has a house, believing this is the only way he can get her to marry him. The wedding is held. Immigrant families from the neighborhood gather for a joyous celebration.

Everything was fine up to this point. But then the bride finds out that the house she thought was theirs belongs to someone else. Her happy smile vanishes. She had always been a cheerful, lighthearted girl, but now she sinks into gloom.

They begin their married life in a small, shabby apartment. On the wall they carve little notches with a knife, a record of their determination, no matter what the sacrifice, to save enough money to buy a house. Then a child is born.

As the movie continued, the events unfolding on screen became more and more harrowing. Early one morning the mason comes home drunk, having spent the night with another woman. On his way up the stairs of the apartment building, he decides to punish himself. He swings his open palm down on the pointed tip of the newel post.

No! Father caught his breath and quickly turned to look at his daughter. The book he had bought for her on the way to the theater was raised in front of her face. She had instinctively lifted it from her lap, as though merely closing her eyes would not be enough to block out the scene. Clever girl, he thought, breathing a sigh of relief.

The mason continued to suffer one misfortune after another, and with each frightening scene the book on the girl's lap rose, then fell again. Each time, her father let her know when the scene was over. "It's all right now," he would whisper. "You don't want to miss this part."

Near the end, when the mason fell into the pit, Father stole another look at his daughter. Once again she was hunched tensely behind her book. This time the book remained up through the entire scene, while the roar of the falling concrete and the sound of the mason's screams filled the theater.

Suddenly the screen fell silent, and the girl peeked tremulously from behind her book. The mason was nowhere to be seen. His bereaved wife stood all alone, utterly stricken.

"Did . . . did he die?" the girl asked in a tiny voice.

"Yes," he answered.

Father recalled all this as he watched his daughter work at her sewing. That book had really come in handy then, he thought. It had helped her get through the movie without having to watch the scary scenes.

In the same way, his daughter had been spared knowledge of what had happened in her own home on that morning long ago. She was still an infant at the time, and could not have known the meaning of her mother's deep sleep. An invisible hand had gently covered her eyes.

8

"Hey Dad," the older boy said. "Tell us something that begins with *s*."

"Something that begins with *s*?"

"Uh-huh. *S-t*."

"*S-t*?"

"*S-t-o-r-y*. A story."

"What about a story?"

"We want you to tell us one."

"I don't know any stories," Father protested.

"You do too."

"I can't think of any."

"How about the wild boar story?"

"But I've told you that one lots of times."

"That's okay."

Father had run out of excuses. "During the summer," he began, "boars always sleep. They stay at home in their dens, lying on big soft beds made of thatch, and all they do is sleep and sleep and sleep. Thatch—that's what the old hunter who told me this story called it—is a plant that grows in the mountains. Besides using it for beds, the boars make roofs out of it, to keep off the rain when there's a storm and to shade themselves on hot, sunny days. It works very nicely, both ways. So the boars just lie around sleeping in their cozy little thatched houses, day in, day out, all summer long. If that isn't the easy life!" he exclaimed enviously, glancing from the older boy to the younger.

"The old hunter told me, though, that you can't eat boar's meat in the summer. It doesn't taste good. So I guess maybe it's not such a good idea to sit around doing nothing after all. You see, when they butcher a summer boar, there's always a layer of fat as stiff as a board right under the skin. In fact that's what the hunters call it—a 'board.' And they say a boar with a board isn't any good because you can't eat the meat. But actually, the board has a special purpose. It helps keep the boar's energy inside its body so that it can sleep the whole summer long."

"That's why badger's fat is better, right?"

"Right. Badgers are the opposite of boars. They sleep through the winter, which means they have a lot of fat then and almost none in the summer. Badger's fat is really good. If you take some from just under the skin and heat it in a pan, you get a smooth, clear oil. Oh, by the way, there's another special name the hunters use: 'cukes.' That's what they call baby boars, because they have patches of fur on their backs that look just like big, fat cucumbers."

"That's kind of cute," the older boy said.

"That's kinda cute," the younger quickly repeated.

"Mmm, I thought so too. Now, one of the boar's favorite foods is earthworms, of all things. To think that an animal that big would go for worms—when they're known to gobble up a whole patch of sweet potatoes in a single night! The old hunter was really shaking his head over this one. He never could understand why such a big eater would take a liking to tiny little earthworms. And they like spiders and mud snails, too. They dig up the snails with their snouts, just like the worms, but it's a mystery how they eat them because they never leave any shells behind. They must either take them home to eat, or else they swallow the whole thing, shell and all. The hunter said he didn't imagine snails would taste very good with the shell on them." Father tilted his head thoughtfully, then shrugged, "Who knows what they do?"

He went on: "Hunting boars can be pretty rough, I guess. When you walk through the snow looking for tracks, your feet get soaked and clumps of snow fall on you from the branches overhead, and after a while your stomach starts to growl. An important thing to know when you're looking for tracks is that boars always travel the same paths. Maybe they're just the methodical type, or maybe they're actually afraid of something—I don't know. But in any case they always follow exactly in each other's footsteps. So no matter how many boars have gone by, it looks like only one. That's how consistent they are.

"One time a terrible thing happened because of this. At the power station in the mountains there's a sluice for the water that turns the generators, and it has a log lying across it for a bridge. One snowy morning the workers at the plant found three dead boars washed against the sluice gates. They went up along the sluice to see if they could find out what had happened, and when they got to the log they discovered there was an icy spot about halfway across. What had happened was the first boar to come along that morning had slipped on the ice and fallen into the water. Since the sluice is made of concrete and the sides go straight up and down, the boar had no place to climb out, and it got swept away by the current. Then the second one came along, and, because it followed the first boar's tracks onto the log, it slipped at the same place. After a while a third one came and fell into the water just like the others. Poor things. The men couldn't tell whether the boars had come one right after the other or a long time apart, but they could see what had happened from the way the tracks ended in the middle of the log."

"They should've watched out better," the older boy said.

"They should've watched out better," his younger brother echoed.

"That's right, they might have been okay if they had only stopped to think, 'Hey, wait a minute. The tracks don't go all the way across.' But they didn't, I guess. Well then, let's get back to the story about the old hunter meeting up with the wild boar."

The boys leaned forward. This was the part they had been waiting for.

"When he was in the mountains one day, the hunter came across a boar's den—made of thatch, as I said. He went home and told three of his hunter friends about it, and without letting anyone else know of their plans they got ready to go back for the kill. You see, you have to have at least three or four hunters to get a boar. If you try to do it alone, the boar will always get away. On the day of the hunt—remember, this all happened before the hunter was as old as he is now—the four of them set off for the mountains early in the morning. As it turned out, there was another group of hunters that had somehow gotten wind of their plans and had left even earlier. But the old hunter and his friends didn't know this yet, and they hiked on and on through the underbrush toward the boar's den. They came to a small cliff and started climbing it, when all of a sudden they heard a panting sound and boom!—"

Pretending he was the hunter crawling up the side of a cliff, Father jerked his head back.

"Just as the old hunter started to pull himself over the top, he found himself face to face with a giant boar. Talk about being caught off guard! They had all assumed the boar would be fast asleep in its den! The hunter immediately ducked down and reached for the rifle slung across his back. And the startled boar retreated, too, almost as quickly."

Now Father acted the part of the wild boar, first leaning forward as if poking his head over the edge of the cliff, then hastily pulling back.

"The hunter thought the boar had decided to run back the way it came, and if he didn't hurry it would get away, so he started to scramble up after it. But *whoosh!*—the boar flew right past his head, landed with a tremendous skid at the bottom of the cliff, and went crashing into the underbrush below. By the time the hunters turned around, all they could see were the broken branches where the boar had disappeared, and, farther on, the churning of the undergrowth as it ran off."

"Wow!" the older boy exclaimed.

The younger boy sat speechless, his wide eyes glued to his father's face.

"What had happened was that the other hunters, the ones who had gone earlier, had already shot at the boar and put it in a panic. That's probably why it made such a desperate leap. So when the old hunter thought the boar had taken off in the other direction, actually it had only backed up a little way to get a running start for the jump." Father broke into a laugh for a moment but then finished the story with a straight face. "The hunter said someone else finally shot the boar a week or so later. And that's the end of the story."

9

Their uncle came to visit them from the town where they had lived before moving to their present home. He brought with him a bag of walnuts for the children.

"What a nice gift," Father said afterward. "We couldn't spend money on nuts for ourselves—they're too much of an extravagance. But as a gift for someone with children, they're perfect. A real treat. A chance for the children to have something we couldn't normally afford."

But how would they divide up the nuts? Mother decided as follows: the girl could have seven, the older boy five, and the younger boy three. That would still leave two, so she and her husband could have one each.

The older boy went to get the hammer and quickly finished off his share. The younger boy ate all of his, too, with Mother's help to crack them open. Mother waited to eat hers until the following afternoon when she was at home alone with the younger boy. Father slipped his into his pocket; he still had it when he went to work the next day, but lost it somewhere the day after.

The girl decided to save hers for a while. She put them in a drawer in her desk, and took them out one at a time to polish them with a piece of felt. She wanted to bring out their shine.

A few days later she told her two best friends at school about the nuts. "They were a present from my uncle when he came to visit," she explained. "Do you like walnuts? If you want, I'll bring you some tomorrow."

"Sure," they said. They both liked walnuts.

Should she give them each two, or only one? she wondered. If she gave them two, they could rub them together in their hands to make a grinding noise, and they'd have more fun with them. But if she gave each of them two, that would leave her with fewer than half of her original seven. She wasn't sure she liked that idea. She enjoyed watching the walnuts roll around when she opened the drawer, and it just wouldn't be the same with only three nuts left. To give two would be better, of course. There was no question of that. But even one was better than nothing.

When she was getting ready for school the next day, she took four walnuts from the drawer and dropped them into the pocket of her skirt.

At school she ran into one of her friends. "I brought the walnuts," she said, reaching into her pocket. She still hadn't made up her mind whether she would give one or two.

"Here." She held out a single walnut.

"Thank you," her friend said gratefully.

That afternoon she walked home with her other friend, Ikuko. As they passed through the school gate she handed her a walnut.

"Thanks," said Ikuko.

"Try this. It's fun," she said, taking the other two nuts from her pocket and rubbing them together.

"That's neat," Ikuko said. The girl lent Ikuko one of her walnuts. Ikuko rubbed the nuts together for a while as they walked, then gave back the one she had borrowed.

"Not very long after that," the girl later recounted to her father, "we went by a place where some men were working on the road. We still had the nuts in our hands, but I guess I wasn't really paying attention because all of a sudden Ikuko said, 'Hey, you dropped one of your walnuts.' So we turned around to look for it right away, and guess what. We hadn't gone back more than five or six steps when one of the construction workers said, 'I bet you're looking for a walnut, aren't you?' and started laughing. He said he'd already eaten it and showed us the shell broken right in half."

"And the nut was all gone?" Father asked.

"Uh-huh."

"Was he still chewing?"

"No, he wasn't. He'd already swallowed it. It couldn't have been more than a couple of seconds."

"Mmm."

"What I want to know is how could he have cracked that hard shell? With his teeth? We told him he was mean and just came on home, but we were really mad."

"I can imagine," Father nodded. After a pause he said, "I guess the nut must have rolled right in front of him—right where he happened to be looking."

10

The goldfish seemed to have grown since it first joined the family. Its stomach had filled out; the faint patches of red were now a deeper hue; and with each passing day it looked more and more like an adult fish. Everyone enjoyed watching it dart briskly around its bowl on the sunny windowsill.

"I don't think I've ever seen such a peppy goldfish before," Mother said.

"Yes, we should count ourselves lucky," Father replied. "Let's hope he stays that way."

Every other day Mother changed about half of the water and sprinkled in a pinch of salt, and every third day she gave the fish some bread crumbs or pieces of crackers or cookies. When the children wanted to feed it, she made them take turns, and she kept track of the days to ensure they didn't feed it too much or too often.

Father did not help with the fish, but from time to time he would go into the children's study and watch it move about in its bowl. Such balance! he marveled. With the slightest flick of its fins and an occasional twitch of its tail, the fish could hold itself perfectly still, going neither forward nor backward, for as long as it wished.

He and the children had recently made a second trip to the fishing pond. This time, however, the little tin bucket proved useless, for they failed to catch even a single fish. Nor were they the only ones to come up empty-handed; nobody else's luck appeared any better, at either of the ponds.

As evening approached, the air over the pond grew heavier and heavier.

"This time it looks pretty hopeless," Father sighed. "No one's getting anything." Even changing the bait seemed a waste of effort. Still, he stuck it out at the same spot until the hour they had paid for was up.

The fish he had caught the last time now became more precious than ever. There was a big difference between catching one fish and catching none at all. To have hooked that one fish almost began to seem like a special meeting of fates.

An old man wearing a hunter's cap started to put his gear away. "I should've known better than to come today," he muttered grumpily as he left. "Fishing's never any good when the wind's out of the east."

A few minutes later they were all given a start. Over at the other pond, a boy who had been watching his father fish fell into the water with a loud splash. Everyone turned to see the fisherman pulling his son out. The child, soaked from the neck down, looked to be about ten years old.

A gentle wave of laughter spread among the few people remaining at the pond. The incident dispelled the oppressive mood that had descended over the place, and everyone relaxed again.

Frustrated and tired from an afternoon spent in vain, the man had apparently started to doze off. When he leaned over against his son, the boy had lost his balance and tumbled into the water.

Having retrieved his son—instead of a fish—from the pond, the man could hardly go on fishing. The sun was low in the sky as the two left for home, the hapless boy sloshing awkwardly along behind his father.

11

"I wonder what's wrong with this thing," Father mumbled to himself. "It manages to flower all right, but it always looks so scraggly."

On Sunday morning he had stepped out into the yard to take a closer look at the lilac bush. His eyes moved from the long, spindly branches, to the clusters of tiny, purple flowers, and to the ground underneath the bush.

He had planted this bush five springs before—the year after they had moved to this house. But once it had reached a height slightly taller than he was, it had stopped growing. It never developed a main trunk; instead, it had split at the base into a mass of skinny branches that fanned out toward the sky.

He had originally hoped it would grow large and full enough for the children to hide behind when they played games of hide-and-seek. This no longer seemed likely.

He was still contemplating the lilac when a band of street musicians came into view down the road. The man at the head of the troupe pranced about nimbly in time with the music, turning first one way, then the other.

He keeps people's attention that way, thought Father. If he walked along normally, there wouldn't be anything to watch.

From where he stood inside the fence, Father continued to follow the dancer's movements as the band moved closer. Suddenly he saw that the dancer was not a man at all, but a woman—a rather skinny woman dressed in a man's clothes and made up with white greasepaint.

Behind her came a second dancer in a similar outfit, only this one actually was a man. Third in line was a woman in a black beret playing the clarinet. Next came the drummer, beating with exaggerated flourish on the rack of gongs and tom-toms strapped to his chest. A trumpet player wearing a radioman's cap brought up the rear.

The procession came to a halt. The three musicians continued playing while the two dancers went from house to house passing out handbills.

The older boy had come out of the house to watch from the side of the road. Now the drummer approached him and said something. The boy stared back, but his lips did not move.

Why didn't he answer? Father wondered. What could the man have said?

The group slowly moved away again, and the boy came back into the yard.

"Did the drummer say something to you?" Father asked.

"Uh-huh."

"What did he say?"

"I had my fingers in my ears," the boy said, "and I was pushing them in and out to make the music sound real loud and then real quiet." He demonstrated as he explained, putting his fingers to his ears again. "So the man said if I had to plug my ears like that, I shouldn't come so close, I should go somewhere else."

"I see," Father nodded.

"I guess he thought I didn't like their music," the boy grinned.

12

On Sunday evening Father took out his sketchbook and began to draw a picture of his daughter. She had gotten ready for bed after an early bath, then settled down on the tatami in the front room to read. She saw what her father was doing and tried her best to sit perfectly still for him.

"Are you getting stiff?" he asked her after a while.

"No, not particularly." She sat with her legs flopped to one side and the book open in her lap. The big toe of one foot peeked out from behind the other knee. Father started sketching the toe.

"No, that's too big, I guess," he said, mostly to himself.

"What's too big?" the girl asked.

"Your toe."

"It better not be," she giggled.

"Do you remember your grandpa?" Father asked as he rubbed the toe out.

"A little," she nodded.

"I was just thinking of the time he told me to make a drawing of your feet."

"My feet?"

"Uh-huh."

"What for?"

"It was a day or two after you were born."

"Why my feet?"

"He said it'd be fun to have later on." He started outlining the toe again. "All I had with me was my address book, so I drew a little sketch in that. Just the bottoms of your feet. I suppose it got thrown out somewhere along the way."

"Too bad."

"Yes, I wish we still had it. You'd get a kick out of it. With my knack for losing things, I wonder if Grandpa really thought I'd keep it all this time. . . . Hmm, I guess this hand isn't quite right, either." He started to reshape the hand holding the book. "I remember how impressed Grandpa was with the hospital room. He kept saying it would make a great apartment, and that they should rent it out to us."

"Can I move my legs a little now?" the girl asked.

"Sure, go ahead. It really was a nice room. A quiet room, perfect for reading. The windows faced the nurses' dormitory, and every once in a while we'd see one of them dash across the street through the rain. I remember there was a big paulownia tree by the front entrance . . . Why can't I get these fingers right? The more I work on them the worse they get."

The girl looked up and glanced at her father's sketchbook.

"That day," he went on, "as I was leaving the hospital, I ran into your grandpa coming through the rain, wearing a hat but without an umbrella. He was on his way to see your mother. We stepped under the eaves to talk for a couple of minutes, and do you know what he said? He had never been to a maternity ward before; he had never visited anyone who'd just had a baby. So I decided to go back to the hospital with him. Later, when we were leaving, he told me not to worry— every day a baby lives it builds up that much more strength to survive. You see, we were having a terrible time getting you to nurse. You kept falling asleep as soon as you got the nipple in your mouth, even when one of the nurses pulled on your ear. We didn't know what to do with you."

The girl giggled sheepishly.

13

"Guess what we found at school today," the girl said at the dinner table. "A mole cricket. We were digging in the flower bed, and—"

"Another mole cricket!" exclaimed Mother. "Yesterday it was your brother who found one. He comes in the door after school, and, before I even have a chance to ask him how his day was, he dangles this ugly creature in front of my face and says 'Look, I brought you a present.'"

"You should've seen her jump," the boy said gleefully.

"Of course I jumped. How many times do I have to tell you? You can bring home anything you like as far as the front door, but I won't have you bringing bugs into the house."

"So-o-rr-y."

"So what did you do with the mole cricket in the flower bed?" Father asked.

"Mine was in the sandbox," the boy said.

"The sandbox? You mean you brought it home all the way from school?"

"Yep."

"When we caught the one in the flower bed," the girl said, "we held it like this and asked it, 'How bi-i-ig is so-and-so's brain?' and it would sort of wiggle in surprise and spread its front legs."

"Whoever thought *that* up?" Father wanted to know.

"We all thought it up together. When you say your own name, you say 'BI-I-IG' real loud," she said, putting extra stress on the B. "Then it spreads its legs way far apart, like this. But when you say someone else's name, you say the words real soft: 'How big?'" This time she lowered her voice to a whisper. "Then it only moves its legs a tiny bit." She demonstrated with her arms as she spoke.

"You're making this up, right?" Mother said.

"No, it's true, it was like the mole cricket really heard. So we started doing the same thing as the cricket, and spread *our* arms real wide, too, when we said our own names."

"As if the poor thing wasn't startled enough already," Father said.

The girl seemed endlessly amused by the way the mole cricket squirmed in surprise. She went through her "How bi-i-ig?" antics several more times, transforming herself from little girl into mole cricket and back again, then collapsing in a fit of laughter.

"How bi-i-ig?" the older boy said, moving his arms like his sister.

"How bi-i-ig?" the younger boy imitated.

"*So-o* big."

"*So-o* big."

"All right, all right," Father said when they all started doing it together. "That's enough. Let's have some quiet for a change. Please."

Even now, in the deserted schoolyard where the children had played that day, the mole crickets would be quietly burrowing their way through the sandboxes and flower beds.

14

Two stuffed toys, a tiger and a rabbit, shared the wide windowsill where the goldfish swam in its bowl. The tiger lay on its stomach, its legs thrust forward. Its head was tilted to one side so that its nose almost touched the ground, and it looked as if it were scrutinizing the movements of some industrious ant. The rabbit, wearing polka-dotted pants, faced the opposite direction. It lay on its back and stared up at the sky.

During the daytime, the two animals sat like this on the sill. Then, when night came, they were taken off to bed by the children. The younger boy always got the rabbit—there were never any quarrels about that. But the older boy and the girl had to take turns with the tiger, and many an argument broke out when one or the other of them missed a day.

One night, Father was getting ready for bed in his room at the end of the hall when he heard the children's voices rise to a fighting pitch. A moment later his wife intervened: "All right, now, who had it the day before yesterday? And yesterday? No, no, you both know the rule—forgetting doesn't count."

It was their own fault if they missed a turn, she explained, as she had so many times before. They could not demand their turn the next day. If that were allowed, neither of them would be able to count on their regular turn anymore, and there'd be no end to the fighting. If they forgot, it was just too bad. They would have to wait for their next turn.

How had this all started? Father wondered. How long had they been having these squabbles?

Sometimes several days went by without either of the children remembering to take the tiger to bed. Since neither of them could recall who had had it last or how long it had been, even their mother couldn't settle whose turn it should be. Eventually, to make sure this didn't happen again, she had begun keeping track by marking the calendar with the children's initials.

Father shook his head as he got under the covers. It was beyond him why they would want to take something like that to bed with them. *He* had slept alone when *he* was a child. And he had taken it for granted that everyone else did, too.

The children's dispute finally came to an end. That night, the tiger would sleep with the girl.

"Lucky stiff!" the boy grumbled loudly.

As Father picked up one of the books lying at the head of the bed, his thoughts drifted off to another stuffed toy they had once had—a puppy, neither so small nor so soft as the tiger the children had just been fighting over. He recalled the Christmas morning, more than ten years before, when he had found the puppy standing beside his baby daughter's bed. The tall, husky puppy had seemed so enormous next to the tiny figure of the baby.

Now what did she go and buy something like that for? he remembered thinking to himself.

Only a few minutes earlier, when he first awoke, he had been equally surprised to find a box, neatly tied with a ribbon, sitting beside his pillow. The box had contained a fedora.

Had he said he wanted one of these? He couldn't remember, but perhaps he had, sometime or other, and his wife had taken him seriously. Or perhaps he had only commented on how nice someone else's looked.

How much did hats like this cost? He really couldn't imagine.

He had never considered buying one for himself, or envisioned himself wearing one to the office, so he'd never had cause to explore the hat section of the department store. His knowledge of hats was pretty much limited to the corduroy cap he got out in the summertime. But that was one of those things you could roll up and stuff in your pocket—it hardly counted as a real hat. The only other hat he had ever worn was a boater, in his student days. He remembered having to hold it with one hand on top to keep it from flying off as he raced to get on the train before the doors slammed shut.

He knew he hadn't paid very much for that boater. But fedoras were in a different class altogether. It must have cost a small fortune. Why had his wife made such an extravagant purchase without consulting him? She knew they didn't have that kind of money to throw around.

Sitting up in bed, he tried on the new hat. He liked it, the way it gently pressed against his head. But he wasn't sure what position he should wear it in. If he pulled it down too far, his head would push out the crease on top and make it look like a bowler instead of a fedora. How did other people wear them? He would have to pay more attention from now on.

He returned the hat to its box and closed the lid.

Since it was a holiday, he could sleep later than usual if he wanted. But the surprise of the hat had left him wide awake. He decided to go ahead and get up.

The quiet of morning filled the house. Outside, clouds hung heavily in the sky.

It was then, when he poked his head into the next room to see if his wife and daughter were awake, that he had had his first glimpse of the toy puppy.

For several moments, all he could do was marvel at its magnificent size and beauty. In any display of stuffed toys, this puppy was bound to reign as king of beasts. Once you had seen it, all the other toys would look like mere knickknacks by comparison.

Clearly it had been made to last. It could probably hold a child on its back without collapsing.

But once again he wondered about the cost. Although he knew even less about stuffed toys than about hats, he could guess it had been expensive. What could his wife have been thinking, spending so much money on a toy like that? With all the daily expenses they had to worry about, she should show a little more sense.

He would have to give her a little scolding, he decided. In fact, he would do it right then and there. So what if it was a holiday? It was already later than usual and time she got started on breakfast.

He called her name, but she slept on without so much as a stir. His wife was one of those people who always looked as though they hadn't had enough sleep, and at night she was lost to the world the moment her head touched the pillow. She seldom dreamed, and was never wakeful. But when the alarm went off the next morning, or when he called her, she would be up in an instant. In all the time they had been married, he couldn't remember having had to call her twice.

"Hey, wake up," he said again, reaching over to shake her shoulder. All of a sudden he noticed that what she had on was not what she normally wore to bed.

As Father lay reflecting on that Christmas morning, he thought again of the puppy. It had proved to be just as sturdy as his first impression had suggested. The girl had played with it for a long time, riding on its back, hanging on with her baby fists clutched tightly around its soft, fluffy ears. She had started doing this even before she learned to walk. When their first son came along, he had played with it, too, bouncing up and down on its back no less gleefully than his sister. But it had still held up as good as new.

Later, when they moved to their new house, the puppy had come with them. Father remembered packing it to be shipped with the other baggage.

"The fedora was a different story though," he sighed. *That* he had lost almost right away. At a movie theater. He had put it on his lap during the show, only to forget about it when he stood up to leave. He was all the way outside before he noticed, and by then it was too late. One of the ushers had kindly gone to retrieve it for him, but came back saying the theater was too crowded. He had had to give it up for lost.

15

When the boys asked for an *s* again one evening, Father told them another story about the old hunter.

"Next to hunting," he began, "the old man's favorite pastime is fishing. He became a hunter first, and he's been making regular trips into the mountains for more than forty years, since he was a young man. Then about thirty years ago, when he moved to the town where he lives now, he took up fishing. He liked the town so much, he's lived there ever since, and he's spent a lot of time at the nearby river ever since, too. He got started fishing, he says, because he found a good river-teacher there."

"A river-teacher?" the older boy laughed.

"That's right. Maybe you've only heard of schoolteachers, but there are river-teachers, too—and mountain-teachers, and even ocean-teachers. A long time ago, this river-teacher had worked as a raftsman for a lumber company. You see, when a lumber company cuts down trees, up in the mountains, the logs are tied together into rafts so they can be floated down the river to the lumber mill. The raftsman is the person who steers the raft down the river, through the rapids and between all the rocks and things sticking up out of the water. It's a really dangerous job. Anyway, after this river-teacher had worked as a raftsman for a while, he decided to settle down in one of the towns along the river and become a fisherman instead. He knew that river like the back of his hand. No one could match him. He could tell you exactly how many fish there were and what they were doing or which way they were swimming anywhere along the river, even in the roughest and deepest places. If you were fishing with him and he said, 'One more,' that meant there was only one fish left in that spot. And he'd be right!"

"Wow!" the older boy exclaimed.

"Wow!" the younger boy mimicked.

"That's incredible," the first added.

"The old hunter couldn't get over it either. He said he'd never heard of anyone who knew so much about rivers and fish. The river-teacher's name was Katsujiro, but since his father's name had been Katsuzo, everyone called him Little Katsu. People still called him that when the hunter met him, even though he was an old man by then."

The older boy laughed when Father said "Little Katsu."

"The problem was that since Little Katsu depended on catching fish for his living, you could never believe what he told you. If you asked him where was a good spot, he would lie and send you off someplace he knew was lousy. The hunter got to be his best friend, and they would drink together almost every night, but he still couldn't get a straight answer out of him. For instance, he might ask if today was a good day, and Little Katsu would say, 'No.' Well, that would turn out to be a lie—the days he said 'No' were in fact the best days. So pretty soon the hunter tried doing the opposite of whatever Little Katsu said. If he said 'No,' the hunter would set out for the river. And sure enough, Little Katsu would be there."

"So he had to listen to him backward," the older boy said.

"That's right. With a teacher like Little Katsu, that was how you learned. Even then the hunter got tricked a lot, so he tried something new. Instead of asking Little Katsu directly, he would sneak up to his house and peek in to see if he was at home. If he found him puttering around the house or just taking a nap or something, he knew there was no sense in going to the river."

"'Cause he knew he wouldn't catch anything even if he did," the boy said.

"Uh-huh. Now, I said Little Katsu lied a lot, but actually there were some things he didn't lie about. Like how to cast a net so it would spread out the way you wanted it to. Or what's the best way to tie the hook to the line. Or how when you're fishing for dace and get a nibble you have to give the line some slack instead of pulling it in right away as most people do.

"It was lucky for the hunter that Little Katsu told the truth about these things. Otherwise he might never have learned how to cast the special sweetfish net that's used only on that river and nowhere else. It's about fifteen feet long, like a huge ribbon, and getting it to spread out just right is pretty tricky. If it goes into the water in a straight line, like this," he drew a line with his finger, "the fish will get away. They can swim right around it. To keep them from doing that, you have to make the net hit the water curved like a bow. Like this." He indicated the curve with a sweep of his arms.

"Like this?" the older boy said, making a similar arc.

"Like this?" his younger brother imitated.

"The reason it makes a difference, you see, is that sweetfish can't turn around very well. When they bump into the net, they just wriggle a little to one side or the other and keep trying to push ahead. That means if both ends of the net are curved back like this, then the fish are forced to swim toward the middle." Father cupped his left hand and poked at it with his right index finger to show how the fish bumped against the net and kept swimming forward until they wound up trapped in the center. The boys paid close attention.

"But if you just leave them there," he went on, "the fish eventually get turned around and find their way out. So, to make sure that doesn't happen, the old hunter swims down underwater to where the net is and breaks their spines."

"What's 'spines'?" the older boy asked.

"Right about here." Father patted the back of his neck. "Then later, after he's got quite a few, he brings them in all at once. He says he used to catch thirty, even forty, in a single night back when he first started fishing. On nights like that he wouldn't even notice how cold the water was. Until he got home, that is. Then he would start shivering like crazy. He'd take a good hot bath and jump into bed with the covers pulled all the way up over his head, and he still couldn't stop shaking. Even in the middle of summer. But you know what? No matter how bad the shivering was, he'd be right back at the river again the very next night. It's hardly a wonder he developed so many aches and pains as he got older, but he just shrugs and says, 'That's the way it goes.'"

"Tell us about the fox," the older boy broke in again.

"Okay. That happened when he was snagging, which is another way to catch sweetfish. Instead of a net, you use a line with a lot of hooks spaced three or four inches apart, and you snag the fish by their gills. Sometimes you can catch five or six all at once. With this method, too, the best fishing is at night, especially when the river is swollen and muddy after some rain. You can haul in dozens.

"Anyway, one night when the old hunter was snagging out in the middle of the river, a fox came along the bank and stopped to watch him. For a long time it just stood there like a little statue, not moving a muscle." Father got on all fours and made a fox's face, then continued. "Now, the hunter wouldn't have minded about the fox except that his basket of fish was sitting on the bank. You see, he had two baskets for the fish he caught—a small one that he tied around his waist, and a larger one that he left on the riverbank. Whenever the small one filled up, he would go back to shore and empty it into the larger one. The problem was the fox had stopped only a few steps away from this larger basket."

"Chase him away!" the older boy cried.

"Chase him away!" the younger boy echoed.

"You can imagine the hunter got pretty nervous about the basket. He picked up a rock from the riverbed and threw it hard at the fox, thinking that would surely send it scampering. But no, the fox just ambled a few steps to one side, stopped, and turned to eye him again. Then after a few moments it sauntered back toward the basket."

"Throw some more rocks!" the older boy said.

"That's right. He picked up another rock and yelled 'Beat it!' as he hurled it off. But the fox wasn't any more impressed this time than the first. The old hunter said he had never seen such a lack-adaisical fox. Then, just as he was trying to decide what to do next, the fox grabbed the basket in its snout and trotted away."

"Too-o ba-a-ad," the older boy said sympathetically.

"Too-o ba-a-ad," the younger boy repeated.

16

"Hey Mom, Ikuko and I are going to make donuts this afternoon, okay?" the girl asked one Sunday, a little before noon.

"It's fine with me," Mother nodded.

"She said she'd bring the ingredients."

"She doesn't have to do that."

"That's what *I* said."

"I'm sure we have everything you need."

"I know, I told her that, but she insisted."

Ikuko arrived around two, bringing with her a bag of flour and an egg. She was a cute, cheerful girl, who never seemed to stop smiling.

"Can I help?" the older boy asked.

"There you go again," Father admonished. "Always getting into other people's projects. For girls, making donuts is like doing homework for school. You'd be bothering their studies."

"But I want to do some homework too."

"Look, there's not enough room in the kitchen for all three of you to work in there at the same time."

"Yes there is," the boy whined. He stuck out his lower lip in a pout. His eyes filled and a tear or two trickled down his cheek.

"All right, you can help," Mother agreed. "But don't get carried away now. Understand?"

"Oka-a-a-y," he promised. A smile had already spread across his face. The switch from sad to happy was just that quick.

Father looked on as his wife got the children started. Then, having nothing better to do, he decided to go lie down for a while.

"Make them small," he said as he stood up to leave. "They're better that way."

In the back room he folded a cushion in half to use as a pillow and stretched out on the tatami. Even from there he could hear the voices in the kitchen.

"Stop taking so much," the girl scolded the boy. It seemed he had gotten carried away after all.

Then his wife was saying something. That was the voice of the woman he had married, he thought to himself as he listened. That was how she sounded when she did things with the kids.

For some reason he was reminded of the muffled sobs he had once heard, a long time ago. When had it been? Oh yes, it was in their old house. He was taking a nap upstairs late one Sunday afternoon—he even remembered using a folded cushion for a pillow, just like now—when all of a sudden he began to hear what sounded like a woman crying. He lifted his head to listen more closely, but the sound stopped. Then, while he was still puzzling over what to make of it, it started up again.

Was something wrong? Who could it be? Why would anyone be weeping?

Going downstairs, he found their second child fast asleep on the baby bed and his wife rinsing some spinach at the kitchen sink. Their daughter had gone out to play.

"Did you hear anything?" he asked his wife.

"No, not that I noticed," she replied, turning around with a bright face.

"That's strange. I could have sworn I heard something. That's why I came down—to see what it was."

What could it have been, then—that sound of short, broken sobs? Something being jostled by the wind, perhaps, rubbing against something else. But why had it sounded to him so much like his wife's voice?

He went back upstairs, but the sound did not return.

Father now lay on the tatami in the back room staring into space as he thought over the incident that had puzzled him so. His wife had had no cause for weeping then. And in fact she *hadn't* been weeping.

"This one's mine," the boy's voice broke through his thoughts. "I put a mark on it so I could tell."

A few moments later someone began to laugh. Then they all laughed.

Footsteps came running down the hall and the door slid open. It was the younger boy. "They're done. It's time to eat," he said, and went dashing back toward the kitchen.

Father got up and followed. He found the others at the low, round table in the front room, the donuts divided up onto several small plates. There was an extra plate for him.

"Mmm-mmm, perfect!" he said between bites. "Just as I said, the small ones are best." He finished the donut and sat back to watch as the others ate theirs.

"Have some more," his wife urged.

"No thanks. One's enough for me." He pushed his plate toward the children.

"That was fun," the girl said as she took her last bite.

"And delicious," Ikuko added, finishing hers.

The boy, too, was down to his final bite, when his sister suddenly cried out, "Wait! Save a little piece!" But it was too late. The last bit had vanished into her brother's mouth. "Ohhh well," she said, disappointed.

"What's the matter?" Mother asked.

"We forgot to save any for the goldfish."

The boy tapped his cheeks as if to prove that the donut was completely gone. Not a single crumb remained, either on the plates or on the table.

17

"We listened to the New World Symphony in music class today," the girl said one evening near the end of dinner.

"How nice!" Mother said. "Did you like it?"

"It was beautiful."

"Yes, it really is a beautiful piece."

"But you know what? When the teacher told us he was going to play it, the boys all groaned and didn't want to listen. Only the girls wanted to hear it."

"Why? What did the boys have against it?" Father asked.

"I don't know. All they said was 'B-o-r-ing. B-o-r-ing.' I guess they didn't think it would be much fun. They must have liked it more than they expected, though, because once it started they all listened quietly."

"Do you get to choose the music you listen to?" Mother asked.

"Uh-huh. Every once in a while the teacher asks us what we'd like to hear and makes a list on the board. One time, not too long ago, a lot of people wanted the *New World* Symphony. But he didn't have it taped yet."

"Oh, so you listen to a tape," Father broke in.

"Uh-huh. He's got lots of different music on tapes."

"I see."

"Anyway, today he came in and said he'd finally had a chance to record the *New World* Symphony the other night, so let's all listen to it. But first he explained that the beginning wasn't recorded very well—he hadn't had time to adjust all the knobs before the symphony started because he forgot until the last minute that it was going to be on the radio that night; he only barely got the tape recorder set up in time. And he said there was a place in the middle where we would hear his son's voice."

"Did you?" her brother asked.

"Uh-huh."

"What did he say?"

"I couldn't tell. Something like 'Ahhh-yooo.'"

"Ahhh-yooo?"

"I couldn't really tell, it went by so fast."

Several evenings later the girl had another story.

"In Ikuko's class," she began, "they listened to *Invitation to the Dance* today. The teacher told them beforehand that the composer—I think his name was Weber—had dedicated it to his wife, and that it was a flowery sort of piece."

"So that's what you call it," Father said.

"Then after he started the tape, he explained what was supposed to be happening at each place in the music." She had begun to speak a little faster, as she always did when she neared the best part of the story. "Well, evidently, there's a place in the middle where the music stays kind of low for a while and then gets high, and the teacher explained that the low part was where the men go up to the ladies and ask, 'May I have this dance?' Then when it came to the high part, he started to tell them that that was where the ladies turn all red and say, 'Ohhh, something-or-other.' But just as he said 'Ohhh,' his false teeth came loose, and they almost fell right out of his mouth!" Unable to hold back any longer, she burst out laughing.

Her parents stared at her in disbelief.

"His false teeth?" Father asked.

"It's really true! They almost fell out!" She laughed so hard that tears came to her eyes, and she had to hold her stomach. Before long her father began to laugh, too, and then her mother and the boys. They laughed and laughed, unable to stop.

Finally the older boy asked, "So what did the teacher do?"

"Ikuko said he turned the other way and fixed them in a real hurry," the girl answered.

18

A bagworm the older boy had been keeping in a small cardboard box disappeared.

At the time, Father did not yet know about the bagworm. No one had thought to mention it to him. It was not until afterward that he heard the story.

The boy had originally found it on a tree in their neighbor's yard when he and a friend were gathering nuts to use as pellets in their toy guns. His friend told him that if he stripped the worm and put it in a box with some leaves and bits of paper, it would make itself a new nest in about three hours.

The boy brought it home and did as his friend had said. But when he peeked into the box that night, the bagworm had not moved. The next morning it still hadn't moved.

He then forgot about the worm, and three days went by before he thought to check its box again. This time it had crept into a corner and begun building a little tent-like shelter on its back. The boy poked at the half-finished canopy with his finger. To his surprise, it flipped right off.

A day or two later he found the tiny creature crawling across the floor of the study. This time, too, it had a tent on its back, about the same size as the one before. The boy carefully returned it to its box.

He neglected to check on the bagworm for several days again after that. When he finally remembered, it was no longer in the box. With his mother to help him, he scoured the floor of the study from under the sewing machine to behind the toy basket, but to no avail.

Then one evening about two weeks later, Mother went into the study and found the bagworm in a new nest on the wall, a short distance below the picture of the star children.

"Here it is!" she exclaimed in surprise.

The lost worm had made itself a new bag out of the persimmon twigs and newsprint scraps the boy had given it, plus bits of lint it had gathered on its own. Patchwork though it looked, it was a perfectly good nest.

Where could it have been hiding all that time? Father later wondered. Someplace no one would find it, that much was clear. Perhaps behind the bookshelf, where there was plenty of lint it could use to make a nest. Then, when it had finished weaving its new quarters, the worm had crawled out to a bright, sunny spot near the southern windows.

The boy was in the bath shooting his water gun at the walls and ceiling. Caught up in his game, he had stayed in much longer than he should have.

"Hurry up and dry off and come on out here. We've got a surprise for you," his mother and sister called to him.

Little imagining that the "surprise" would be his bagworm, the boy jumped out of the bath and dried himself as fast as he could.

The last one to learn about the bagworm was Father. He had gone out that evening and did not get home until late, long after the others were in bed; it was the next morning before he finally heard about the bagworm from his wife.

Out-of-doors, he had never given bagworms a second thought. But there was something rather curious about a worm that built itself a shelter when it was inside a house with a solid roof and ceiling overhead.

"I wonder what it has in mind," he said to his wife. "Does it intend to set up housekeeping there, do you think?"

"It certainly looks that way."

He noticed a tiny piece of bright red paper stuck to one side. Had his son put some bits of construction paper in the box too? Or was this something the worm had picked up in its travels around the room?

At the other end of the bay window from where the two stood inspecting the bagworm, the goldfish swam quietly in its bowl. It nibbled for a moment at some moss that had formed along the edge of the water, then lost interest and turned away.

CRABS

*t*he boy in the Cézanne room discovered some crabs living in the stone fence against the embankment behind the inn. What a find! Since he was supposed to be taking a nap, he watched them from the window for a while. But finally he couldn't sit still any more.

"I'll be right back," he said. "I just wanna see." He ran to get his shoes from the entrance and climbed outside through the window.

Instead of coming back as he had promised, though, he went to get a tin can from the innkeeper's wife and found a stick he could use to pin the crabs down when they tried to escape into the nooks and crannies among the rocks. Armed with these tools, he kept shuffling back and forth in front of the fence—rather like the crabs themselves, you could say.

Soon the innkeeper's son came along wearing a sports cap, and the two became friends. Since the Cézanne boy was only in the second grade, while the other was quite a bit older (they found out later he was in the fifth grade), becoming friends didn't mean they had a great deal in common to talk about. But the Cézanne boy couldn't get up enough nerve to grab the larger crabs even after he'd nabbed several of the small ones, so the older boy caught the big ones for him. Living by the ocean had given the innkeeper's boy a much darker tan.

After a while, the Cézanne boy's older sister (she was in the sixth grade) came outside with their little brother, and they joined the crab patrol with the others.

Inside, the children's parents lay on the tatami. Their mother had dozed off—she could fall asleep anytime and anywhere. Not so their father: he would close his eyes for some rest only to find himself staring into space again a few minutes later.

The couple had brought their children to this small fishing village on vacation. They'd risen that morning in darkness and set out before any of the other houses were awake. It had been hard labor getting the children and all their baggage safely onto the train. They had to be sure to get seats so they wouldn't have to stand up for hours and hours en route, and that meant they had to be in line early at the station.

Ever vigilant, they had to move quickly and without misstep. Everyone in line was their competitor and foe, and everyone in line viewed them the same.

Alas, alack, no one said life was easy. But did it all have to be like this?

The father, who lay in the Cézanne room restlessly opening and closing his eyes, had asked for four days off from work so he could take his children swimming at the beach.

Next to the Cézanne room on the near side was the Braque room, and on the far side was the Renoir room. There were two more rooms on beyond that, but no one had gone to find out the names.

It was an artists' inn—this explained the room names—where the modest, unpretentious atmosphere let you relax instead of putting you on your best behavior. There were few enough rooms that no one was far from the entrance, so you could come and go easily. And best of all, the rates were low.

Everything about it was perfect for artists who wanted to settle in for a spell to paint.

The sky was mostly overcast and they found the water a bit too cold. When they got back to the inn, the boy went crabbing again. This time only his little brother joined the hunt.

"What're you catching?"

Two girls in light summer kimono poked their heads from the

window of the Renoir room. The question had come from the older of the two.

"Crabs," the boy answered curtly, still tip-toeing along the stone fence.

"Show me."

The boy took his tin can over to the window and thrust it in front of the girls.

"No!" the older girl screamed. She pushed the can away without really even looking.

The boy rolled his eyes and returned to his place at the fence. His little brother tagged along behind.

After a while, the girl called again.

"What're you catching?"

"Crabs," the boy answered without looking around.

"Show me."

The boy went to show her the can again.

"No!" she pushed it away.

The boy rolled his eyes and turned back to the fence. She had asked to see, so he couldn't very well ignore her, but when he went over to show her she screamed "No!"—as if he were doing something mean and she were trying to get him to stop. "What's going on, here, anyway," his face seemed to say as he returned to the fence.

It wasn't long until she called again.

"Show me!"

"Girls!" the Cézanne father thought scornfully. But he couldn't very well call out to his son to just ignore the girl. If he did that, the girl's mother and father would hear. In fact, since only a single layer of sliding doors separated the rooms, they might hear even if he barely muttered it to himself under his breath.

Besides, the Renoirs seemed like such a quiet and polite couple. They had arrived with their family that same day, barely thirty minutes after the Cézannes.

A small disturbance took place in the Cézanne room before dinner.

"Time to go home," the little brother said. No one was making any preparations to leave no matter how late it got, and he'd finally decided to speak up.

The others explained that they weren't going home; they would be staying at this inn for the next few days. But that only made him more adamant.

"I wanna go home. I wanna go home," he insisted, his voice turning to tears.

The things you never expect!

It was because the boy had never slept away from home before. In his mind, even if you went somewhere during the day, you always returned home to sleep.

"It's like a sleepover," his sixth-grade sister said cheerfully. "Pretty soon we'll have dinner, and then we'll go for a walk, and after that we'll all come back here to sleep. When we're at home, we sleep at home. When we go someplace far away on the train, we get to sleep over at an inn. That's what this place is called."

He was crying because he didn't understand the idea of sleeping over. Somehow they all had to make him understand.

What if we lost our home and became homeless wanderers? the father thought in dread. Then we'd have to sleep in the woods or by a river or anywhere we could.

It took quite a while for the boy to stop crying. In the end, though, he had no choice but to accept that you could sometimes sleep away from home.

The Renoir room remained quiet throughout the disturbance.

The Cézanne family went for a walk before going to bed that evening.

First they headed for the beach where they'd swum that afternoon, to look at the ocean at night. All they could really see was that the ocean was dark, so they didn't stay long. Remembering they had intended to buy some small fishing nets, they retraced their steps.

Partway back to the station from the inn was a little shop that sold nets for children. Much of the shoreline nearby was rocky, and when the tide went out lots of little fish got left behind in small pools among the rocks.

Each boy got his own little net.

As they started walking back toward the inn, inside one of the houses facing the road they saw a bare-chested man sitting on the tatami with one knee propped up, talking to a woman. Being a fishing village, it was not especially unusual to see men wearing no shirts.

The man and the woman sat talking like any fisherman and his wife.

But after passing by the house, the Cézanne father turned to his wife and said, "Wasn't that man a foreigner?"

"I think he was," she said.

"So you saw him, too?"

"Yes. I'm sure he wasn't Japanese."

"That's odd," the father said, tilting his head.

The man had dark skin and thinning hair. The woman—she *was* Japanese—seemed about the same age as the man. Neither young nor beautiful, she looked like any other fisherman's wife.

And the two sat talking like any Japanese couple might do on a night when it was too hot to sleep.

"For being a foreigner, he sure looked like he was in his element, didn't he?—sitting there bare-chested, on the tatami, with one knee up."

"He certainly did. He looked like he really belonged."

When they reached the inn, they found their bedding laid out and the mosquito nets hung. The Renoir family was already asleep.

The second day was chilly, with a brisk wind. The fishermen stayed in and mended their nets rather than go out to sea. By afternoon the waves had grown even rougher, so it was not a day for swimming.

The Cézanne family went down to the beach once to have a look, but quickly gave up and retreated to the inn. The sister was especially disappointed because she had just started to learn the crawl stroke. She could go about five yards now if she kept her face down, and she was anxious to practice how to breathe at the same time.

The older brother went to see if the boy who'd helped him with the crabs yesterday could play, but he soon returned by himself with a big stack of borrowed comic books. After that the children buried their noses in comics, and the room fell silent except for the low voice of their mother reading to their little brother. Father did nothing. He quietly contemplated the sight of his family sprawled about the room, reading.

Just look at that boy, he thought. Get him reading comics and it's like he's disappeared from the face of the earth. If I had something of my own to do, I'd forget he was even here.

"And that's the end," his wife said after a while. "Now it's time for a nap." She set the book aside and closed her eyes. The room became completely still.

Father picked up one of the books lying beside his son and began to read. When he had finished the one, he did not pick up another. He closed his eyes to rest but soon found himself looking around the room again.

The older boy's voice suddenly broke the silence.

"Can I open this?" He had his hand on one of the sliding doors between Cézanne and Renoir.

"What's wrong?"

"One of my crabs got away."

"One of your crabs?"

"The biggest one. He's in the next room right now."

The Renoir family had gone out.

"If I don't hurry, he'll get away. Can I go and get him?"

"Wait a minute. You can't just go in when they're not there."

"But all I want to do is get my crab."

"I know, but it'd be rude to go in without asking. How did he get over there, anyway?"

"I don't know. He got away when I wasn't watching."

"It makes it hard, that he got away clear into the next room."

"If I don't hurry he'll go even farther," the boy cried, his eye still pressed to the narrow space between the overlapping doors. His father came over.

"Where is he?"

"Right there."

"Where?"

"Look, right there, you can see him."

"Oh yeah, I see him."

The crab was sitting just barely inside their neighbors' territory.

"So can I go and get him, Dad?"

"Bring me your net a minute." Taking the net from the boy, he poked the handle through the opening between the doors. It worked. The crab scuttled back toward them and came through to their side.

"There, grab him!"

"You grab him, Dad."

The crab sidled warily along the bottom edge of the door.

"Hurry up and get him, Dad."

"He's your crab. You get him."

"But he's too big. I'm scared."

"Scared? If you're scared of them you shouldn't be catching them in the first place."

Father reached for the crab but pulled back when he got close.

"See. You're scared too," the boy said.

While the two of them were dawdling, the crab nearly escaped again through the space between the doors. The boy's sister came over and trapped him with the net. The largest of the tiny crabs was returned safely to the tin can.

On the night of the second day, the railroad company sponsored an outdoor movie in front of the station. The Cézanne family went to see it.

The villagers had brought straw mats along to spread on the ground and sat fanning themselves as they waited for the show to start. The early arrivals were mostly children and grandmothers.

First came two short films advertising the railroad, and then the new stationmaster gave a little speech. Even though he stood on the bed of the truck that held the movie projector, it was too dark to see his face. When he had finished, he hopped down from the truck, threaded his way through the standing crowd, and circled around the back of the station to his office. Apparently he was on duty and had only taken a few minutes off to come and greet the crowd.

After a newsreel and a cartoon came the main feature, a samurai drama, but by this time the boys were too tired to stay awake, so the Cézanne family decided to head back to the inn. On the way they crossed paths with the three maids from the inn going off to see the movie together.

Back at the inn, the Renoir family had already gone to sleep.

According to one of the maids, the man in the Renoir room taught junior high art. He had come here last year, too—to paint.

He left the inn with his wife and children first thing each morning, and came back just in time for dinner. After dinner, they went out again. They didn't linger on and on in their room or spend their day in idleness.

By all appearances, the man had come here to work.

The Cézannes were quite the opposite. Their whole purpose in coming was to loll about and be idle.

At first they didn't know where the Renoir man went to paint.

But on the morning of the third day, they hiked up the beach a short distance beyond their usual swimming spot, and crossed over by ferryboat to a small island offshore. They found the man with his easel out on the tip of a rocky promontory, where centuries of waves had eroded the boulders into myriad shapes.

There he stood, painting, atop a great boulder.

Back near the ferry landing, his wife and two daughters sat in the shade of a tree, patiently waiting for the head of their household to finish his work.

That day the skies remained partly cloudy during the morning, but then the clouds burned off, leaving nothing to shade the fiery summer sun. The Cézannes spent the first half of the day on the island, trying out their new nets on the fishes darting among the rocks; the second half, they returned to spend at their usual spot.

This was in fact the family's last day at the beach.

The daughter practiced her crawl over and over, trying to learn how to turn her head and breathe in time with her strokes, but she had trouble getting the hang of it. The older boy searched in crevices among the rocks for hermit crabs hiding in the sand.

The younger boy dug up the beach at the water's edge to build a dike against the incoming waves, but after a while he just sat down on the sand and watched the people in the water.

The father spent most of the afternoon swimming and helping his daughter with her crawl. Once when he looked back toward the beach, he saw his younger boy's head slowly nod to the right and then suddenly snap back straight. The boy had fallen asleep sitting up.

A portly woman was watching from a little way off, looking quite amused.

The father called to his wife nearby. "Hey, will you look at that?"

"My goodness," she chuckled. "He's taking a nap right on the spot, with his towel around his neck."

The boy's older sister noticed him, too, and let out a gentle laugh.

Another family with children came to stay in the Braque room. They had a boy who looked about kindergarten age and a girl much smaller. The man appeared to be an office worker rather than an artist. Like the Renoir couple, he and his wife gave the impression of a quiet and polite pair.

The Cézannes decided not to go out anywhere that night so they could get to bed early. Everyone was exhausted from their full day at the beach.

The Braques went nowhere either. No doubt they, too, had left home with their suitcases before dawn in order to line up at the station an hour early.

When the Cézanne family had returned to the inn earlier that evening, they had found the man from the Braque room sitting on the bench by the entrance to the inn's garden wearing only his underwear. A lean man, he looked quite worn out. He sat lethargically, with his head rolled back against the thick boards of the bench back.

As usual, the Renoir couple set out for a walk with their daughters as soon as they'd finished their dinner. By the time they returned, the Cézannes were already in bed under the mosquito nets. They had left their door open.

"I wonder if they've put our beds out yet," they heard the Renoir man say as he went by. A moment later they heard him heave a disappointed sigh.

They were tired, too, just like the others. But they quietly waited for the maid to come by.

"Shall I put out your beds?" she asked.

"Yes, please," the mother responded.

The Cézannes were all nursing painful backs from having suddenly spent a whole day under the blazing sun. Gasps and groans escaped every time someone rolled over in bed. They had turned out the lights but were having trouble getting to sleep.

The Braque room remained noisy as the boy and his little sister fought over something they both wanted.

"Where's Mom?" the boy asked.

"She's doing some laundry," his father said.

The Renoir room had now fallen silent.

After a while the Braque boy announced, "It's time for the Lion Quiz!"

"Keep your voice down, now. The people next door have already gone to bed."

"Okay. Question number one: What starts with *m* and blooms in the morning?"

"Morning glories."

"That's correct!"

The Cézannes laughed under their breaths—all except the smallest, who had fallen asleep.

"Question number two."

"Shhh."

"What walks on land and starts with *d* and *c*?"

"Something that walks on land?" his father mumbled, sounding half asleep. "Hmmm. Something that walks on land, you say?"

The Cézanne boy started to whisper the answer, but his sister stopped him.

"Your answer, please!" the Braque boy pressed.

The father mumbled something no one could quite catch, but then they heard the boy call out clearly, "I'm sorry. That is *not* correct!"

"I think Dad's had enough, Son," the man said.

The Braque room fell silent for a time, but shortly after the mother came back from her laundry, the boy started singing a nursery song.

The words went like this:

> Long ago there was a duck,
> A duck so big and strong;
> Everyday he swam the sea,
> Ate fishies all day long.

After that the refrain went "Laa-la-la laa-la-la-la," repeated four times. The way the boy sang the slow and gentle melody, it was hard to imagine anything more likely to lull his father to sleep. Especially the "Laa-la-la laa-la-la-la."

"Keep it down, now," the boy's father murmured. "All the other rooms are already sleeping quietly."

But as soon as the boy had finished the verse, the Renoir girl started in on the same melody. She had not been asleep after all.

Her lyrics were different, with the duck changed to an ostrich. The ostrich wanted to cross the river, but the water had risen and he couldn't get across.

When she finished a verse, the Braque boy broke out in his quiz show voice again:

"Thank you for a very fine performance!" he said.

His voice carried easily through to the Renoir room, so the girl went on with a second verse. (This was the girl who kept asking to see the crabs the other day.) Her voice rang out clear and sharp compared to the boy's. Perhaps too clear and sharp.

Her mother could be heard gently trying to hush her.

When she'd gotten through the fourth verse, the Braque boy started singing along with her—only this time with considerably more gusto than before. But his song was still about a duck, while the girl's was about an ostrich.

"We're surrounded!" the Cézanne boy exclaimed.

"Shhh!" his sister said.

The sleepy father in the Braque room had apparently given up trying to stop the boy and decided to let him sing himself out. Once he even joined in with the boy for a line.

Eventually the song about the duck and the song about the ostrich both faded away. The children in all three rooms had finally fallen asleep.

The grown-ups had been quiet, so there was no telling whether they were still awake. At one point, the woman in the Braque room, sleeping closest to the hallway, whispered something to her husband over by the window. No more voices came after that.

The father in the Cézanne room recalled the bare-chested foreigner they'd seen talking under a dim light bulb, sitting on the tatami with one knee up.

I wonder if he's sitting there like that again tonight, he thought. Right about now.

BIRDS

*f*irst thing each morning they dashed out of the house calling, "To the Viper Trail!"

Father and sons—Akio in the fifth grade, Ryoji in the first— jogged down the path along the cliff to a grassy field at the other end, where they did their calisthenics before coming back home. This had been their daily routine since the beginning of winter vacation.

They had never done anything like this before. It all began one morning when Father marched into the boys' room and shouted:

"Out of your bunks and on your feet!"

After opening the windows, he turned back toward the boys, who were still wriggling around like caterpillars under the covers.

"Assemble in front of the barracks! Five minutes and counting!" he called, his pitch now lower but his voice no less intense.

"Out of your bunks and on your feet" had sounded fine, but this second order seemed a bit off. It wasn't what they'd said in the navy when Father was in training twenty years before. To make it like the navy, he should have said:

"Assemble in front of the barracks! Five minutes sharp!"

Everything was "Five minutes sharp!" in the navy, no matter what they did.

What had come out of his mouth this morning, though, was

"Five minutes and counting!" And now as he repeated the phrase silently to himself, he decided it didn't sound so bad. He liked the longer rhythms that made it less of a bark.

To his amazement, the second command actually got a rise. Akio turned over in bed to look at him.

"What'd you just say?" he asked.

"Assemble in front of the barracks, five minutes and counting."

This time Father said it in a more ordinary voice, but even so Akio leaped out from under his blankets in a flash. Quickly unbuttoning his pajamas, he called to Ryoji in the bed against the opposite wall.

"Hurry, Ryoji, hurry."

The younger boy continued to hide under the covers, pretending not to hear.

"Come on, Ryoji. It's five minutes and counting," Akio pressed.

Passing Kazuko's door, Father contemplated waking her as well but decided to let her sleep. The boys had gone to bed around nine, but his ninth-grade daughter had been awake until after two, studying for her upcoming high school entrance exams.

After waiting a few minutes, he went to put on his shoes in the front foyer. He heard one of the boys run down the hall to the back door and dash outside. The other followed, almost noiselessly.

When Father opened the front door, Akio was already standing at attention a few feet away. Ryoji hurried to join him, pulling at the zipper of his jacket and kicking the toes of his sneakers against the ground, trying to force them on. Soon they stood shoulder to shoulder.

"Heels together!"

"Close that mouth, Ryoji!"

In their matching jackets and denims, the boys gave Father a salute.

"Get those fingers together. Your thumb, too."

Ryoji had closed his mouth as commanded, but he could barely keep a straight face. Now Father needed to teach them what to say.

"Say 'All assembled, sir!'"

"All assembled, sir!" Akio repeated, still holding his salute.

"Good. To the Viper Trail!" Taking the lead, Father started jogging toward the path but almost immediately lost the sound of footsteps behind him. He turned around to find both of the boys peeing into the bamboo grass at the side of the road.

"So much for military discipline," he muttered to himself. He waited impatiently while the boys peed on and on, gazing out over the valley as if lost in a dream.

This was how their morning routine had begun. When Father had marched into the boys' room barking out navy commands, all on a whim, he had hardly expected to so capture their imaginations.

Sometimes on Sundays and holidays the boys got up early and put on their clothes and snuck out of the house on tip-toes. But they usually gave this up during vacations—especially when it was cold.

More typically, if you pulled off their quilts, they clung to their blankets, and if you pulled off their blankets, they clung to their sheets. Then, when you took away their sheets as well, they clung to their pillows. A pathetic sight indeed.

If you managed to get one of them completely uncovered and started in on the second, the first promptly retrieved his sheet and covers and wrapped himself up again.

Yet the same two boys had responded dramatically to that rather odd-sounding command he had inadvertently invented:

"Assemble in front of the barracks! Five minutes and counting!"

It had taken him completely by surprise.

Even with only two of them, when they stood shoulder to shoulder at attention, waiting for their next command, it actually began to feel a little bit like an "assembly" of troops.

Of course, the boys' response had not come completely out of the blue. Shortly before the beginning of winter break, Father had taught Akio how to salute. He'd also taught him "attention" and "at ease."

"Good, good," he had said as he adjusted the angle of the boy's arm and straightened his fingers together. "When you stand at attention like that, you look like a whole new person."

"A whole new person?"

"I'd hardly recognize you, you look so sharp, so smart."

"It's true," Mother agreed. "What a difference it makes!"

Akio had trouble with Father's version of "at ease." At school, "at ease" meant standing with your legs a little bit apart and your hands loosely clasped behind your back. He demonstrated for them.

"That's how they do it in other countries," Father noted.

Akio had already gotten so used to the school's "at ease" that his legs moved apart and his arms moved back automatically as soon as he heard the command. On the other hand, when he tried his father's Japanese-style "at ease," he looked like he might topple right on over onto his face. He was supposed to keep his right foot in place and slide just his left foot forward at an angle, but he couldn't quite get his balance right. Even after he mastered "attention" and the salute, he kept tripping up on "at ease" no matter how many times he practiced.

Father also put him through "right face," "left face," and "about face," but these were apparently the same as Akio had learned at school.

Father sat with his legs under the *kotatsu,** putting Akio through his paces. Akio came to attention and gave a crisp salute each time he was commanded, but when it came to facing left or right he sometimes turned the wrong way and burst out laughing. It was hard to tell whether he did it by mistake or on purpose.

"Stop laughing," Father said. "You know very well which is right and which is left. And even if it's by mistake, you should keep a straight face. Now, which is your right hand?"

"Uhhh, let me think."

"Which hand do you use for your chopsticks?"

"Uhhh, let's see, my chopsticks go in . . . which was it?"

"Now listen, Akio," Father said sternly. "A long time ago in China there was a famous commander who could make his troops move any way he wanted. The king said to him, 'I want you to show me how you do it. But the condition is, you have to show me with women troops.'"

"Weird king!" said Akio.

"'Fine,' the commander said, and the king brought out a hundred and eighty beautiful women. The commander divided them into two companies."

"That'd be ninety each."

"That's right. He chose the two most beautiful women to be the captains of the companies. Then he addressed all the troops, saying, 'Do you know where your chest is, where your right and left hands are, and where your back is?' 'Yes,' they answered. 'Then when I say "front," look toward your chest. When I say "right," look toward

---

*A *kotatsu* is a low, quilt-draped frame with a firepan or a heat lamp under it for warming one's legs, usually with a square board placed on top to serve as a tabletop. A key source of warmth in the traditional Japanese house without central heating, it becomes the center of most family activities in the winter.

your right hand. When I say "left," look toward your left hand. When I say "back," look toward your back.'"

"That sounds simple enough."

"That's right. It's simple. Things like this always work best when you keep them simple. After very carefully explaining it to the hundred and eighty women several times, the commander struck his battle drum and shouted 'Right!' and they all laughed."

Akio burst out laughing.

"There you go. They laughed just like that. The commander said, 'That was my own fault because I didn't explain well enough,' and he went over the directions with the women another time. Then he hit the drum again and said 'Left!' and they all laughed."

"They laugh a lot."

"Now the commander said, 'If they don't do what I tell them because they don't know the command, then it's my fault. But if they don't do it even when they *do* know the command, then it's the captains' fault.' So right then and there, right in front of the king, he cut off their heads with an axe—the two most beautiful women, who he'd made captains."

"Yeowks! That's scary!"

"The king begged him not to go through with it, but the commander wouldn't listen. That's how some people are. So, now, which is your right hand?"

"This one."

"And your left?"

"This one."

"And you won't mistake them again?"

"No sir."

This had taken place only a short while before winter vacation.

2

The small neighborhood eatery served everything from western-style platters to ramen, and they delivered, too. Looking over the menu posted on the wall, he ordered a bowl of ramen topped with stir-fried vegetables. It was late, and there were no other customers.

Earlier that day he had checked into his publisher's employee dormitory in order to work without distraction on a manuscript that had to be finished before year's end. Supper had left him craving something more, and he had stepped out to buy some fruit or cookies for a snack. Instead, this little restaurant had beckoned to him from across the trolley street.

At home he never had to worry about getting hungry, knowing he could have something to eat any time he wanted. But when he spent a night or two away from home like this, not only did he have to decide for himself what to have for his meals, he also had to think about what to do if he got hungry again before bedtime.

While he waited for his order, the door from the street slid open and a man came in—apparently a neighbor rather than a customer. He started talking with the proprietor, who was busy behind the counter.

They spoke about a funeral they'd both attended that day for someone from the neighborhood. The proprietor mentioned several people he hadn't notified because he didn't think he should, but said he had notified everyone in the old block association.

What he called "the old block association" was evidently the neighborhood group they had belonged to during the war, before firebombings had leveled the entire area.

A young man returned from making a delivery and soon brought a steaming bowl of ramen to the table. Brimming with soup, it was too hot to eat right away.

"I was one of the bearers," the neighbor said. "People really get heavy when they die, don't they?" His tone suggested the deceased had not been a particularly big man.

"That's right," said the proprietor. "Any man with a wife and kids is going to get heavier when he dies."

Listening to their conversation, he picked up his chopsticks. Now that the food was ready, all the room he thought he had in his stomach seemed to have disappeared, but he dipped his chopsticks into the soup and lifted some noodles to his mouth.

The proprietor and the neighbor were still talking about the funeral when he left the shop.

3

"You wake up to a bugle?"

"That's right. You're sleeping soundly in your hammock, and then gradually you start hearing a bugle."

The Viper Trail sloped gently downhill at first, but then a pond came into view farther down on the right and the trail started back up. Father and Akio and Ryoji ran the first part and walked the rest. Ryoji showed no interest in his father's navy stories and tended to lag behind.

"Hustle up, Ryoji," his father or older brother would call back.

With their exercises on the grassy knoll, too, Ryoji went through the motions begrudgingly, as if to say he only did them because he had to. As if actually he couldn't care less about such nonsense.

"The first *pup-pup pu-rup-pup* comes to you in your dream, but then it starts to get clearer, like something slowly rising to the surface from the bottom of a pool of water, and you finally can't ignore it any more."

"Po-o-or Dad."

"Huh? Oh, no, there's no time to feel sorry for yourself. You're not supposed to do anything until the bugle is finished and you hear the command, but then, the moment you hear the command, you have to hop to. Out of your hammock, all lined up with the others."

With a sudden sharp fluttering of wings, two turtledoves flew up from a clump of grass at their feet and headed straight off over top of the path.

"And then comes 'Assemble in front of the barracks'?" Akio asked.

"No, not yet. First you have to strip to the waist and do a dry-towel massage—rub yourself down real hard. So you can't wake up early and secretly put your shirt on ahead of time, while you're still in your hammock. They've got it set up so there won't be any funny business like you and Ryoji tried yesterday."

When he had gone to wake them up, he had found them already dressed in bed, pretending to be asleep with their covers pulled up to their chins.

Father thought of the time he'd seen his own father like that— by all appearances sleeping peacefully. But that had been in a strange room, and Grandpa had by then drifted beyond the help of anyone but strangers.

"After the dry-towel rubdown comes 'Hammocks away.' You have to roll up your hammock and wind the rope around it so tight that you can stand it up straight on the ground. When you're done you give it to whoever's on duty for stowing them in the shelves up by the ceiling, and then hurry outside. I remember the captain always stood by the door timing us with his watch, but I don't recall how many minutes he gave us to get outside."

"And what if you didn't make it?"

"He'd sock you across the face."

"What about you?"

"I always made it on time."

"So you never got socked across the face. That's lucky."

Sometimes after their exercises, they did shoulder rides around the field. First father would crouch down for Akio to sit on his shoulders, then Ryoji would climb up onto Akio's shoulders, and then Father would slowly stand up.

Carrying just one of them was nothing, but with two it wasn't so easy. One time he strained so hard trying to stand up that he popped the pin on his belt buckle.

After standing up, he slowly circled the field as if they were an acrobatic family in the circus. When they were done, Ryoji flipped backward with his legs still over Akio's shoulders.

"One! Two!"

And they were all back on the ground.

4

The light gray suit Grandpa wore the day he died was still quite new. It became Father's.

A drop or two of blood had left a small stain on the lapel. Even after rubbing with ammonia and benzene, it wouldn't all come out.

The dizziness and nausea that led to Grandpa's final decline had occurred once before, at home, when he was washing his face in the morning. Going straight back to bed, he called for Grandma to bring him a razor.

"He started hacking away at his earlobes, and he got blood all over the quilt and all over his pajamas and all over the blankets," Grandma related later. "I had a terrible time getting everything clean again."

Great big earlobes like Grandpa's were a sign of good fortune, everyone had always said, but now they bore a tangle of scars from the razor blade. He had tried to administer his own bloodletting, but that time it had not been the cerebral hemorrhage he feared.

When Grandpa died, Father took charge of the clothes he'd been wearing, and Mother was the one who worked on the stain with ammonia and benzene. Grandpa's wallet came with the suit, in the inside pocket of the jacket, and while the suit remained in his keeping, Father borrowed money from it little by little whenever he ran short. Eventually he borrowed it all.

When Grandma finally asked him to return Grandpa's clothes to her, he showed her the wallet.

"It's all gone," he said.

Grandma didn't say a word. She had no idea how much the wallet had contained. She could have asked all kinds of questions, but she didn't.

After sending the suit to the cleaners, Grandma gave it back to Father to keep. Grandpa had been a bit heavier than Father, but they were the same height and the same in the shoulders, so Father could wear the suit without alterations.

Before this, too, Father had gotten more of Grandpa's clothes than any of his brothers. Partly it was because Father got his first regular job right after the end of the war, when everything was so hard to come by. But it was also because they had the same build.

And besides, Father had always preferred his clothes a little on the baggy side, rather than cut to fit closely.

5

The brass band now struck up "Jingle Bells." The warm sun shone drowsily on the white paint of the lifeboats.

A group of deckhands in their work clothes had gathered near the bow to watch the band. Below, on the lowest level of staterooms, a dark-skinned man wearing a fedora leaned out of a porthole, tugging with much excitement at the paper tape he held. On the bridge the captain was speaking with a svelte, well-dressed passenger. On the deck below them stood two stout grandmothers carrying on an animated conversation.

The company logo graced the smokestack: a golden crown superimposed on a red and blue background.

Many of the thirty-seven passengers on board were bound for Brazilian ranches, where they intended to settle permanently. Their well-wishers on the pier—a woman with a baby on her back and two other small children in tow; a large group of family members; a group that seemed to be friends from work; and so forth—held Japanese flags imprinted with the message, "Best Wishes for Bold Beginnings."

On deck stood a young couple, both of them waving large Japanese flags and holding several strands of paper tape. They exchanged a word or two now and then, but mostly remained silent.

Two women watched over the couple from the pier. The younger of the women explained to the reporter friend Father had come with:

"That's our brother. He's the youngest of seven in our family, and he's going to a ranch in Paraná run by Japanese immigrants. He really insisted he wanted to go, so what could the family say? He's been president of our local young men's association ever since graduating from high school, and he only got married after he decided to go to Brazil. We just had the wedding the other day. Our parents are gone, but our oldest brother does a good job of filling their shoes, and he made all the arrangements."

The older sister's eyes brimmed with tears.

Following several loud cheers came the traditional three-beat applause, and then the brass band started playing "Auld Lang Syne."

As the ship slowly moved away from the pier, a cloud of balloons rose from the bow and floated up over the crowd of well-wishers. Father reached up and grabbed a yellow one.

As though unable to tear themselves away from the last view of their loved ones, some of the people on the pier watched after the ship until it was no more than a tiny speck on the horizon. One little girl was crying in great sobs at her mother's side.

Father gave her the yellow balloon.

6

During vacation, Akio had been borrowing books from Kazuko's shelf to read. One day he asked:

"Who do you like best, Kazuko? Liu Bei or Guan Yu or Zhang Fei."

"What do you mean? I have no idea."

"Who's your favorite?"

"I read that book so long ago I've forgotten."

"I like Guan Yu. And Zhao Yun."

Akio was reading the Chinese war epic *Romance of the Three Kingdoms*. He went to ask Mother the same question.

"Who do you like best?"

When she wouldn't respond to his question either, he proclaimed in a loud voice:

"Here stands Yan-ren Zhang Fei!"

They could tell he didn't know what *Yan-ren* meant.

"*Yan-ren* means 'person from Yan,'" Kazuko explained.

"Oh."

"What did you think?"

"I didn't know."

"*Yan-ren* isn't actually part of the man's name," Kazuko went on. "It's the same as in our own war tales, you know, when the warriors step forward and shout out their names. 'Here stands so-and-so, fifth son of so-and-so, from the province of so-and-so.'"

She explained it very well, Father thought. Akio now took a wide-eyed, glowering stance intended, presumably, to cow the enemy, but he might as well have stuck to the nonsense of Yan-ren Zhang Fei for all the ferocity he managed. And a subsequent event served to confirm all doubts about his heroic stature.

"Oh, I'm sorry. I didn't bring in the evening paper yet," Mother said one night after dinner. "Could you run and get it, Akio?"

"Wha-a-at?"

"What do you mean, 'Wha-a-at'? I only asked you to get the paper."

Akio looked up at the transom. It had long since grown dark outside.

"Now, step to."

"But I'm scared."

"Scared of what?" asked Kazuko. "Since when did you turn into such a sissy? There's nothing to be scared of."

"But it's out there."

"What's out there?"

"A ghost," he blurted out, his face turning red.

"Don't be silly," Kazuko said, suppressing a snort of laughter. "There aren't any ghosts out there. There's no such thing anywhere."

"But there is," insisted Akio.

"Where?"

"Right by the mailbox."

Everybody burst out laughing. Even little brother Ryoji had no use for such foolishness and laughed as hard as anyone.

"Cadet Ogawa!" Father barked. "Atte-e-ention!"

Akio stood up.

"Salute!"

Akio managed a salute, but it was nothing like his crisp salutes at their morning "assemblies."

"Right face! . . . Forward march! On the double!"

Akio lifted his legs in running motion, but moved backward.

"Cadet Ogawa!"

"Yes, sir!"

"Destination mailbox, straight ahead. Forward march!"

This time Akio moved forward, but, after opening the sliding door and getting as far as the kitchen, he issued his own "about face" and came back.

"And you call yourself a man?" said Kazuko. "I think you'd better demote him, Dad. No one who acts like that deserves to be called a cadet."

"No! No!" said Akio.

"Then be a man and go get the paper."

"I'll leave this open," said Akio, pushing the sliding door all the way open and turning on the light in the kitchen. "Don't anyone dare close it, and don't turn off the light either."

"Okay, we promise. You needn't worry," Mother said.

Akio put up two fingers like antennas by his ears. "Beep, beep," he said, and ran for the front door.

Almost immediately he returned in a stampede of panicky footsteps.

He made a second attempt. This time he emitted no signals before going. They heard him turn on the light in the front foyer.

"Is there anybody there?" he shouted to no one but himself. "Is there anybody there? Answer if there is."

Just when it seemed he would pull it off this time, he came thundering back in an even greater panic than before.

On his third attempt he finally made it all the way to the mailbox. Then he flew back into the house, shrieking, like a man with an angry bull on his tail.

7

For Christmas three years ago, Akio gave Father a homemade board game with acorns for playing pieces. Kazuko gave him a wallet made of a heavy black fabric. Akio was in second grade then, and Kazuko in sixth.

Akio's "game board" actually consisted of no more than a sheet of drawing paper with a path drawn on it in pencil. The object of the game was merely to move your acorn along the path without falling off, but you had to do this with a special wand made from the ball-shaped lid of an old cosmetics bottle attached to a wire handle. Holding the opposite end of the handle, you had to pin the acorn down with the bottle top and drag it along. It proved to be a lot trickier than it looked. The slippery acorn kept jumping the track.

Akio had drawn a gate at the start of the winding path, and at the other end stood a tall castle.

One acorn would have been enough, but he included a large supply of spares in a plastic bag. He had gathered them in the woods on his way home from school some time before, but they had been stashed away in the drawer of his desk along with a jumble of other treasures.

The wallet from Kazuko came with a card: "Merry Christmas! Notice how big I made it. That's so it can hold lots of money," it began. "But watch out for pickpockets. I put in two hook-and-eyes to fasten it shut. Your name is inside. The extra cloth is for repairs in case it gets torn. Kazuko."

She had completed her signature by drawing a little round cartoon of her face next to her name.

Father undid the two hooks and looked inside. On a white patch sewn to one corner were his name and address written with traditional brush and black ink. Some basting stitches held a small scrap of extra fabric in place. She had thought of everything.

"Where did you get the fabric?" he asked.

"I saved some pieces I got from Mom. You know when she made her half-coat? Leftovers from then."

He remembered Kazuko telling him this, but its significance hadn't really sunk in. He had assumed it was just another piece of leftover cloth she'd gotten from her mother to use for making doll clothes and such, and thought nothing more of it.

The wallet was too floppy for actually carrying around in his pocket. Instead, though unfortunately it meant contradicting Kazuko's hope that the wallet would hold lots of money, he deposited in its soft folds the sixteen acorns her brother had gathered in the woods, and tucked it away on a shelf in his bookcase.

The two had gotten together to give him gifts before this as well, but he no longer remembered what they had been. They were the kind of thing that quickly vanished into oblivion once Christmas day had passed. This time, by putting all the spare acorns in Kazuko's wallet, perhaps he could keep at least the acorns from scattering so soon to parts unknown.

The following spring, the family had packed up their belongings and moved to a new house, disposing of a lot of old junk in the process. But the black fabric wallet holding the acorns arrived safely along with the bookcase and books.

A few days ago, Father took the wallet from its place in the bookcase and looked inside. Of the sixteen acorns, one had split in half and burst its shell, but the rest remained safe and sound.

He'd been prompted to dig out the wallet after going with Kazuko on an errand to the station that afternoon. As they left the house, Kazuko had put on a black half-coat.

"What's this," he asked, indicating the coat.

"It's Mom's."

"I thought that was bigger," Father said. "But it's your size?"

"Uh-huh."

"You didn't alter it or anything?"

"Unh-unh."

Kazuko hadn't asked Mother about the coat before she took it. She probably borrowed the coat regularly and didn't need to get permission each time. Father simply hadn't noticed before.

"So that's Grandpa's old inverness."

"Uh-huh. You got it from Grandpa, and then you gave it to Mom to make into a half-coat."

Father remembered that part. Sometime or other his wife had asked, "Do you think you'll ever wear the inverness you got from your dad?"

"The inverness?" he said offhandedly. "No, I don't suppose I will. I never go out in kimono."

"Then could I have it?"

"What for?"

"I thought I'd make a half-coat."

"Sure. Go ahead."

"Really? Thank you. Your dad hardly had a chance to wear it, and you hardly wore it either, so it's practically brand new still. And it's such nice material. It seems a shame to leave it hidden away in a box."

When she came to show him the completed coat, he thought: I shouldn't have let her have it.

Even if he never wore it, even if it meant leaving it in mothballs in its storage box forever undisturbed, he should have kept the inverness. Just because he didn't wear it didn't mean he didn't need it anymore.

All the other clothes he'd gotten from his father were now gone. The inverness was the only piece of clothing he had left for a keepsake.

"Isn't it nice?" Mother said.

The big, heavy inverness had grown pitifully small and seemed to rest almost weightlessly on her shoulders.

It was easy enough to make something large into something smaller, but, once you had done that, you could never restore it again to its former size.

I shouldn't have let her have it, he repeated to himself.

Now Kazuko was wearing that same half-coat, and it fit her perfectly—as if it had been made for her to begin with.

It was then that he had remembered the wallet from three Christmases past.

"Ohhh," he said in sudden comprehension.

"What?"

"Never mind."

When Kazuko had said she'd gotten some scraps left over from the half-coat, she'd been talking about this coat. Why hadn't he made the connection before?

"Come on, tell me."

"No, it's nothing."

I'll have to hunt out that wallet when I get home, he thought. The last I knew, it was in the bookcase somewhere. I'm sure it must still be there, holding those acorns, safe and sound.

8

It had rained hard during the night.

The bamboo brush and tall grasses along the Viper Trail hung heavy with water. Though the three joggers sidestepped as much as they could, their pants quickly got soaked below the knees. The wetness felt cold against their legs.

As they came back up toward the house after their usual exercises, Akio halted his steps.

"Wait here a minute," he said and waded into a clump of withered grass along the path. Ryoji followed close behind.

"Hey, we got one!" Akio cried.

Father went to see and found a small bird hanging upside down in a small mist net stretched across the underbrush.

"We got one!" Ryoji shouted again excitedly.

When Akio tried to get hold of the bird to extricate him from the net, he pecked ferociously at his fingers. He might be small, but he had a lot of pluck.

There were streaks of black and white around his eyes, and his wings were dark brown. None of them could recall seeing a bird like this before.

The net had snared both the bird's wings and his legs, and Akio was having trouble getting him loose.

"Ouch!"

Grimacing but not letting go, he worked gently and deliberately to remove the delicate threads.

"Where'd this net come from, anyway?" Father asked. "When did you set it up?"

"Kawai gave it to us. At first we put it in the grass over there, but we didn't catch anything in three days so we moved it here."

"When?"

"Last night."

Father had known nothing of it. The trap was about the size of a Ping-Pong net.

"I often see birds around here, so I thought it might be a good place and gave it a try."

"I wonder how long ago he got caught," Father said.

"I wonder."

The threads holding the bird's legs had all come loose, but the ones caught around his shoulders seemed hopelessly tangled.

"What a mess," Father said. "Maybe we should just cut that part."

"Do you think so?" Akio said.

"Yeah, let's cut it. Ryoji, go to the house and get a pair of scissors, would you?"

When Ryoji took off at a run, Akio shouted after him, "And bring the bird book, too!"

"Oka-a-y," Ryoji called back.

"You know what's really weird?" Akio said. "I dreamt about this trap this morning, before you came to wake us up. I wondered whether moving the trap had done any good and went to look, and sure enough, there were a bunch of birds frantically flapping their wings."

"Like this bird?"

"No. Bigger. About the size of pigeons, and colored kind of like baby chicks."

"How many?"

"First I saw three and thought, Wow! And then I saw some more flapping away at the other end."

They were fitting birds for a dream, Father thought. Gay and pretty.

"I got all excited, with my heart pounding, and then the door opened and you came in and shouted, 'Out of your bunks and on your feet!'"

A moment later they saw Kazuko and Ryoji running toward them from the direction of the house.

9

The bird guide gave them their answer right away: They'd captured a lively little meadow bunting.

They brought the bunting home. The two parakeets they'd had as pets from before were father and son, but lived in separate cages. Now the two were moved in together to make room for the bunting.

The wild bird immediately attempted to fly away, only to smash his head against the top of the cage and tumble to the bottom. Again and again, flying first in one direction, then another, he searched the entire cage for an opening. Several times he fell into the water dish, or flapped against the feed container and sent millet seed scattering across the floor.

"When you see something like this," Father said, "you realize just how domesticated the parakeets are. In all these years, I'd never really thought about it, but look at the difference! If you think of the parakeets as polished white rice, the bunting is like the original brown rice."

"That's what we can name him," Akio said. "Brown Rice."

"Now wait a minute. We haven't decided we're going to keep him yet."

"Can't we, Dad? Ple-e-ase?" Ryoji said. "I mean, Akio went to a lot of trouble to catch him. . . ."

"It's not so simple," Father said, "Look what the book says. 'Lives in mountains in summer . . . visits lowlands in winter . . . nests in small trees and shrubs . . .' They're used to living in a tree somewhere and getting up early to scavenge for food among the grasses in the meadows. I don't know if it's a good idea to try to keep one as a pet."

"But it says people do keep them as pets sometimes," Akio noted.

"Sure, if you really know what you're doing. But what if he dies? It'd all be for nothing."

"That's right," said Kazuko. "Look at the poor thing, smashing into everything. He even bumps into the bars he's supposed to perch on."

"I still think we should keep him." Ryoji said. "Ple-e-ase."

"I'd heard the name often enough," Mother said, "but I never knew what a meadow bunting looked like. With those black and white eyestripes, he looks a little like a raccoon."

"You're right, you're right! He looks like a raccoon!" Akio and Kazuko both laughed.

"I wonder what he sings like?" Mother said.

"The book says *chipi-chipi tsut ti-ti-tit,*" Akio said.

"*Chipi-chipi tsut ti-ti-tit?*"

"Right. You know, I've heard birds singing kind of like that. Down by the S curve and in the woods by the cliff."

"Really?" Kazuko seemed a bit dubious.

"Uh-huh. I've heard them singing. It's not quite *chipi-chipi tsut ti-ti-tit,* but it's pretty close. Just a second. I'll get the encyclopedia."

"It would make sense," Father said. "You can pretty well figure, if this bird is the first thing to land in the trap like this, he's probably got a whole flock of friends out there. Isn't he a fine-looking bird, though?"

"He is. He really is," Mother and Kazuko agreed.

"With a face that says 'I'm a child of the earth,'" Father added.

Akio brought back a volume of the encyclopedia.

"I found it! I found it!" he cried.

The entry included a picture of a meadow bunting perched on a tree branch.

"Let's see," Akio said as he began scanning the article, reading little bits aloud as he went. "'Eats insects and seeds. . . . Builds nest of withered grass, weed stalks, and roots, on the ground or in the branches of saplings and shrubs; shaped like—'"

"What does it say about its song?" Kazuko interrupted.

"Hold on. '. . . shaped like an open bowl.' And, let's see . . . 'Its song is a *chit-tsu chit-tsu chit-tsu chi-i-it*, usually from high in the tree tops.'"

"What did the other book say?" Father asked.

"*Chipi-chipi tsut ti-ti-tit.*"

"I suppose it's kind of similar," Father said.

"There's more. What's this, Dad?" Akio asked the reading of a character he didn't know.

Father read it for him. "It means 'commonly,'" he added.

"'Commonly remembered as *sweet-sweet, where-where, here-here, see it—see it.*'"

The others started exclaiming their recognition as soon as he began reading it.

"Oh, tha-a-at."

"*That's* what it is?"

"So it's *sweet-sweet, where-where.*"

Everyone laughed. They'd all heard *sweet-sweet, where-where* lots of times in the nearby hills, but they'd always thought it came from the white-eye.

The first part of the song came through clearly as *sweet-sweet, where-where,* and then the *here-here, see it—see it* part raced by in rapid fire. They'd had fun seeing who could imitate the fast part best. Little had they known they'd been mimicking Brown Rice and his fellow buntings.

"'Known as fine vocalists,'" Akio read on, "'and often kept as pets.'"

"I want to keep him," Ryoji said.

"Well, shall we see how he does, then?" Father had begun to relent.

"I suppose we could," Mother said. "We can keep him for a day and see if he starts to settle down."

By the time the family had finished breakfast, the new bird had stopped throwing himself every which way against the cage. He seemed to have figured out what the perch bars were for and actually landed on them from time to time. By noon he was pecking at the millet seed Akio had scattered for him on the bottom of the cage.

That night, the father parakeet in the next cage sang a line that sounded remarkably like *sweet-sweet, where-where, here-here, see it-see it*. Edging as close as he could to the meadow bunting's cage, he had been studying his new neighbor with great curiosity all evening. This parakeet had lost his mate a year ago after they'd produced a total of eighteen baby parakeets.

Before going to bed, the boys put a fresh dishcloth in the meadow bunting's cage. The bare floor of the cage looked so cold, but it was too late to go out and gather dried leaves for his bed.

The next morning, when the three came back from their usual "assembly" and exercises, Kazuko was out in the yard blowing empty millet hulls from the parakeets' seed container.

"How's the bunting?" Akio asked.

"He's got his feathers all puffed out, like he's angry or something."

"I wonder what's wrong," Father said. They went inside to have a look.

The bird sat in the corner of the cage with his feathers puffed out in a ball and his face buried in his feathers—like a person with the collar of his overcoat turned up.

Possibly he was just sleeping. But every so often his body gave a little shudder.

He sat directly on the bare floor instead of on the dishcloth the boys had given him before bed. And though yesterday he had been rapidly opening and closing, opening and closing his tail feathers, now he just sat there bunched up in a ball.

"Something's not right," said Father. "And I don't think it's that he's angry."

"Maybe he's sleeping," Akio said.

"I don't know. Do you really think that's how buntings sleep?"

In the next cage, the father parakeet sat on the upper bar, beside the nesting box, while the son sat on the lower. Every time the father moved toward the feed container, the son went into a tizzy and drove him away. Hopping down to the greens holder brought the same result.

The hapless father had had one of his tail feathers pulled out, and it lay on the floor.

"Something must really be wrong with the bunting," Father said as he finished his breakfast. "Maybe he caught a chill. Maybe he got too cold and he's freezing to death."

"You could be right," Mother said. "The temperature dipped pretty low this morning."

"Without his usual nest of dried leaves," Akio nodded, "he didn't have anything to keep him warm."

"But what can we do?" Kazuko said.

Father remembered a book he had in his bookcase and asked Mother to get it for him. "It has a story about a Scotswoman who rescues some birds freezing to death in the snow under her eaves and nurses them back to life. Maybe we can try what she did."

"Oh, yes, I remember," Mother said. "You read it, too, didn't you, Kazuko?"

"Uh-huh."

Mother soon came back with the book. Father opened it to a chapter titled "When Winter Came" and found the story of the birds.

"Every morning we found more birds nearly frozen to death," he read. "Some were dead. In fact, at a glance, most of them appeared to be dead—all stiff from the cold. But when I took them inside and warmed them by the fire in a covered basket, many of them came back to life."

One time she had ten birds in her basket, of all different kinds.

"Stonechat, greenfinch, dusky thrush," Father read down the list. And then, to his surprise, "Snow bunting."

"A bunting!" everyone said at once.

Another time she carried the frozen birds in her basket to the bedroom and laid them around a kerosene lamp. Turning the flame way up high, she gently fanned warm air down on them with her hands. Before long the birds started chirping, all around the circle—weakly at first, and then stronger and stronger.

"But I remember there was another time," Father said, "when she used a hot water bottle instead of a lamp. It must be farther along." He scanned ahead quickly, looking for the next episode.

"Here it is. Here it is," he said.

There was a jar her children used when they played house. She filled this jar with hot water and wrapped it in some flannel, and on top of that she laid the half-frozen birds drifting precariously near the boundary between life and death.

She also mixed a little brandy with some warm milk and fed it to the birds with a medicine dropper.

"Can we use a regular hot water bottle, then?" asked Mother.

"I'd think so. I'm sure it's better to use a real hot water bottle if you have one. It even says in the book that the problem with her makeshift arrangement was that the water cooled down right away, and she had to keep changing it over and over."

Mother brought the hot water bottle and filled it with water from the kettle on top of the kerosene heater.

"Shouldn't we cover it?" Mother said. "He could get burned."

"Do you think so?"

"It'll still be pretty hot even with the cover."

"Then let's cover it."

Akio took the bird from the cage and lowered it onto the hot water bottle on his knees, keeping it cradled in his hands. Without moving, he waited to see what would happen.

When the bird made a tiny movement, he took his hands away. Now the bird lay directly on the hot water bottle, hunched over limply in a heap. His feathers were no longer puffed out like before.

Kazuko went to her room to get a piece of wool she used as a shawl for one of her dolls and draped it over the bird.

"I don't suppose we have a medicine dropper around, do we?" Father asked. "The woman in the book used a medicine dropper to give the birds some warm milk. With a spot of brandy."

"A dropper, a dropper," Mother repeated as she tried to think. "We must have some kind of a dropper around somewhere."

No one could recall seeing one around.

"Or maybe something else that would work like a dropper," Kazuko suggested.

"I know," Akio finally broke the impasse. "The little glass dropper for my old eye drops."

"Oh, that's right," Mother said. "Do you still have them?"

"I think so. Probably."

"Great!" said Father. "That's exactly what we need."

"I'll go look. Be right back."

Akio gently slid the hot water bottle from his knees to Kazuko's. By this time the meadow bunting had rolled over sideways on his warm bed. He didn't move a feather, not even when Kazuko gently touched him on his woolen shawl.

Mother went to the kitchen to warm some milk, while Ryoji followed Akio. Only Father and Kazuko remained to watch over the bird on the hot water bottle.

He lifted his head and stretched his mouth open, once, twice. Then he dropped his head and did not move again.

"Oh, no. Did you see his eyes?" Kazuko said, looking up. "He rolled the whites of his eyes. They looked really weird."

The bird remained motionless, with both legs stretched out behind.

"I found it, I found it, just where I thought," Akio said as he came rushing back to the room with a small glass dropper.

10

Two years ago, at Christmas, Akio gave his father a cane made from a tree branch.

It was a sturdy cane, just the right thickness, fine grained and straight. Akio had rounded off the end into a handle that fit perfectly in his father's palm, and beneath the handle he had carved the characters for "Ogawa" with his pocket knife.

"Do you know what kind of wood it is?" his father asked.

"No, I don't."

"I wonder what it could be."

It wasn't a kind they saw much.

"Swinging on a branch is easy," Akio said, "but it's not so easy to hang onto a branch and try to cut off the end of that branch at the same time."

"I suppose not."

"You have to push hard enough for the saw to cut, but you can't push so hard that you lose your balance and fall when you finally cut through."

"Mmm, I see."

"It wouldn't be so bad if the branch were down low, but this one was way up high. It was scary."

Akio's gifts to Father before this had generally been insubstantial, fleeting things that quickly got broken or lost. This gift, however, would not likely suffer such a fate—unless Father himself were to absentmindedly leave it somewhere by mistake.

"It's very nice. Thank you," he said. He held it different ways, first trying out the feel of the handle, then brandishing the cane itself in his hand.

Afterward he never actually took it with him when he went out. He kept it in the umbrella holder by the front door, untouched and gathering a thin layer of dust. But if he should make up his mind to use it, it stood ready to serve at any time. It was a good sturdy cane, and he knew it wouldn't go anywhere, so he could rest easy and not worry about it.

Last Christmas, Akio gave Father a wooden shot glass. He had cut off a small block from a tree branch and hollowed out the middle with a hand chisel.

Kazuko gave him a flask of whiskey. Obviously the two children had collaborated and intended him to drink the whiskey out of the wooden shot glass.

"Remember the day when I cut my wrist here with a chisel?" Akio said, extending his left arm and pointing at the scar.

"Uh-huh."

"I did it carving this shot glass."

"So *that's* what it was."

One evening about the time it started to get dark, Akio had come into the house saying he'd jabbed himself in the wrist with a chisel.

"You'll be sorry someday if you're not more careful," Mother scolded as she dressed the wound in the kitchen. "What if you'd cut an artery?"

By the time Father came to see, she was wrapping the wrist in a gauze bandage.

"Chisels are scary," Mother said. "It's so easy to lose control."

Father had not seen how bad the wound was. "You shouldn't let yourself get hurt so easily," he said sternly.

"I didn't get hurt easily."

"*This* is what you call easily."

Akio remained silent.

"You've heard me say this before. Your body and all its parts are given of your parents," Father said.

"That's right," Mother immediately seconded. She completed Father's quotation from the Chinese classics: "Guarding them from injury is where filial piety begins."

"Which is to say, don't let yourself get hurt so easily," Father repeated his earlier admonition. "Listen. Just because it's your own body doesn't mean you're free to hurt it however you want. From the hair on your head to the tips of your fingers, this body is a gift given of your parents, and it's your responsibility always to try and try and try not to get hurt. That means you shouldn't go around scraping yourself here or jabbing yourself there all the time."

Little had he imagined Akio's injury occurred while carving a gift for himself.

Father poured some whiskey from Kazuko's flask into Akio's wooden shot glass and took a sip. It smelled faintly of sawdust.

"It has the fragrance of fresh wood," he said. "Not bad at all. Except that I feel like I'm getting cheated by the wood soaking up the whiskey."

11

"I'm so nervous my peart is hounding," Akio joked into the little microphone, not realizing the tape recorder was already running. Then he got his cue.

"Huh?"

Now he choked up and seemed to have lost his tongue, but he quickly recovered and began:

"Recorded in January 1963. That's all."

They paused the tape for a moment.

"First we will have a duet by Mom and Kazuko," he resumed. He passed Kazuko the microphone.

"O lilies in the garden,—"

As they started singing, Ryoji made a noise.

"Quiet!" Akio hissed.

"O blossoms on the fence,—"

Ryoji started laughing.

"Shh!"

"This is the day—" The two ignored the skirmish between Ryoji and Akio and sang on. "—I last gaze on you."

Ryoji finally fell silent and just the singing continued.

Ryoji had been pestering the others for several days to make a tape together. "If we don't do it soon, vacation will be all over," he said.

This was true. And once school started, it would be back to getting dragged out of bed early and whining about it being too cold as he stood on his bed and pulled on his shirt.

"Thinking of you, my tears wet my knees," they sang in harmony, with Mother taking the high note and Kazuko the low. For the final "This is goodbye, O my home, sweet, home," they came together on the same note, repeated the line twice, and that was the end.

With the tape paused, they decided Ryoji would be next, with "The Lone Ranger." There had been a time when no amount of coaxing could have gotten him to do anything for the tape, but recently he'd become more willing.

Akio gave the introduction. "Now we will have Ryoji's 'Lone Ranger.'"

"Er . . ." Ryoji wasn't quite ready when he got the microphone. He cleared his throat with a quick cough and began.

"Hi-yo Silver!"

He did fine through "With his faithful Indian companion Tonto," but then skipped "the daring and resourceful masked rider" and went straight to "Return with us now." Kazuko came to the rescue and prompted him with the missing line to get him safely through "Return with us now to those thrilling days of yesteryear." This should have brought him to the final "The Lone Ranger rides again!" but he forgot this line, too. Now that his own turn had actually come, stage fright seemed to have got the better of him.

This time it was Akio who dived in for the rescue—though in this case instead of simply prompting Ryoji he shouted out the line in Ryoji's place. The flustered Ryoji ended his turn in a great hurry, his usual boldness nowhere to be seen.

"Next, Dad will sing 'On a Winter's Night.'"

A pause followed Akio's introduction. Father held Kazuko's song book from school in his hands.

"Clo-o-o—"

The first line was "Close by the burning light," but Father had started out too slowly on the opening note, and his voice had changed pitch up and down two or three times. He turned bright red as he stopped and tried to keep from laughing.

The laughter immediately spread to the children.

"Hurry up, hurry up," Akio said amidst the laughter. "Come on, Dad. Hurry up." The other two were laughing too hard to speak. Even Akio was still laughing, and his words came out in spurts, riding the waves of the others' laughter.

"Come on, Dad. Try again," Kazuko finally managed to say.

They stopped the tape and laughed without holding back.

"You laughed first!" they accused one another.

"Oh, I can't stand it! My stomach hurts!"

When they had all laughed themselves out, Father got ready to try again. The tape began turning. Kazuko sang "Clo-o-o" in a low voice to give him his pitch, and quite as though this had given him energy he had not had before, Father started in.

"Clo-o-se by the bu-u-rning li-i-ght—"

This time he got through the first line in good form—not as slow as before, and not too fast either. He gave no sign of losing control.

But in the next line, "Upon a cloak, my mother sews," he start ed to fade at "Up-," got even weaker at "-on," and just barely squeaked through "cloak" before petering out completely.

The family looked on silently, hoping Father would somehow manage to recover under his own strength and go on with the song. But like the first time, all he could do was hold his breath and try not to laugh.

Kazuko started laughing first. "That's okay, that's okay," she said. "You were doing fine."

"Hurry up," Akio said.

"Upon a cloak, my mother sews," Kazuko quickly sang, but her attempted rescue came to no avail. Father could not make a sound.

They turned off the tape again. After a short break, Father decid ed to try it once more from the beginning.

"Now, no more laughing, Dad," Akio said. "Okay?"

"Okay."

The tape started spinning.

"Clo-o-ose by the bu-u-rning li-i-ght," he sang, but he had done better on his second attempt. He carried the first note too long, and it came out sounding forced and heavy.

He somehow held on through "Upon a cloak," but then fell apart. The rest of the line deteriorated into laughter: "My mo-ho-ho-ha-ha."

Everyone started laughing and couldn't stop. It was his own performance they were laughing at, but Father laughed just as hard as the others.

Ryoji started shouting, "Hurry up, hurry up," but no one could hear him above the din.

To run out of steam like that in the middle of a song and, finally, not be able to go on singing—was that something like it would be when he died? Father wondered. Would the scene be like this one, with his family surrounding him and rooting for him to hang on, to not give up?

Kazuko took the microphone. "Next is Akio's coyote howl."

When he was going off to do his homework, Akio's howls came quite naturally. But it wouldn't be so easy when he didn't have anything to howl about.

The theme song of a cartoon they'd seen on television had a family of four coyotes sitting on top of a mountain howling together at the moon. After each chorus of howls came a refrain:

"We're just poor as poor can be."

Akio had especially liked this part of the song and took to repeating it—though he'd simplified the chorus of howls.

"I wish you wouldn't use those lyrics. People could get the wrong idea," Father had said. That left just the howls.

"Wait," Akio said, and again, "Wait." Then, with his eyes closed and his voice trembling mournfully, he cried out four times:

"Aooooo. Aooooo. Aooooo. Aooooo."

12

"Kawai told me the other day," Akio said as they returned from the grassy field after their morning assembly, "that he saw two baby turtles in the stream that runs by his house, but when he tried to catch them, they both took off like lightning, and he couldn't believe how fast they moved."

"Were they swimming?"

"No, they were where the water's only like a thin film on a bed of mud."

Father had been to the stream once with Akio and Ryoji. It flowed along the foot of a slope, shaded by a stand of trees that darkened the water.

"He also saw a loach in the water right close by," Akio went on, "and at first it didn't move even when the turtles went scurrying away. So he thought he'd go after the loach instead, but by the time he looked again it was gone."

Kawai was a farmer's boy, and when he wasn't in school he had to help with chores like cleaning manure from the stalls in the barn or hauling blocks of salt for the cows.

"Another time he saw a turtle way up in the hills."

"Just one?"

"Yeah, just one. This one was a grown-up turtle, dragging himself along like he could barely keep going, and he didn't run away even when Kawai came up close."

"I wonder where he thought he was going, walking in a place like that?"

"Yeah, I wonder," Akio said. "Maybe he got lost." He turned around and called to Ryoji. "Hurry up."

Swinging a stalk of brush bamboo he'd picked up, Ryoji had fallen far behind. As usual, he hurried to catch up a bit when he was called, but then quickly dropped back again.

13

A bookstore, a clothing store, an eel restaurant, a hardware store, a sweet shop—he walked down the street glancing into each shop as he went. The shopping district in front of the station bustled with year-end activity.

In the next shop he passed, a man and his still boyish son were fitting a lid onto a plain wooden box.

He wondered for a moment what they could be making such a box for, but then saw the shop's sign: it was a coffin-maker's shop.

The lumber seemed quite thin. What kind of wood would it be? Cedar, perhaps? In any case, it probably wasn't their best coffin. No doubt they made a sturdier one, too, with heavier planks. Surely they did.

By this time he had walked well past the shop.

He'd once read an article in the paper about an elderly Englishman, living alone, who was so proud of the coffin he'd chosen to be buried in. It was a coffin made of oak.

The man had bought it thirty-four years before and polished it without fail every day since. It must have been a truly magnificent coffin.

According to the article, he set it in the shade of a tree in his yard and took naps in it on hot summer afternoons. What sort of a tree would it have been? An ancient one, no doubt, with a broad trunk, and thick-leaved branches spreading coolly out over the yard.

The man wanted to see what he looked like in his coffin under the tree, so he called in a photographer to take some pictures. Now, *there* was an idea!

But how had he posed for the pictures? With his eyes closed, as if in the midst of his nap? Or turned toward the camera, with a big smile?

He passed by the shop again on his way back. The coffin-maker and his son continued at their work, and the boy was smiling and saying something to his father.

14

"There goes Bogie, lecturing Frosty again," Mother said.

"Really!" Kazuko said. "He sure does it a lot."

"It always sounds like he has something so important to say."

Bogie was the name of the older parakeet, the one who'd lost his mate, and Frosty was his son. Bogie and his mate had produced hatch after hatch of baby parakeets, faster than the family could find new homes for them. In the end, the second cage had gotten so crowded that they'd asked the man from the pet store to come and take all but one baby away.

Frosty had stood out among his siblings for one particular characteristic: at night, when all the others slept shoulder to shoulder on the perch bar, he alone went off into a corner and slept clinging to the side of the cage. He was imitating his father, and, in fact, the corner where he went was directly opposite the place where his father clung to the side of *his* cage each night.

"It's amazing how they can sleep that way," Father marveled.

Bogie had plenty of room in his cage. His mate more often than not spent the night in the nesting box, so he could have chosen to sleep anywhere without being disturbed. Yet, for some reason, he always went to that particular corner to sleep in that oddest of positions. So Bogie himself could be called eccentric. But it seemed even more eccentric for only one of his offspring to adopt the same habit all by himself.

"Maybe Frosty's a bit feeble in the head," they all concluded. Their unanimous agreement that Frosty should be the one to stay behind when the others went to the pet store owed to his having singled himself out like this.

Even now, Frosty continued to mimic his father in the next cage. When his father twisted his head down to scratch among his feathers with his beak, Frosty would do the same. When his father walked around the wire walls of his cage using his beak as a third foot, Frosty did the same. When his father ate greens, Frosty ate greens. When his father came to the side facing Frosty's cage, Frosty came to face his father. With their cages set right next to each other, they'd be practically beak to beak.

And it was at such times that Bogie would launch into an extended diatribe.

"I wonder what he's saying."

"I wonder. It sounds like he's really giving him a piece of his mind."

Frosty would remain silent throughout. He was no baby anymore. He was old enough to be a full-fledged father himself, and physically he was no different from Bogie. But he had never become a father because he had never been given a mate.

Since the time Bogie first came into the family three years ago, the gentle slope from the crown of his head to the nape of his neck had grown slightly more angular, and he seemed to be thinning out a bit on his forehead. When you looked at Bogie alone, it wasn't particularly noticeable, but when you saw him face to face with Frosty, you could tell right away who was whose "old man."

Occasionally the roles were reversed, with Frosty doing the talking while Bogie listened.

"What could two single men have to talk about so much?" Father wondered.

"Really!" Mother seconded with a smile.

At night, the sound of the two parakeets' breathing rasped through the darkness.

15

Two more days and vacation would be over.

In the morning, when Father opened the door to the boys' room, a stuffed rabbit fell from above. It missed his head and skimmed past his face.

He glanced from one bed to the other. Both were empty.

"Hey, where're you hiding?" he said, before hearing a low, suppressed titter behind him.

Crouched together behind the dresser were two sheet-monsters, one large and one small.

The head of the small one was shaking, and the tittering came from there. Soon the other sheet started shaking, too.

Part way down the Viper Trail they came upon three bamboo pheasants playing in the withered thatch-grass.

Father was in the lead, with Akio right behind. Whatever the pheasants had been doing together in their little cluster, they all took off at once just as Father passed by.

Normally, bamboo pheasants didn't take off all at once like that. One would fly up, and then there'd be a pause as if the next were counting one . . . two . . . three before taking off. There'd be another pause, and another would take off. It would catch you by surprise each time another one flew up out of the grass.

Oh, there's another one, you'd think.

But that was when you saw them from farther away, not when you startled them up close like this.

"Such pretty colors!" Father thought. The flash of color from the feathers on the pheasants' breasts as they lifted into the air lingered in his eyes.

16

That evening Father went to visit a friend who'd grown up in the country. He told him about the meadow bunting the boys had caught in their mist net.

"Oh, yeah, we used to call them dummy buntings," the man said. "They're so easy to catch."

Father had never heard them called dummy buntings before. It made the bird that puffed itself up and died after only one night in their home seem all the more pitiful.

"Dummy buntings, huh?"

"I used to catch them all the time when I was a kid. Thrushes and buntings—that's what we usually got. But we didn't use mist nets. We used kachunks. We'd set them up on our way to school and check them on our way home. Sometimes, we'd set three traps and catch something in all three."

An interesting name, "kachunks." Father wondered how they had gotten such a name, but the man who grew up in the country said he didn't know.

"'Let's do some kachunks,' we'd say, and gather all our friends to go and set the traps together. The bamboo whipped down like a club, and it killed the birds, but we kept setting them without thinking anything of it—I don't know why."

A brother much older than him—the one who eventually inherited the family—preferred mist nets and was famous for how he flushed birds into the traps.

"He'd set the trap where the birds gathered in flocks and stick his head out from behind the bushes on the opposite side. The way he stuck his head out was really good, and the startled birds would all fly right into the trap. But it seemed like there was nothing to it if you used nets, and that's why most of us favored kachunks."

All you needed for a kachunk was some bamboo, some string, and a rock to use as a weight. Then you tied it to a tree in a place where you thought birds might come.

The man drew a diagram, explaining how the bird came up and tripped the release, which made the flexed bamboo whip back into a straight position. Though Father could see well enough that the bamboo was supposed to slap down on the bird from above, he couldn't quite understand how the trigger worked.

The man hadn't made traps like this in fifty years, but he still remembered every detail and could explain the system as clearly as if he still made them all the time. His short, stubby fingers moving across the diagram as he talked reminded Father of how his own dead father's fingers had moved.

They were down to the last day of winter vacation.

After breakfast, Father showed Akio the diagram he'd gotten the night before and repeated the explanation. Akio caught on right away—kids were a lot quicker at things like this. But he, too, had trouble with the part Father had memorized without actually understanding.

That afternoon, munching on dried persimmons from Mother and carrying a knife, Akio and Ryoji disappeared into the woods behind the house.

A while later Father followed. The woods sloped up the side of a hill. From the underbrush came sounds like a person walking—like dried leaves crunching beneath a person's feet.

"What's that?" he wondered, stopping to listen. The birds singing in the trees all sounded like meadow buntings. *Chipi-chipi tsut ti-ti-tit. Chipi-chipi tsut ti-ti-tit.*

Well, what do you know! he exclaimed to himself. All the birds in these woods were buntings. The woods were filled with the friends and family of the bird they'd brought home—that poor little fellow who'd given two big gasps, turned the whites of his eyes, and then fallen eternally still.

The sounds from the underbrush stopped. Had it been an animal of some kind? Lots of rabbits lived in these woods. Weasels, too. And a year ago, Akio's friend Kawai had found a baby badger drowned in the pond nearby.

Now he heard the sounds of someone coming down from the grove of young pines. He whistled, and a whistle came back. It was the whistle Akio called Ryoji with, even at home. In the bathroom or anywhere, this signal would bring Ryoji running.

"Where are you?"

"Over here," he said.

Akio emerged from the undergrowth carrying his kachunk. Ryoji followed, lugging a good-sized rock.

"Does this look right?" Akio asked.

"You made it already?"

"Uh-huh."

"The bamboo's awfully thin."

"I know, but it still hits pretty hard."

"Think so? Well, give it a try, anyway. You sure didn't waste any time."

"We didn't have any rice seeds, so I brought some of the parakeets' food."

"That's fine. Now, where do you want to set it up?" Father looked back toward where he had heard the leaves rustling. Whatever had caused the rustling, it had been over there, beneath that tree. And it could very well have been a bird instead of a rabbit or a weasel. Maybe it had sounded like something bigger only because everything else was so quiet.

"Let's try over here," he said, leading the way, stepping as softly as possible. "Here," he said. "Right around here."

Dry leaves thickly carpeted a small hollow, but he didn't see anything that looked like a nest.

"A minute ago something was making noises right about here," he said. "I couldn't tell what, but something."

"Which tree should we tie it to?"

"Let's try this one."

Directly above the hollow stood a tree that wasn't too big. Akio tied the bamboo to the trunk near the ground, and weighted it with Ryoji's rock. For the part that neither Father nor Akio had understood, they improvised: a small stick would hold everything in place until a bird came after the millet seed, and then as the bird pecked away it would naturally bump the stick and knock it down, setting off the trap.

This was Akio's idea, and it looked promising.

The toughest part was figuring out how far back to bend the bamboo. If it hit too hard, the bird would die; if it didn't hit hard enough, the bird would get away.

"All we really want to do is knock him out for a while," Father said. "There. How does that look?"

"It's hard to know, isn't it, Dad?"

"Yep, it's hard to know."

They decided to leave the bamboo relatively slack. Then they scattered a little more millet seed by the entrance to the trap.

"We want the bird to think, Hey, here's some millet. And here's some more. And wow! There's lots more back here," Father said to Akio.

17

In the morning Mother came to wake Akio and Ryoji. Vacation was over.

This morning there could be no "Assemble in front of the barracks!"—they had to go straight to breakfast. But in the breakfast room, both boys stuck their legs under the *kotatsu* and lay back on the tatami to catch a few more winks.

"Come on, boys, sit up and eat."

Mother's voice brought them both upright. Up until this morning, they were halfway down the Viper Trail by this time, ready to stop running and start walking.

"Ohhhhh," Akio groaned. "I sure wish it was the beginning of vacation instead of the end."

"Me too," Ryoji said.

"You can wish all you want, but you can't turn back the clock," Mother said. "It won't be long till spring break, though."

"How many days?" Ryoji immediately wanted to know.

"Until spring break?"

"Uh-huh."

"I don't have time to count them now. Just hurry up with your breakfast."

Akio let out a coyote howl, then a second, and then a third as he headed out the door with Ryoji.

"Well, they're off. I wondered if they'd make it."

"Those were great howls," said Kazuko. "He should have done them like that when we made the tape."

Even as they spoke, Akio came running back.

"What'd you forget?"

"Ryoji's shoe bag."

"It's right here. He brought it as far as the door but then left it behind. You have your own, don't you?"

"Yeah, of course." Akio ran off again.

Father thought of the kachunk and went to have a look, but for some reason could not find it. Even when he started over from where he'd entered the woods the day before and tried to retrace his path through the trees exactly, he still failed to come out at the hollow where they'd set the trap.

Akio and Ryoji got home around noon.

"We went to check the kachunk," Akio said. "The bamboo was down, and a bunch of feathers were scattered around."

"Some of the millet was gone, too," Ryoji added.

"Feathers?"

"Uh-huh. Tiny, soft feathers. All scattered."

"The bamboo must have been too slack."

"Yeah, it was too slack, so even though it snapped down like it was supposed to, the bird probably just flapped its wings and got away."

"I guess we loosened it too much."

"Yeah, we loosened it too much."

Later, Father went with the boys to see. This time they found the place without any trouble.

Bird's down was scattered on the fallen leaves. Much of the millet seed still remained.

At supper that evening Akio suddenly said, "We should have pulled it tighter."

"Pulled what tighter?" Kazuko asked.

"The kachunk," said Ryoji.

"Oh, that."

"We really should have pulled it tighter," Akio said again.

WOODSHED

*I*t had barely begun to sprinkle when I first arrived at the inn, but it turned into a steady downpour just moments after the innkeeper had led me out the other side of the dirt-floored entryway and through the garden to the small cottage where I would stay. I could hardly step out for a look around town in this kind of weather.

The one-room cottage stood apart from the main building of the inn, next to an old storehouse. When I opened the curtains I found myself looking through the branches of an apple tree at a neighboring farmer's vegetable field.

"If this keeps up," I mumbled to myself, "I'll have to stay right here all afternoon." My watch showed a little past two-thirty.

I put my coat on a hanger and sat down at the *kotatsu*. The cord stretched up to the light fixture overhead.

The cottage was apparently of a more recent date than the rest of the inn. The tatami still smelled fresh, and the ceilings and walls looked almost new. Instead of the outbuilding of an old country inn, the room suggested something more like the night watchman's quarters of a junior high school, and the small vanity table set against the wall seemed oddly out of place.

I felt a bit let down. When I'd first seen the well-weathered building from the road, I had envisioned being shown into a quiet, restfully old-fashioned room. Also, now that it had started to rain in earnest, being separated from the main building meant I was completely cooped up. To make matters worse, the room had neither a phone nor a call button. It was simply not a very convenient arrangement for anything.

After a short while I heard a door open and close. The sound seemed to come from directly behind my room. I heard some voices.

Perhaps the cottage was set right up against the neighbor's house, I thought.

Then there were other noises. It sounded like a farmer putting things away in his toolshed.

What could be back there? I wondered.

Voices came again, and I tried to make out what they were saying, but they broke off almost right away—like some insignificant exchange between family. Then silence.

Across the back wall were a closet and a cupboard. At one end of the cupboard was a set of drawers. They were inlaid and obviously belonged to a different age, as if a piece of the main building had wandered astray and found its way here. I opened them, but they were empty.

If I'd known this would happen, I could have stayed on the train. I could have waited until evening to get off and find an inn, instead of stopping practically at midday in this tiny town. In fact, I might even have chosen to go straight back to Tokyo without stopping anywhere, since I had already accomplished most of what I'd planned to do on this trip.

But it had seemed worth a stop of one more night to have a look at this forgotten post town along the old highway, left behind by history. I wondered what such a town might be like. My impressions from the short walk between the station and the inn, though, were of a run-of-the-mill small town with nothing to distinguish it from any other.

Stretching out in front of the station was a street lined with small shops. At the other end, it intersected with the main highway that ran through town. Both streets were deserted, perhaps because of the rain.

"You'll find the inn around the corner next to the dentist's office," they had told me at the station.

I turned the corner rather dubiously. It did not really look like a street where I would find an inn. Nor, at first glance, did the house I saw next to the dentist's office actually look like an inn.

When I opened the sliding door and stepped inside, the house was completely still. The large-framed man who came out to greet me seemed unaccustomed to dealing with guests. There was a clumsy sort of formality in his manner as he responded to my inquiries and showed me to my room.

And no one had come to look in on me since.

I thought of the girls' school students who had been on the train. Apparently they had just come from their graduation ceremonies, for they were all carrying those long, cylindrical diploma cases.

If I had only stayed on that train, I thought to myself, I'd be a long way down the line by now. And if I had gone all the way to the transfer station and changed to the express for Tokyo, then what time would I have gotten home? I might actually have made it before dark.

I realized I was becoming a bit homesick. But even though I could easily enough find out when the next train would come, I wasn't about to pick up my bag and go trudging back to the station through this rain. I simply wasn't up to it. Besides, I had already arranged to stay here. I couldn't very well turn around and leave now.

2

The front door slid open and a woman entered carrying a tea tray.

"I'm sorry to have kept you waiting," she apologized. "With this rain all of a sudden, I had to drop everything else to take in the laundry."

I remembered seeing a woman frantically removing laundry from the bamboo clothes rack in front of the storehouse as I came through the garden. It had been this woman. In contrast to the robust, rugged-faced man who had greeted me at the door, she was a slender woman with a fair complexion and delicate features, and she spoke with a note of reserve in her voice.

She set out a padded robe along with a light cotton kimono. "I'm sorry," she said a bit hesitantly, "but may I ask what level of service you had in mind?"

"What would be the usual?" I asked.

After first remarking how the price of food and everything else was going up these days, she apologetically explained that they'd had to set the minimum at such and such an amount. But in spite of her preface, the figure she stated turned out to be surprisingly low.

"And what does that include?"

"Oh, I'm afraid it really isn't anything to speak of," she replied. She was probably only being modest, of course, but somehow she managed to make it sound as though she meant it.

"How much higher can one go then?"

"There's no set limit, really."

"Well, let's see . . ."

"I can arrange for whatever you like," she said with a smile.

"Let's see," I said again, still wondering how high I should go. It certainly did not help for her to leave the matter entirely up to me like this.

"I can really decide on any amount I like?"

"Yes sir." She waited for my decision, kneeling attentively across from me, but since she had not given me any clear notion of what to expect, I remained at a loss. After several moments of silence, she added, "Though, as you may well imagine, we can't give you anything very fancy at a place like this." She seemed a bit embarrassed.

"Oh, never mind that," I quickly replied. "Really, just so long as I have a little something to go with my saké."

A look of relief came over her face. It seemed she wasn't trying to get me to name a price much higher than the basic rate she had mentioned at the beginning. She had left it to me because she genuinely did not know what price to set.

The thing to do was to guess an amount high enough that I could be sure I wouldn't go hungry, but not so high that she would have to worry about going to extra lengths. I made a stab and stated a figure. "And for the saké," I added, "what's the local favorite?"

She named two local brands and explained that one was sweet and the other dry. The one they had on hand was the sweet.

"The sweet?"

"Yes. We used to serve the dry one, but we switched to the other ever since my husband got sick."

"He likes to tip a few, does he?"

"Yes, and sometimes a few too many, I'm afraid. It hasn't been good for his health," she said, sounding embarrassed again. "The doctor told him that he'd be at least a little better off if he switched to a sweet saké, so we started serving that to our guests, too."

"I suppose he meant because people who really like to drink tend to prefer the dry."

"I imagine so. But my husband still drinks quite a bit, even after he switched to the sweet—though I guess it has to be a lot less than before because he doesn't go *out* to drink anymore."

She explained that her husband worked for the railroad and for many years had commuted to a large city farther down the line.

"I guess at the bars there he could always drink as much as he wanted, because even if he didn't have any money with him they'd let him run up a tab. It ruined his health in the end. Finally, when he got really bad he asked to be transferred to the local office here, and now he only drinks at home."

"He didn't have to go to work today?"

"No, it's his day off."

She said she would call the liquor store and have them bring by a bottle of the dry saké for me.

After asking me what time I would like my dinner served, she got up to go out, but paused at the door.

"Shall I leave this open?" she asked, indicating the sliding shoji between the room and the small entrance hall.

"Please," I said. It would give me a nice view of the garden through the glass in the outer door.

Before long the rain turned to snow and began to cloak the garden in a soft layer of white.

3

The innkeeper came with my dinner shortly after dark. He had started some charcoal in a small brazier and brought with it all the fixings for me to make my own sukiyaki. Outside, the snow continued to fall.

I placed the meat in the hot cast-iron pan and then gradually added the vegetables and tofu and noodles, talking aloud to myself as I went.

"I suppose that ought to do for now."

"Maybe a tad more soy sauce."

Between ingredients I set down my chopsticks to sip at my saké or pour myself another cup.

When the innkeeper came back with the rice and soup, I asked him for another server of saké and invited him to share it with me.

"Thank you," he said, breaking into an amiable smile. "As soon as I've got things under control in the main building."

Eating and drinking alone made me fidgety and bored, and before long I couldn't tell whether I was already bloated or still needed more to drink. It seemed a shame, now, that they had gone to special trouble to order the dry saké just for me. I'd been paying more attention to the pan and hadn't even noticed what I was drinking. And besides, the sukiyaki sauce had gone from sweet to salty and back again so many times that my palate had been rendered effectively senseless.

After bringing my second server of saké, the innkeeper did not reappear for some time. It made me wonder what he'd meant when he'd referred to getting things under control in the main building. Had he meant other guests were waiting to be served their dinners? My room stood apart from the main building, so I didn't know whether there were other guests—especially since I had been shut up here ever since two-thirty.

The place might not look much like an inn, but it did face the main route through town and it did have a sign out front. Perhaps an itinerant tradesman had seen it and decided to stop for the night. Or perhaps there had been another traveler like myself, who had gotten off at the station and asked directions to the nearest lodgings.

The innkeeper came in carrying two more saké servers on a tray, and made himself comfortable with the easy manner of a man accustomed to spending time in drinking establishments. With his preferred brand of saké in the house for a change, he had apparently had his wife warm two servers for his own enjoyment, and brought them along to share.

He lifted one of his servers and filled my cup. I returned the gesture by pouring for him from my own, which still had quite a bit left in it. Then he began to speak.

"Around here," he said, "the houses that have big tall oaks or pines growing out front are the old houses. They have latticed or solid wood front doors like you don't see so much anymore, and when you go inside, a standing screen separates the entrance from the rest of the house."

In my hurry to find the inn before the rain got any worse, I had failed to notice whether or not there was a tree in front of this house. And although I did remember opening the latticed door, I couldn't recall seeing a screen in the entryway.

"But since there were two big fires that burned down the whole town, even the oldest houses don't go back all that far. This one was built after the second fire. If my father were still living he'd be in his nineties by now, and he said he was born in this house, so it must be close to a hundred years old by now. No one really knows. The old records were lost in fires, too.

"There used to be a barrier gate here, and apparently the livery was right next door to us. This was the biggest house around in my grandfather's day, so when anybody important came through they always stayed here—even before my grandfather got permission to turn the place into an inn in 1882. We had two horses, and employed two maids and a manservant. But my grandfather liked his drink, I guess: he drank himself into debt and lost the family fortune.

"One of the neighbors was a moneylender. Their house was built like a storehouse, really dark inside. My father said he used to hear them counting money when he walked by outside."

I asked the innkeeper what the main building was like. He told me there were four guest rooms—all eight-tatami size, and all with an alcove and a large closet. Each of the alcoves had a main shelf made of a single, broad and thick slab of wood cut to six feet, and each had a built-in cupboard. The shoji were made of zelkova wood. The fittings would once have been considered quite extravagant.

"The inn was in its worst shape when my father took over, but even then the bedding we used always had our mark on it. This whole area used to belong to the shogun during the Tokugawa period, and today people still carry on a kind of feudalistic pride. Especially for marriages. The better families always insist on matches with better families. A lot of them aren't so well off anymore, but no matter how poor they get they always make a fuss over blood. I told you how the older houses have big oaks or pines out front, but sometimes we joke with each other that the trees keep on growing while our pocketbooks keep on shrinking. . . .

"Our roof here is kind of unusual. The rafters aren't strong enough to support tiles, and tin wouldn't work either, so it's a shingle roof with chestnut shingles. Originally we used rocks to hold down the shingles, but the shingles started rotting under the rocks, so after that we decided to fasten them down with strips of bamboo from the grove out back."

I could picture in my mind the snow falling out of the dark sky onto the chestnut-shingled roof. The whole roof would be blanketed white by now.

"This cottage used to be our woodshed before we remodeled it."

So that was it. I hadn't guessed a woodshed myself, but the place did have something of that feel to it.

"There isn't much to see or do in these parts, but for some reason we seem to get a lot of young couples, so about three years ago we decided to fix up a new room out here to give them a little more privacy."

The couples came from the city, he said, about an hour away by train. With all the things they could do in the city, it seemed almost backward that they would want to come out to a little place like this, but that was what they did.

I recognized the city as the one his wife had spoken of earlier, where he'd gotten into problems with his drinking because the bars would let him run up a tab when he didn't have any money.

"The way I figure it, if you want to make ends meet in this business anymore, you have to attract the younger people; you can't just cater to the old folks. Of course, there's not a whole lot we can do with a place like this. You can say it's quaint and rustic or it has history or whatever, but you can only make so much of a virtue out of oldness. When it gets to the point where even those of us who live here don't quite know what to think of the place anymore, how can we expect our guests to like it? I'd hate to think they're going away in the morning wondering how we can call ourselves an inn. Until now, my job with the railroad has kept me away an awful lot, so I couldn't do much around here; but I'll be retiring next year, and after that I'm hoping I can do some serious work on the place."

He went on to describe the new bath he'd had put in last year.

"I didn't think we should wait till next year to do something about the bath and toilets, though. It can be fatal for an inn if the bath and toilets aren't nice. They can ruin your reputation in a minute. So I decided we should go ahead and have a new bath and toilets put in. But when I actually started making the plans, I saw right away that we couldn't do both with the budget we had. One or the other had to wait. I thought about it awhile and figured, well, nice toilets are nice, but so what? Everybody has nice toilets. But you can really make an impression with a new or unusual bath. People will go away feeling better about the whole inn. So I decided we would build new toilets next, but the bath was more important for right away.

"I wanted it to be a place where you could really relax, with a big dressing area, and plenty of room for washing off, and a tub you could stretch all the way out in. A bath that would make our guests feel a bit pampered—feel almost as though they had come to a fancy hotel in some big hot-springs resort. That way, even if they didn't think much of our old-fashioned rooms they might change their minds and decide it's not such a bad place after all. Whether they were one of those young couples on a date or some traveling tradesman on his rounds, they'd go home feeling like they'd made a rare find.

"But then when we showed the plans to our builder and told him what kind of materials we wanted him to use, he shook his head. There's no way, on this budget, he said. Make it smaller. The bath doesn't have to be so big to be nice. I said, unh-unh, it's got to be this big, it has to feel grand. But he still didn't see the point. Why did the bath have to be so grand all of a sudden? Well, he had a point, in a way. Why just the bath? But I insisted, and he finally agreed to build it the size we wanted—only we would have to buy the tiles separately and lay them ourselves. So I had my high school boy help me, and the two of us did all the tilework."

The innkeeper, who had seemed so stiff and formal when I first saw him at the front door, had really loosened up once he started talking. We continued to pour for each other as we talked.

"I have three boys, but only the youngest is at home with us anymore. The oldest went away to work for the Forest Service, and then got married and settled down there, so he won't be coming home. Actually, when I asked him about it once, he said he'd come home when he retired. But by then my wife and I will be long since dead and roaming the banks of the River of Three Crossings. The second boy married into a fabric dyer's family in Kyoto, and he's taken up that line of work.

"I'm hoping we can get the youngest one to marry a local girl and stay here to carry on the inn. He says he wants to go to college, and I've told him he can, but that means he'll go away somewhere and he'll probably wind up finding a wife and staying there like his brothers. I doubt he'll want to come back to run a tiny country inn. If we let him go to college, I know there won't be any two ways about it. So we're trying to think of something to keep him from going, to keep him at home. Running an inn like this really isn't for a couple of old folks. It's for someone young. The old folks can set by the kitchen fire and drink tea, but they shouldn't be going around serving the guests. They take away from the allure. That's why we want to try to keep our youngest boy at home."

Moving from one topic to another, the innkeeper told me that in this part of the country people were buried rather than cremated, which meant their family burial plot was much larger than usual.

He also explained that the inn didn't have the usual concrete foundation dug several feet down, but instead was built on slabs of rock laid right on top of the ground, so in the winter when the moisture in the ground froze and expanded, the building got all out of whack.

"One time it'll be this place, another time somewhere else—I don't really know why. Maybe even under the same house, the soil is different between here and there. It wouldn't be so bad if the whole house got lifted up evenly, but it never seems to work that way."

His father had had to go through a lot of hard times from being so poor, but he had never turned to drink to wash away his troubles.

"Then I turned into a drinker, in spite of him, and so he never gave me anything until he died. I suppose he was afraid I would follow in my grandfather's footsteps and lose the house and everything. I can hardly blame him for it, considering what he'd been through. Still, no one can say I've squandered the family fortune on drink the way my grandfather did. I haven't exactly made the inn prosper, either, but I haven't lost it, even if I do like my drink. I figure that's doing pretty good, all in all. That's what I tell my wife, anyway."

The saké was all gone. I felt like I'd been listening to the innkeeper for a long time, but when I looked at my watch I found it was only a few minutes past eight.

"I'm afraid your soup has gotten cold," he said.

"No, no, it's fine."

"Well, when you've finished eating, please help yourself to the bath. We really should have offered you a chance before dinner."

He told me the bath was around the corner of the gallery skirting the main building, and then got up to leave.

He paused by the outer door. "At this rate, it looks like it'll snow all night," he said.

"Do you think so?"

He stepped out and slid the door shut behind him.

When I awoke the next morning, bright sunlight was filtering through the closed curtains. Outside, the neighbor's vegetable patch and apple trees were all covered with snow.

On my way to the washroom I met another man wearing one of the inn's padded robes. With a toothbrush in his mouth, he was watching some carp swim about the little pond in the garden.

AZURE SKY

"*A*nd when we turn here," Yomogida said as they rounded the corner, "we'll see the Kishigami Clinic." He pointed down the street at a walled compound with a large gate.

"That place?"

"Uh-huh, that's the place. Do you remember?"

Kazuko looked up at the western-style building within the compound. "No, I don't," she said.

"I wonder if Dr. Kishigami's still with us?" Yomogida said as they turned another corner before actually coming to the clinic gate. "I don't recall ever hearing that he passed away."

"Oh, I remember this street," Kazuko said.

"I once ran all the way up this street with you in my arms. Straight for Dr. Kishigami's. You were still in diapers."

"I know," Kazuko smiled. "I had some kind of a fit, right? And you went into a panic and grabbed me and took off running. Mom told me about it."

Yomogida paused his steps. "When I got to right about here, a small turd came tumbling out from under your baby kimono and made me stop."

He couldn't remember exactly where, but it had been more than halfway. Between his house and the clinic was just this one straight street. He had charged up this street as if running from fleet-footed Skanda.

He was a young and inexperienced husband then, in the fourth year of his marriage. Kazuko had seemed listless, so they took her temperature, and it was a hundred. Figuring she'd probably taken a chill from kicking off her blankets, they put her under the *kotatsu* quilt. But the next time they took her temperature the thermometer said a hundred and two. With a fever like that, they thought maybe it was her bowels and gave her an enema.

The first enema had no effect, so they decided to try a second— perhaps one wasn't enough. But as Yomogida was waiting for his wife to get it ready, Kazuko's eyes glazed over in a glassy stare.

"What did the doctor say?" Kazuko asked.

"I told him you'd finally had a bowel movement on the way there and now you were all right, and he just said 'Well, well.'"

Kazuko laughed.

Considering how agitated he was, Yomogida wondered that he'd even noticed the turd. But just at that moment, baby Kazuko had started to cry, and her rigid figure softened in his arms.

"So the doctor didn't do anything?"

"There wasn't anything left to do."

"Not even some medicine?"

"He might have given us something later, but right then I came home without anything."

"Walking?"

"Yeah, no more running," Yomogida said with a laugh.

Actually, he had charged up this street in the same kind of frenzy one other time as well, but *that* was something he couldn't talk about with Kazuko.

The memory of that other time had come back to him the moment they'd turned the corner toward the clinic. Until then, he had merely been thinking this was the shortest way to the house where they used to live.

All the while they talked about the turd falling out from under Kazuko's gown and making her better, the events of the other time never left his mind.

"You must have been a fast runner," Kazuko said. "You still are."

"For short distances, yes. In intramurals I remember running in the 800-meter relay and winning. I was pretty fast, I guess."

"You look like a real powerhouse when you run."

"I do?"

"Uh-huh. I didn't know you could go so fast."

Even now, he would sometimes challenge the children to a race.

"But when it comes to long distances, it's a different story," he said.

"Really?"

"A complete washout. In middle school we had a 2000-meter race that everyone at school had to run. You might think two thousand isn't all that much, but it took only a fraction of that to make me feel like I was going to die."

Kazuko laughed. "Really? I don't think I believe you."

"It's true, though. In the navy, too, we once had this race where you had to run a long way carrying full gear. It was squad against squad, so you couldn't drop out—the whole squad had to finish in good time. For that race I felt like I was going to die even before we started."

"So, what happened?"

"I keeled over in no time at all. I didn't even make it half way."

"Did you get in trouble?"

"No, fortunately it was such a sweltering hot day that even people who normally would have finished fine were dropping like flies. It was a wonder anyone finished at all, actually, and they had to call the whole race off."

"Sounds bad."

"Nobody even noticed who dropped out first."

"Did you pass out?"

"No, I didn't pass out. I quit while I still had my senses."

"That's good," Kazuko laughed, then went on. "I'm the opposite. I can hang in there pretty well in the long races, but I'm no good at the dashes. In all our field days in elementary and junior high, I never did better than third."

Kazuko had just finished tenth grade. The last time she had accompanied Yomogida on a visit to his hometown was five years ago, when she was in fifth. In the intervening years, Yomogida had come by himself a number of times, and he had come with his wife when memorial services were held for his father, but this was the first time he had come with Kazuko since she'd grown as tall as her mother.

It was also the first time while out walking with Kazuko that he had recalled those two headlong dashes from his old house to the clinic.

Which of the two had come first? Was it the time he held little Kazuko in his arms, or the time he raced off all by himself? Both times had been in winter, and, if memory served, not very far apart. The time he had made the dash alone he remembered clearly. It was on Christmas morning. But had the other time come before that, or had it come after?

Wait: it couldn't have been before. Late that fall his oldest brother had died in the hospital—died without ever seeing forty. All the relatives had come to stay at his parents' house next door, which shared a yard with Yomogida's house, and things had been pretty chaotic until the funeral was over.

His dash with Kazuko wasn't right after that. He could be sure of that because he remembered talking to his mother when he brought Kazuko back all better.

His mother had sensed something wrong and come to see if there was anything she could do. He recounted the whole story—from the first enema not working, to racing off in a panic before the second was ready, to the turd that fell out from under Kazuko's kimono. She rejoiced that the crisis had passed so quickly.

"Thank goodness," she said. "Thank goodness."

In his memory, his parents' house was quiet then. But it didn't feel like the quiet that came with sighs of relief just after his brother's services were over. It seemed later, when they'd all grown used to having it quiet again.

So perhaps it hadn't happened the same winter after all, and he only thought it had because he remembered Kazuko sleeping under the *kotatsu*. Perhaps it had happened a whole year after he'd run to the clinic alone.

The entire length of the dash with child in arms came back to him like a scene in a movie, but try as he might, he could not sort out where to place that scene within the days and months of his past. Everything about his life at the time seemed wrapped in a haze, and his memory of it unreliable.

On neither occasion had he met anyone along the way. Even in the daytime, the street saw so little traffic of any kind that the toddlers of the neighborhood could safely use it as a playground. With no one to worry about bumping into, he'd been able to run full tilt, giving it everything he had.

* * *

"And this was our house, right?" Kazuko said.

"Uh-huh."

They walked past the house where they used to live. Ten years had passed since Yomogida and his family left this house and moved to Tokyo.

Storm panels covered the upstairs windows. The two Chinese tallow trees by the front door still remained.

Instead of feeling nostalgic, Yomogida simply wanted to pass by as quickly as possible—because of his daughter beside him.

A man with his same build (though not quite as heavy as he was now) and his same face (but with a younger complexion and thicker hair that perhaps made him look like an entirely different person) had once lived in this house. And with him had lived a young wife and little girl.

2

"Congratulations! You and your new bride must become one both in body and in spirit as you build a wonderful new life together. You must truly believe that in marriage one plus one makes not two, but a single boundless unity."

The man who said these words to Yomogida had been his predecessor in the job he found when he came home from the navy in the fall of the year the war ended. His name was Kutani, and he had resigned from the firm in order to return to his hometown, but before he left, he and Yomogida had worked together as colleagues for a little over a month. Yomogida had developed a warm regard for him.

On the evening of his departure, Yomogida went to his house to say goodbye, taking with him a farewell gift of steamed bread and potatoes. He had nearly forgotten to go.

"Oh, that's right," he remembered in the midst of dinner. "This is the night Mr. Kutani leaves."

The day before, when they parted at the office, Yomogida had promised that unless something unexpected came up he would stop by to say goodbye. Now he hurried through the rest of his dinner and set out, worrying that he might already be too late. He was relieved when the house came into view and lights were still burning both upstairs and down.

"Come on in," Kutani greeted him. "It's still a real mess. I suppose I ought to tell you to leave your shoes on, but . . ."

In a room littered with short bits of straw rope, an empty seaweed canister, some dust-covered beer bottles, a blackened cooking pot, a broom without a handle, and a chopsticks case, Kutani had been packing the things he would carry with him on the train into a rucksack.

"I'd hoped to finish sooner," he said, "so we could just sit down and talk when you came. But it turned out at the last minute that I could send some things I thought I'd have to leave behind, and I had to borrow a bicycle cart to haul everything to the depot. Then I spilled the load three times at the railroad crossing, which made it take even longer. I didn't get to eat until I had a combined lunch and dinner just a few minutes ago."

He had sent his wife and child home earlier, before the war was over, and remained behind by himself in this house in the city.

"Oh, I know. Here," he said, extracting a beer bottle from his rucksack and pouring into a teacup.

"What is it?" Yomogida asked.

"It's nothing special. Just . . . just call it water. It's all I have to offer."

The teacup held a clear but slightly amber liquid. No doubt it was the saké he had set aside to drink on the train.

Without taking off the navy-issue raincoat he wore, Yomogida sat down in a clear spot on the tatami and sipped the saké. He felt like he had returned to his student days, not really so long before, when he'd helped a friend move out of his boarding house.

Kutani went upstairs to do something and soon began singing "Let's Go Over the Hills." The song had been popular when Yomogida was a boy. After a while someone went by on the street outside whistling "Until the Day of Victory." When Yomogida started singing along in a low voice, the singing from upstairs switched to "Until the Day of Victory" as well.

When Kutani came back downstairs he was carrying a blanket tied up in a wrapping cloth.

"I have to run next door for a minute, but I'll be right back. I'm all out of time, so I'll have to ask them to finish cleaning up for me."

He poured Yomogida a second cup of saké and went out.

When he came back, he had the nameplate from his front door in his hand. Carved in large characters it said "Kutani Ryotaro."

"There's a story behind this nameplate," he said. "At first I made do with one of my business cards. But when my father came to visit, he had trouble finding the place because the characters on the card were so small. He doesn't have very good eyesight. So he ordered a big nameplate with big characters and brought it to me saying now he'd be able to tell where I lived."

He stuffed the nameplate into his rucksack.

"This bottle of red ink is my own personal bottle I brought with me when I came from my last job to this one. There's still a little left, so I'm taking it with me as a memento."

This, too, he pushed into his rucksack.

What if it were to break? Yomogida worried. He wondered if taking the red ink along didn't have more to do with parsimony than sentiment.

Next came an old teacup.

"This belonged to the first set of teacups my wife and I bought when we got married," he said. "I think the set had five cups, originally, but now this is the only one left. My wife says I should throw it away, but I'm keeping it as a memento."

That's more like it, Yomogida thought. But he still couldn't help wondering if all this talk of mementos wasn't actually a cover for basic parsimoniousness.

Then Kutani brought out a large bundle with a rope crisscrossed around it, and set it down in front of Yomogida.

"I hope you don't mind, but I'd like you to take this."

"What is it?"

"Charcoal. I had this much left over. I'm sorry it's such a load to carry, but please take it and use it up."

The bundle wasn't so big that a confirmed skinflint couldn't have taken it along. That was probably why he'd tied it up with a rope. But now he was giving it to Yomogida, so maybe the charges of parsimony were off the mark after all.

Kutani also gave him some leftover manuscript paper, and five tickets to the subway and tram. Of course the tickets would have been useless in his hometown.

He poured him a third cup of saké.

"No thanks," Yomogida said, but Kutani poured anyway.

Finally he unscrewed the light bulb, put it in the empty seaweed can, and wedged it into his rucksack.

"That's it," he said. "Let's go."

After stopping to say goodbye at the house of the senior member of the block association, two doors down, Yomogida and Kutani set off down the darkened street. Kutani shouldered the bulging rucksack, and carried the wrapped-up blanket in his hand; Yomogida carried the bundle of charcoal.

It was then that Yomogida told Kutani he had gotten engaged.

"Well, well! Congratulations!" Kutani said. "But I'm disappointed I won't get to meet the bride. If you had told me sooner I might have been able to share some things with you from my own meager experience."

They reached the station and parted at the ticket gates.

"Well, here's to good work and good health for both of us. Far apart, but one in spirit," Yomogida's departing colleague said.

Eighteen years had passed since then. No one had ever sent or brought word of what happened to Kutani Ryotaro after he'd returned to his hometown. What kind of work had he found? Did he remain at the same job today? Did he still live in the seaside town he'd gone home to, with his wife and his now-grown child, in a house with "Kutani Ryotaro" carved big and bold on the nameplate by the door? And the teacup that he had taken along as a memento because it was the last of a special set—would it, too, have gone the way of the others by now, or had it somehow survived without ever chipping or breaking?

Yomogida was married two months after seeing Kutani off at the entrance to the station—in January of the New Year. And after that he had forgotten all about this former colleague of his who'd gone back to his hometown.

He had forgotten all about him for a long time.

Shortly before coming with Kazuko, during her spring vacation, on this trip to visit the family grave, Yomogida had come across Kutani Ryotaro's name while flipping through the pages of some old diaries. A picture of his former colleague immediately rose up in his mind.

Yomogida had also found in his diary the words his colleague had spoken about marriage as he trudged, rucksack-laden, toward the station. The words leaped back into Yomogida's consciousness over the expanse of eighteen years.

"Become one both in body and in spirit . . ."

"Believe that in marriage one plus one makes not two, but a single boundless unity."

Not "It is so," in marriage, but "Believe that it is so." Yomogida tried to remember how he had felt as he listened to Kutani's words. What meaning would they have held for Yomogida then, as he thought of the young woman whom he had met only once but had consented to take as his bride?

It was Yomogida's father who had suggested the match and arranged the meeting.

Yomogida gazed at the words in his diary as if he were seeing them for the first time. There was something in these words. They contained something important, something that spoke profoundly to Yomogida's experience in the eighteen years since.

He wondered: Did these words, spoken by a married man to a newly engaged man, carry no more weight than the usual stock expressions of congratulations and best wishes one would expect at such times? Or did they carry a more personal significance arising from Kutani Ryotaro's own marriage? What kind of words had they been?

Yomogida had visited Kutani at his home only twice—both times when Kutani lived alone. He had never met his wife or child. On his first visit some ten days before Kutani's departure, he had found the house dark and guessed that he must have gone out to buy his train tickets. He discovered instead that, in spite of the early hour, Kutani had already laid out his futon upstairs and was reading a book in bed.

That time, too, Yomogida's mother had given him some steamed bread and potatoes to take along, and Kutani had thanked him over and over.

In thinking back to those two evening visits now, Yomogida realized they had been like visits to a man who was divorced, or had lost his wife, who now spent his days and nights at home all alone. It seemed rather odd to think that he had received words of encouragement about his impending marriage from such a man.

Perhaps those events had a special, symbolic meaning for Yomogida. He had once come very close to being like Kutani that night—packing up his belongings, all alone, in an empty house.

Very close.

3

Yomogida had not had any breakfast that morning. He did not even know what time it was, now, as he sat at the table in his parents' house next door dishing up his own rice from the rice server. For all he knew, it was already past noon. With the sliding doors shut, the light in the room remained very dim.

"It's ridiculous," his father said in the next room. "We can't have another funeral in this house already."

His mother was there, too.

Barely a month before, a coffin surrounded by a profusion of chrysanthemums had occupied the parlor of this house. In it had lain the eldest son of the family, who had died after a long and painful illness.

"What am I going to tell people? How am I supposed to ask them to all come again, when we just got through having them drop everything to come the first time? There's no way."

How can you say that? Yomogida cried inwardly, stuffing another bite of rice in his mouth to push back a sob.

How can you say that, at the very moment when she lies on the brink between life and death?

In this room, as a child, he had gathered around the table with the rest of his family for many a boisterous and happy mealtime. His father had sat right there, and his mother had dished up their rice over there. That was how it had been all the time until he got married.

Knowing he would cry if he tried to speak, he stuffed some more rice in his mouth. He went on eating, alone, at that odd hour, in a house fallen completely silent.

4

The day was warm, without a breath of wind. The young couple had been married just six days, and this was their first Sunday together. They were walking a country road.

"No one woke me, so Mother and Tamiko were up long before I was, and I was so embarrassed," the new bride said. She wore a bright red coat and navy blue gloves, and clutched to her breast an orange purse and a cloth-wrapped bundle containing a picnic lunch and some donuts.

The couple were on their way to visit a former schoolteacher who had come to their wedding, and they'd brought the donuts along as a gift. The new bride had made them fresh after breakfast that morning, with the help of her sister-in-law.

The country road stretched on and on in a straight line. After a while they turned off to the right along the rim of a large irrigation pond, looking for a place to have their picnic. They came to a shrine with a stand of trees behind it, but as they headed toward it they saw a farmer watching them.

"It's no good," the bridegroom said.

They returned to the original road and walked on. A small village came into view. Just before the first houses, they tried a narrow path that headed off to the left along a little stream. It led them between a bamboo grove and the bank of the stream to a small clearing where the bamboo grass had been cut down.

The bridegroom ran farther on down the path, like a scout on a reconnaissance mission, to see if they were likely to be disturbed. This time everything looked fine. Back at the clearing, they unwrapped their lunch, spread the bundle-cloth by the edge of the stream, and sat down to their picnic.

As they were finishing, two boys and a farm woman came along the path.

The young couple immediately got up and started walking, he leading the way, she following in silence. She knew very well what he was thinking.

Another farm woman came toward them along the path with a grub hoe over her shoulder.

Before long they found themselves back at the original road. On the log that served as a step up to the road, the man turned to his wife.

"It's no good," he said.

"There are too many people around," she agreed. Then she added with a disappointed smile, "We might as well not have come at all."

They started walking again. At this rate they'd get to the teacher's house much earlier than expected.

Even out here in the broad countryside, surrounded by nothing but fields and rice paddies and woods, the newlyweds could find no place where they could be alone together, just the two of them.

Soon some more woods came into view, off to the left.

"We'll try there," the bridegroom said.

Taking a footpath through the vegetable fields, they made their way into the woods. Once again, they came upon a shrine.

The gods are watching no matter where we go, he thought.

Rays of sunlight filtered through the canopy of branches high above, spilling down on them as they walked on between the trees. Farther on, they stopped. He took the bundle and purse from his bride's hand and laid them on the carpet of fallen leaves.

The powder-blue ribbon in her hair was right before his eyes, and a stray hair brushed his nose. Her eyelashes flickered rapidly up and down.

"I wish the earth would quake and swallow us up right here and now," she said, her eyes brimming with tears. She pressed her face to his shoulder.

No sound came from beyond the trees. He wrapped his arms around her and held her tight, but with her coat and kimono and thick, stiffly tied sash in the way, it hardly felt like an embrace.

"I'm in a dream," she said.

From time to time he turned his eyes toward the brightness beyond the woods. Rice paddies and vegetable fields stretched out one after another, and not a person could be seen anywhere.

He started to bring his face to hers once more. Sensing his movement, she opened her eyes wide for an instant, then blinked shyly and buried her face in his shoulder again.

5

Each afternoon Mrs. Yomogida went upstairs to sit in the warm sun and let her thoughts wander while she watched Kazuko play. This had gone on for two weeks now—ever since she had finally been able to leave her bed.

Today she was thinking of last night's dream in which a crocodile had eaten her leg. It was the leg of her burned foot, not yet fully healed. (When she awakened after several days from the sleep she thought would be her last, the bottom of her foot had been badly burned by a hot water bottle.)

She had taken a hot water bottle to bed with her last night because it was so cold. But as her injured foot warmed up, it also began to hurt. Half-dreaming, half-waking, she started to moan in pain.

She was exploring the upper reaches of the Amazon with a rifle slung over her shoulder and five or six natives carrying her gear (it was exactly how she had pictured it when she read about the Amazon in school). All of a sudden she realized she had stumbled into a swamp. Her foot sank deep into the mud, and she couldn't pull it free.

The natives grabbed her arms and tried to help her, but the more she twisted and turned, the tighter the mud gripped her leg. Then one moment the mud in front of her surged as the back of a crocodile rose to the surface, and the next moment her leg was gone.

"I knew it," she thought in despair, "I knew he'd get me." Her body went limp, and she sank deep into the mud.

"Ouch!" she cried, waking up. Under the covers she had reflexively grabbed hold of her sore leg.

It was already growing light. The muscles in her thigh were tight as knots, and she could feel the lump of a swollen lymph node.

Dragging herself from bed, she limped downstairs stiffening her good leg and trying not to use the other any more than she had to. She lit the gas heater.

Now it was afternoon. If only her foot would heal more quickly! Once her foot was better, she could do anything. She wanted to get out of the house. She wanted to take the train somewhere, and look out the windows and watch the scenery go by.

Sometimes she gently pressed on the bottom of her foot through her stocking, and her hand came away smelling of pus. The infection from the burn gave off an unpleasant odor.

This musty smell of decay clung to her tenaciously, and she could not get rid of it. What if she became permanently crippled so she couldn't stand up anymore?

She could hear Kazuko opening and closing desk drawers in the next room.

After a while Kazuko grew sleepy and came to lie down beside her. She promptly fell asleep. Mrs. Yomogida covered her with a blanket.

On her way to the stairs, she glanced into the next room. Dozens of spare pen tips littered the tatami—some gold, some silver, some aluminum, all in a jumble. Kazuko had been taking boxes from the drawer and emptying them on the floor.

As Mrs. Yomogida sorted them and put them back in their boxes, they made her think of knights in shining armor. The scattered pen tips were an army of knights lying wounded on the trampled grasses of the field after a chaotic battle.

When I can go out again, she thought, I'll buy a brand new notebook and start a new diary.

She had burned her old diaries. All of them. Not only the ones from the last three years, but also the five from before she was married.

On a cold day, in the back yard of the elder Yomogidas', next door, she had placed them in the fire one by one, thinking, I won't need to keep a diary anymore.

6

The newlyweds went to see "The Bluebirds." It was the first Saturday in March now, a month and a half since their wedding.

A power outage had delayed the matinee, and they had to wait at the door for nearly two hours.

"What a pain!" the young husband said.

"It's no pain at all," his wife disagreed. "The longer the anticipation, the greater the enjoyment."

The show finally began at about half past four. The only disappointment was that they used recorded music instead of an orchestra.

Because of the delay, running the show without cuts would take until after seven—rather late for a children's theater performance with more children than grown-ups in the audience. So at first the players announced that they would skip the graveyard scene. But a chorus of protests made them change their minds.

Afterward the young couple went home saying the very scene the players threatened to cut had been the best scene in the play.

Chilchil and Michil come out together on the stage, just the two of them. A pale moon shines down over a country cemetery on a hilltop. Chilchil is about to start up the hill to where the rows of wooden crosses stand.

"I'm scared," Michil says.

Chilchil is scared, too. Scared, but trying to be brave.

"Have you ever seen a dead person?" Michil asks her brother. "Where are the dead people? Do they always stay here? Do they come outside on sunny days? Are there little children, too?"

One searching question after another, she asks—afraid she might be left behind all by herself.

Mustering his courage, Chilchil starts walking up toward the dark, cold world of the dead. Michil feels abandoned and helpless and starts to cry.

The clock in the church tower strikes midnight.

With a final burst of resolve, Chilchil runs up the hill into the cemetery. An orange-colored light bathes his tiny figure.

"Hey!" he says. "There's no dead people here."

He'd found instead a world filled with warm, gentle light.

The next best scene was called "Into the Future." A whole crowd of children come on stage wearing long blue robes. They are waiting their turn to be born.

Chilchil and Michil meet the child who's supposed to become their little brother. He has a bag.

"What's in your bag there?"

"My gifts," he answers.

"What kind of gifts?"

"Scarlet fever and whooping cough and measles."

(A big laugh from the audience.)

"And after that?"

"After that I'll die."

"Then what's the point of being born?"

Still sounding very much in high spirits, he replies, "Who knows?"

The time comes for the children scheduled to be born today to ride down to Earth on a boat.

"All right, now. Is everybody ready?" Father Time shouts, and the children start to gather from all directions, one after another, each calling out "I'm ready!" as he comes.

Some of the children are turned away. "It's not your turn yet. You have to wait until tomorrow. . . . You don't go yet, either. Come back in ten years."

One child droops his head and holds back. "I don't want to go," he says. "I want to stay right here." But he, too, must get on the boat.

The play ended a little after seven. The young couple went home through the rain that had started during the show.

7

"When's your night duty?"

"I'm not sure, but probably pretty soon. When I'm on night duty, I bet you'll be lonely, sleeping all by yourself."

For several seconds she said nothing.

"Oh, there I go again," she said with a sigh, "worrying about when you have night duty. I'm hopeless." But then she perked up. "I know. I'll keep the wooden sword by my pillow."

Why did the days go by so fast? the newlyweds often asked themselves. If only the time between seven and midnight were twice as long! That was their wish. In his diary, the young husband wrote constantly about his wife. Everyday, never tiring, all about her.

One evening it was after eleven by the time she finished her bath.

"I didn't expect you to be up still," she said. "I thought you'd be lost in the land of dreams by now."

Unfortunately, he had some work he had to finish by tomorrow morning. She said she would wait up for him, but he told her to go on to bed lest she catch a chill after her hot bath.

When he turned to look at her a little later, she lay on her side, facing his empty pillow, fast asleep.

Her diary lay unopened at the head of the bed. Beside it were a small ink jar and a pen.

As he watched, she wrinkled her brow in distress and her lips made tiny motions as if mumbling something. She looked utterly forlorn.

Slipping quietly into bed, he continued to watch her face. Soon her dream had brought her to the brink of tears, and she started rubbing her eyes.

Softly, he called her name. She opened her eyes on the third call.

"Oh, stop it!" she cried, and buried her face under the covers.

"When did you come to bed?" she asked. "I was going to write in my diary, but I fell asleep staring at the buttons on the back of your navy coat."

8

At night, around eleven, Mrs. Yomogida finished the day's chores and went upstairs. She could hear her husband's deep, regular breathing as he slept in the next room. (She had begun keeping a diary again—in the quiet of night, when she was by herself.)

Having rinsed her face with hot water before coming upstairs, she now sat down in front of the mirror stand to apply some face cream. She spread it evenly, added a hint of rouge, applied lipstick, and dabbed some perfume behind her ears with her finger. Then she stopped.

"Who am I doing this for?"

As the question hit her, tears overflowed her eyes and dropped to her knees.

Oh, how hot were her tears!

They came endlessly, on and on. When they struck her knees, she could feel them all the way to her toes.

In the morning, an ox pulling a nightsoil wagon was tied in front of the house. She started to offer him a long white radish, but got scared and dropped it when he came at it with his big wet mouth.

The nightsoil man laughed. "Don't worry. He won't bite," he said.

"Are you sure?"

She picked up the radish and held it close to the ox's mouth, and he took hold of it with his warm tongue. He had brown eyelashes and pretty eyes.

9

The newlyweds passed through the great *torii* shrine gate and entered the park. The young bride wore a hooded jacket and navy-blue slacks, with a scarf of light-blue silk around her neck.

This was the first Saturday in February. It had started out as a lovely day, but then the sky suddenly darkened as they waited for the train.

Coming out of the station, they had passed several restaurants and coffee shops.

"I'm kind of hungry," the new husband said. "Let's buy some fruit or something to take along."

"Maybe we can find some apples."

They stopped to look in at a small shop but saw no apples, only mandarin oranges.

"That's okay. Let's just go on," the husband said. He remembered that he'd brought along a whiskey flask filled with saké in his bag.

The sky kept growing darker and darker. Few other people were in the park. Barely half a year had passed since the end of the war.

"Let's go over that way."

They cut off across a meadow that rose above the path. It began to sprinkle, and they started running.

"This is what you get," the wife said. "It's your punishment."

It took the husband several moments to realize what she was talking about. On the way there, she had asked if she could read his diary. "No way," he had said curtly, and she had turned sullen. But before long she had cheered up again and talked of other things, so he had already forgotten about the diary.

They were still looking for shelter when the rain began to let up. There was no one else in sight. Tightly holding hands, they pressed ahead over the gently undulating meadow, half running, half walking.

"It's such a nice park!" the wife exclaimed over and over.

The heavy clouds and the approach of evening gave the scenery a dull, almost eerie glow.

The couple came to a small rise sloping down into a wooded hollow and sat down. The husband took out his flask of saké and poured himself a drink using the cap as a cup. The second capful he gave to his wife. Her face showed the effects almost immediately.

In the western sky they could see the top of a mountain still covered with snow. The summit stood out all the more vividly because the rest of the mountain was so dark.

"Isn't it beautiful!" The wife sat gazing dreamily up at the mountain, her lips slightly parted. "I'll never forget this scene, as long as I live." She looked at her husband's flask. "Aren't you going to have any more?"

"Mmm. What I really want right now isn't another drink."

"What is it?"

He put his arm around her shoulder and pulled her to him.

"Let's find someplace more private."

Descending into the woods, they found a small gulch with a

trickle of a stream running through it. As they walked through the trees, they skirted a wide valley to their right. The shiny windows of a building they guessed to be a hotel rose above the trees on the other side. Beneath their feet, pine needles carpeted the ground, slightly dampened by the rain.

The husband came to a spot surrounded by large clumps of tall grass on three sides and trees on the other. His wife had been following a short distance behind, singing in a low voice, but suddenly her voice stopped. Had she hidden behind a clump of underbrush somewhere, ready to jump out at him when he came to look? He didn't hear another sound.

It had begun to grow dark.

He retraced his steps in the direction he'd last heard her voice and found her standing there as if frozen, her face blanched with fright.

With a gasp of relief, she came running.

"I was so-o-o scared!" she said. "I thought we'd gotten separated."

Because they'd walked around in the rain that day, his wife felt cold as ice in bed. To make things worse, she kept rubbing her hands together.

"Stop it!" he said, and she shrank back with a forsaken look on her face.

He slept apart, without even holding her hand. She lay in heavy-hearted silence.

This was what they got for being out so long in February, the coldest month of the year, wandering aimlessly around a deserted park.

10

There was no money left in the house. Never in her life had she been quite this broke before, and Mrs. Yomogida had to think what to do. Her burned foot still troubled her, but she couldn't let that be an obstacle.

She started a load of diapers before waking Kazuko and feeding her her breakfast. All morning she remained on edge, wondering what she would do if the man came right then to collect the electric bill.

After lunch she left Kazuko with a neighbor woman who sometimes came to help, and headed downtown with her red *haori*-coat wrapped in a bundle-cloth. Riding the streetcar for the first time in a month brightened her spirits.

She went to the same shop she had visited before Christmas, when she had sold another red coat to get money for presents. That time there had been a chubby little baby sleeping in a basket, but today the shopkeeper was alone.

When she had had to pawn her things for want of money, she pawned first the things she'd worn in girls' school. Her brown overcoat, her black overcoat, and her hooded half-coat—she had let them all go. She thought it best to try to put that era of her life behind her as quickly as she could.

The hooded half-coat she had designed herself. It had immediately become her favorite, and it had made her especially happy when her husband had said *he* liked it, too, the first time she wore it after they were married.

"You look like a Russian maiden," he'd said. "It's perfect."

Not really wanting to give it up, she had saved it until last, but finally it had had to go. Those were the days when she'd been growing more and more depressed.

After that, nothing else with school-day memories remained.

"How much can you give me for it?" Mrs. Yomogida asked as the shopkeeper examined the red *haori*-coat.

"Fifty yen."

"Fine," she said. Fortunately the shopkeeper had not remembered her face.

The last time she came, on her way home she had stood for a long time looking at a huge Santa Claus decoration covering the side of the department store facing the trolley street.

Santa Claus leaped from the chimney into his sleigh, and the reindeer pulled it slowly away. Then everything went into reverse, and he jumped back into the chimney again.

11

When the young husband got home from work, his wife greeted him in a state of shock. He asked her what was wrong, but for a long time she would not answer.

"I did something terrible," she finally said. She took from her pocket a letter and a small locket wrapped in paper.

The letter was from their go-between's wife. The newlyweds had made a courtesy call on their go-between and his wife three days before, and while there, the new bride had dropped the locket she wore around her neck. She had come home without ever noticing it missing.

The go-between's wife had sent her housekeeper to deliver the letter and locket. She said because they hadn't found it until a whole day later, they didn't make the connection at first, but then when they all put their heads together they finally realized whose locket it must be.

"But you got it back. That's all that matters," the husband said.

His wife shook her head vehemently.

"What do you mean?" he asked.

"There was a picture," she said, opening the face of the tiny locket. "In here. And it's gone."

"Whose picture?"

"Yours. From the navy."

Now *when* had she gone and done that? he wondered. But he shrugged it off. "Oh well."

"I'm so sorry."

"You shouldn't scare me like that. You said you did something terrible so I thought maybe you'd started a fire or something." The look on her face when he first got home had indeed made him fear the worst. "So long as you got the locket back, never mind the picture," he said.

"How can you say never mind, when I lost your precious picture somewhere?"

"But you didn't lose me, so now you can forget it."

"That's true, but . . ." It puzzled her how only the picture could have disappeared when the locket came back. Fretting about that had kept her from doing a thing all day, she told him.

"You're talking about a tiny little picture that fit inside here," he said. "It could have fluttered out anytime at all."

"Where?"

"Onto the ground somewhere."

"Inside the house, you mean?"

"Or in the yard. It's a big house. It could have been anywhere."

No one in the go-between's household would have had any reason to open the locket and steal the picture pasted inside. No one there would have done a thing like that.

Still, it was possible that someone else had found the locket first and taken just the picture. And in any case, it hardly seemed a good omen for the picture to disappear like that.

Later, when the two of them were alone, his wife burst out, "Hit me."

"What are you saying? We don't live in a military state anymore, you know."

"But you have to hit me. I want you to. I mean, really, what could be the matter with me?—losing something like this from around my neck, and not even noticing until someone else finds it and brings it back to me."

"Just forget it. Don't think about it any more."

For several moments she said nothing.

"Two weeks," she sighed. "It's only two weeks since we got married, and look what I've done already. I hate to think what's in store for me down the line."

12

After lunch Mrs. Yomogida went to the market. A typhoon was apparently on its way, and the sky was dotted with clouds like white-capped waves trailing wisps of foam. It looked ominous.

That evening her in-laws next door had visitors. She went to help and joined them for dinner as well.

Washing dishes afterward with her sister-in-law Tamiko, talk turned to Tamiko's husband, who had died last year. Tamiko's eyes quickly filled with tears. In just two months it would be time for the first anniversary services.

Not long ago, Tamiko had brought over her diary.

"I'd like you to look at this, sometime, when you're alone," she said.

She had written a great deal about her husband—about how he held her in the middle of the night when she woke up from a bad dream; about when he took her to the beach; about how he died in the hospital. And about feeling so lonely after his death—even wishing she could die, too.

The diary also told what her husband had said to her the day after they got married:

"I'm going to make you happy for the rest of your life, and that's a promise. So you have to promise to tell me everything, and not keep things bottled up inside when you're lonely or hurting."

13

"I've decided from now on I'm never going to put off my diary until the next day," Mrs. Yomogida declared as she came into the bedroom after her bath and sat down at the desk.

Her husband was reading in bed but soon grew sleepy. She heard him close his book and turned to look at him.

"Tired?"

"I can't keep my eyes open."

"Go ahead and go to sleep, then. I'll wake you up again when I finish."

He dropped off almost instantly.

When he awoke, the lamp was still shining. He looked up from his pillow and saw his wife slumped over the desk, asleep. It had already started to grow light outside.

"Hey!" he called, reaching over to nudge her in the back. She sat up.

"What time is it?" she asked.

"It's morning already, you numskull. You fell asleep over your diary."

"Brrrrr, it's cold."

"It's five-thirty. Come on to bed. You can still get a good hour's sleep."

As she changed into her nightgown she complained repeatedly of the cold. It was only the beginning of April.

She slipped in under the covers, bringing a deep chill with her.

"A veritable Snow Maid," he said.

"I'm so-o-o co-o-old."

He pulled her close and started rubbing her all over with his hands and feet. Her chill spread to him, and a shiver ran through his body.

"If you think you'll catch a cold, you will, so don't let yourself think it no matter what."

"My head aches," she said.

After a while she told him she was starting to feel warmer.

"When did you fall asleep, anyway?"

"I don't know."

"This is absurd. I can't take my eyes off you for a minute."

Finally she seemed to have warmed up, so he stopped rubbing her and let her sleep. Outside the window it had grown almost completely light.

14

In the morning Mrs. Yomogida went to get their ration of flour and stopped at the bookstore on her way home. Flipping through a music magazine, she found a description of a piece called "Adventures in a Perambulator." It went like this:

> First movement: Nurse puts me in my baby buggy and we go for a walk.
>
> Second movement: We meet a policeman. He stops to talk awhile with Nurse.
>
> Third movement: The sound of a hurdy-gurdy comes from nearby. A beggar is turning the crank. The policeman scolds him and he moves on, but then the music starts again somewhere farther away.
>
> Fourth movement: The lake. Waves large and small dance in the beautiful sunlight that pierces the water in thousands of tiny rays.
>
> Fifth movement: Dogs. We meet dogs on the road.
>
> Sixth movement: Dreams. Lying in my buggy, I grow tired and think of my mother. I want to go home. The clicking of Nurse's footsteps behind the buggy no longer seems so reassuring.

She couldn't really tell what the piece would be like but wished she could hear it once. She hadn't been to a concert since she'd gone with her husband on Christmas Eve.

She had fallen while she was out—twice. It must have looked pretty silly, she thought afterward, for the grownup to fall instead of the child. What could be the matter with her, that she would fall like that—not just once, but twice?

That night she didn't do the dishes until after giving Kazuko a bath and putting her to bed, so it was almost eleven by the time she finished.

When she'd gone next door for some firewood to warm the bath, the white daffodils stood out even in the moonless darkness and filled the air with their scent. After taking her own bath and putting everything away, she went back to cut some.

Groping in the dark, she discovered there were only three stems with flowers. She cut just one and put it in a tumbler of water on the table.

15

Several large loquats sat cooling in a cut-glass bowl filled with water. Yomogida's elder brother had bought them on his way home.

It was June of the year Yomogida had gotten married. His mother and father had gone to the other house, and only he and his brother and their two wives remained.

"Do you think my face looks skinnier these days?" his brother asked, setting down his glass of wine. "Downtown today I noticed my reflection in a store window, and I couldn't believe how skinny I looked. So I felt my face with my hands, and sure enough, my cheekbones stick out sharp like this without any meat on them at all."

He pressed his hands to his sunburnt cheeks as he spoke.

"Back when I was on the swim team, I remember weighing one-sixty. I even remember getting teased about having a spare tire once, around the time I graduated. But I doubt I weigh much more than one-thirty now. Where did it all go?"

He'd never suffered from poor health. The loss of weight was from overwork.

What if my brother were suddenly to die, this very evening? Yomogida wondered. Would I cry, regretting that I hadn't been a kinder, more agreeable brother?

"It feels like a night for drinking," his brother said, picking up the wine bottle and taking several long swigs one after the other. He didn't usually drink like this.

(A year ago around this time, they had both been in the service. Yomogida's brother had been in the army.)

"What do loquat leaves make you think of?" the elder Yomogida asked.

"Loquat leaves?" The two wives looked at each other in puzzlement.

"When I see loquat leaves," he said, answering his own question, "I always think of Grandma, who died when I was eight. She was living with our uncle at the old home place in the mountains when she died, and I went there with my dad for the funeral. While I was there, I heard this story."

One day Grandma went to visit a relative in the next village, taking along her school-age grandson. Grandma was seventy-two, and it was a very hot day.

On the way back they came to where a single loquat tree stood in the middle of the rice paddies, and Grandma stopped.

"I'm pooped," she said to the boy. "Let's rest here a bit."

Reaching up, she tore four leaves from the tree to spread on the ground and sat down. They rested for quite a while.

The next day Grandma took to her bed, and two weeks later she died.

"And when they told me the story, they actually showed me the leaves. They'd saved them because they had turned out to be a keepsake of the very last time she'd gone out of the house. But, you know, I've always wondered: Did the boy who went with her bring the leaves back? Or did Grandma bring them back herself?"

His sunburnt face and hands glowed bright from the drink. This was the brother who died two years later.

"To actually see the leaves like that suddenly made me sad. Until then, I hadn't really felt a thing. I was just excited about being able to go on a boat trip with Dad."

16

"Be careful now," Yomogida said. "If you got run over here, they'd take you straight to your grave. We'd have to skip the funeral."

Kazuko laughed.

They waited to cross the busy trolley street, watching the cars race by one after another. The entrance to the cemetery was right on the other side.

A bucket with a bouquet of flowers dangled from Yomogida's hand, and Kazuko held a roll of lighted incense. They had come directly to the cemetery from the train, but left their luggage at the stonecutter's shop where they bought the flowers and incense.

"All right, let's cross," Yomogida said.

They went through a large gateway, and now they were safe. A path paved with stones stretched out straight along the fence.

"We go clear to the end," he said, and began walking. Kazuko would not remember the way since the last time she came, many years ago. She was still a small child then.

"Here we turn right." He looked up at a building that came into view off to the left. "And you don't want to go that way. Make sure you don't find yourself over by that smokestack."

"Stop teasing, Dad," she protested with a little laugh. But then she added more seriously, "I won't. Not if I can help it."

"Now we go this way."

They turned and walked between rows of grave markers.

"I don't remember it being such a big place."

"It's a big place, all right. We go straight this way until we see a huge, tall laurel tree on my side. That's the landmark."

Every time he came this far, his heart started beating a little faster, and his steps unconsciously quickened as if he were on his way to meet someone.

When his eldest brother died and they established the family grave here (they did not have one before), Yomogida's father had been especially pleased by the giant laurel tree that would make it easy for visitors to find the place. For a father discouraged and grieving from the loss of his firstborn son, finding this tree had offered a measure of comfort.

And what had Yomogida been doing at that important time? What had he been doing while his father was busy selecting stones and planning the grave site and deciding on the inscription?

"Look. It's coming into view."

"Oh, yeah, I see it."

When he came alone, he inwardly marked his progress and began addressing his family as he walked: "Look, I'm almost there. I can see the tree now. I haven't been back in quite a while, but I've come to see you all again today." Gazing at the laurel tree that had so pleased his father, he would walk up the path with a flower-filled pail in one hand and a roll of incense in the other.

Today, though, he was thinking of Kazuko, walking beside him. He remembered she had been here when the new grave was first unveiled, in June of the year after his brother's death.

It was a hot and muggy day. Even when he stood perfectly still, he could feel the perspiration dripping down his back inside his suit jacket.

For Yomogida's father and mother it was a season of pain and quiet mourning. But what in the world had Yomogida himself been doing then?

In the family picture taken at the unveiling, Kazuko alone was looking the other way, stretching her tiny arms toward the inscription stone standing next to the main grave marker.

Yomogida's father and mother stood to one side, looking very old. The heat had made them look even older than usual.

Yomogida himself was in the back. After coming for the unveiling, he had not visited again for a long time.

Two years later, Yomogida's father died. That time they didn't all gather around the grave and have someone take their picture. They had done things like that only when his father was still living.

Left behind alone, his mother had not been one to do such things. The family had grown much quieter then.

"There. Now you can really see it," Yomogida said, pointing toward the giant laurel.

"It's beautiful."

"Look how big it is, standing so tall above all the others. Isn't it a great spot to have your grave! Now, wait right here while I go get some water."

"I'll do it."

"No, that's okay."

Taking the flowers from the pail in her hand, Kazuko waited where she was.

When Yomogida came back, he did the things he always did when he visited the grave alone—as if to show Kazuko how they were to be done. He removed the old, wilted flowers from the flower holders and took them to the trash basket, then poured water into each of the holders to wash out the stagnant water, making it overflow until the remaining water was completely clear.

He also washed out the water in the round hollow in front of the grave, and went to throw away several small pieces of litter.

Kazuko went for more water. Going back and forth to the faucet, she poured several more buckets of water over the dark, shiny gravestones. The entire surface of the inscription stone glistened with water. On it, in the first position closest to the edge, were carved Yomogida's brother's name and the date of his death. Next came his father's name, and then his mother's.

"After Grandpa died," Yomogida said, "when we had his name carved here, Grandma said she wanted to have her name carved, too. So we had them both done at the same time."

"Really?" Kazuko seemed surprised that they would do such a thing.

"Only her name, of course. And to show that she hadn't actually died yet, they filled in the carved letters with vermilion paint. It's mostly gone now, but if you look closely you can still see some red spots left."

"You're right."

His mother had died six years after his father.

Kazuko kept going back for more water to pour over the dark, smooth stones.

"That's enough. Stop dumping so much water. The whole place'll turn into a swamp," Yomogida could almost hear his father saying.

A mirror of water remained on the flat top of the main stone, reflecting the spring sky.

"Look. You can see the sky," he said.

Kazuko gazed into the reflection.

Finally they were ready to place the flowers in the flower holders.

"The flowers make such a difference," Yomogida said. "First you get the stones all glistening with water, then you bring in the fresh flowers, and suddenly it's all bright and cheerful."

"It's pretty."

They stood side by side looking at the grave.

"I always like to look at it when it's like this."

The hole for the incense was plugged up. Yomogida tried to clean it out with a twig but the twig broke right away. Kazuko found a small stone chipped in half and carefully dug out what remained.

When they stuck the incense in the hole, the burning tip almost touched the face of the gravestone.

Together they squatted down in front of the grave, folded their hands, and closed their eyes.

17

In the evening Mrs. Yomogida thought she heard a voice from next door and went out onto the veranda to see. A burst of hail was rapidly whitening the ground. She rushed to take in the laundry and then stood watching the large hailstones come down.

"Maybe it was like this when the locusts rained from the sky."

She was thinking of the book she'd read the night before. The story told of an English pilot who crash-landed in a rocky riverbed somewhere in the deserted Mongolian countryside.

He had injured his leg, and he couldn't walk, so when he ran out of food he tried making a kite. But it was no use because there was no wind. He thought all he could do now was wait for inevitable death, and—cool-headed fellow—he simply climbed back into the cockpit and went to sleep, when suddenly locusts began to fall from the sky.

At first he thought it was rain, then the patter grew so loud he thought it was hail. But it was locusts.

How astonished he must have been when he opened his eyes to see a big fat locust sitting practically on the tip of his nose!

And the locust must have blinked in astonishment as well, for in less than an instant it had been seized by the man and thrown into his mouth.

When I came back to life that time, she reflected, I wonder if it was by the same power as the one that rescued the injured pilot with a shower of locusts from heaven.

18

In the afternoon Mrs. Yomogida took Kazuko to the zoo. April showers repeatedly interrupted their meanderings.

They took cover at tea stands during the brief cloudbursts, and when the sun came out again they walked on. The burn on her foot had healed, but Mrs. Yomogida still limped a little, out of habit.

If she pressed where it had been infected she still felt some pain. Dr. Kishigami said it was nothing to worry about, she would get used to it and it wouldn't bother her anymore. But she hadn't reached that point yet.

Two Japanese bears with white, crescent-moon collars shared a single cage. She wondered if they were mates. They both had dark, sad eyes.

Six years ago, when she was still in school and the war was getting worse and worse, she'd come to the zoo thinking she might not be able to see her favorite animals very much longer. She had heard rumors that the animals would be killed once air raids began.

She remembered that sweltering early September day. The polar bears had looked rather well cooked, one of them lying motionless in the lukewarm water of the pool, and the other pacing back and forth on the flat rock beside it.

Over and over and over, the pacing bear took three bobbing steps forward, stretched his neck way out front, then retreated with three bobbing steps backward. He'd apparently been pacing the same spot all day, for the surface of the rock glistened in just that one place.

She watched him awhile, wondering how long he would keep it up, but he never stopped. In the end she became annoyed at his unchanging consistency. Forget it, then, she thought, and walked away. After a few moments she turned around abruptly, as if trying to catch him off guard, but he had not let up.

Later, from farther away, she couldn't resist looking again. He was still at it.

Had those polar bears been killed, too? she now wondered.

In the cage where the lions used to be were two black and white hogs as big as calves. When Kazuko threw in some pieces of rice cracker, a third hog with tusks came rushing out, and all three grunted fiercely as they butted heads in their scramble to get the food.

On a bench in front of the camels' cage sat three Korean women wearing traditional Korean dresses of white and spring green and pink. Their backs were turned to the camels, and they sat quietly, without saying a word.

TWO MEN AND
THE AUTUMN WIND

"Those things really make my mouth water."

Yomogida was on his way out, but he still had some time when he had finished getting ready, so he paused to watch his wife making rolled sushi for dinner.

Mrs. Yomogida knelt on the wood floor of the kitchen in front of the low table she'd brought in from the tatami room. The various makings were arranged before her on the table, and a cypress sushi tub filled with rice sat on the floor to her right. She had bought this tub at the department store just last spring, and the wood still looked brand new. After seasoning it by soaking it for a day and a night in vinegared water, she had given the tub its maiden outing when she made some country-style sushi on the anniversary of Yomogida's mother's death.

Until then, she had had to make do with the largest of her mixing bowls. Unfortunately, its deep bottom made it hard to cool the steaming rice quickly enough when tossing it with the vinegar sauce. The rice tended to stay soggy.

Getting a proper sushi tub had made a big difference. The tub's broad bottom let her spread the rice out in a nice thin layer, and because the wooden sides and bottom absorbed some of the steam as she mixed, the rice came out light and tasty. There's always something better about things that have been used since olden times.

Mrs. Yomogida reached for a sheet of *nori* at her far left. Directly in front of her on the table was a cutting board. On the cutting board she had spread a small bamboo mat, and, on the bamboo mat, a dishcloth. Now she laid the sheet of *nori* on this dishcloth.

Next, she took the rice ladle (she had bought this at the same time as the tub—a large and easy-to-use ladle several times the size of an ordinary one) and lifted some rice onto the *nori*, pressing it down as she evened it out.

Waiting on individual plates on the table were the fillings, each cooked in its own sauce: freeze-dried tofu, *shiitake* mushrooms, shaved gourd strips (the mushrooms and gourd strips were on the same plate), sweet omelette, cucumber strips, and trefoil. Mrs. Yomogida's fingers danced from plate to plate, picking up fillings and lining them up on top of the rice. The long gourd strips had to make a round-trip over and back across the rice to fit.

When the fillings were all in place, she dipped her fingers in a bowl of water and pressed down on the rice here and there. Yomogida asked what that was for, and she said to flatten the spots that weren't even. After dipping her fingers in the water one more time to moisten the far edge of the *nori* (so this edge would stick to the other), she raised herself up on her knees and began rolling the front of the bamboo mat toward the back.

The small bamboo mat, hardly any larger than the *nori*, moved almost like magic in Mrs. Yomogida's hands, and in less than a jiffy everything had been wrapped into a cylinder.

Finally, after giving a quick twist to the dishcloth protruding from each end of the cylinder (this firmed up the rice so it wouldn't spill out the ends), she spread open the bamboo mat and dishcloth to reveal the completed sushi roll.

"I didn't know you intended to go out today. That's why I decided to make sushi," Mrs. Yomogida said after transferring the finished roll to a plate. That made five. "Why don't you have a few pieces before you go?"

"Oh, I don't know," he said vaguely, leaving it unclear whether he would or he wouldn't. "They sure do look good, though."

"You wouldn't want to take any along, I don't suppose," she said. "Since you're going drinking, I mean."

"I think not."

"But you could have a few pieces before you go."

She chose one of the five rolls lined up on the plate and placed it on the cutting board. After wiping her large kitchen knife twice on a wet dishcloth, she began slicing.

"The end pieces here," she said, "taste best. They have lots of the fillings and not so much rice." After each cut she wiped the blade again on the wet dishcloth.

"My dead brother used to like *nori* rolls, I remember," Yomogida said. "When he was on the swim team in high school and they were having training camp, if he went out somewhere and came back late, he used to buy one of these rolls at the shop in front of the station and walk back to camp eating it along the way. He'd chomp on it whole as he walked along the river."

"Really?"

"So when my brother and his friends gave each other nicknames, they called my brother 'Cutless.'"

"Cutless?"

"Uh-huh. He ate the whole roll without cutting it, so he was Cutless."

Mrs. Yomogida laughed.

"I was only in grade school then, but I still remember it. You know, I bet they really do taste better if you eat them whole like that."

"They must!"

"He said he held it like this and just bit off mouthfuls from the end as he walked. Of course, that wouldn't work if it were already sliced. He couldn't have eaten while he walked."

"I suppose not."

Mrs. Yomogida stood up to get a saucer from the cupboard, placed one of the newly cut pieces on it, and held it out for Yomogida. He took it and put it in his mouth.

"Mmm-mmm," he said.

"How about some more?"

"No, one's enough."

His eyes lingered on the rolls lined up on the plate. Their *nori* cloaks had such an inviting sheen, and they looked so plump and satisfying. They'd swallowed up all those different fillings, and yet gave not a hint on the outside, sitting there casually as though they were nothing more than met the eye.

It'd sure be nice if I could take some to Shibahara, Yomogida thought. In fact, this same thought had been going through his mind for several minutes. Shibahara was the friend he would meet at six o'clock today. His wife had died two years before, and he now lived alone with his only daughter, a high school senior.

Yomogida and Shibahara had already met twice during summer vacation. Actually, it was Shibahara who had a summer vacation, since he was a college teacher. Yomogida stayed home all year long, writing stories or thinking about what he would write next, so the idea of a vacation didn't really apply to him. Strictly speaking, that is. In practice, when school let out for the summer and his three children started hanging around the house all day, the rhythms of his own activities quite naturally fell in step with theirs.

The get-togethers of the two men had no particular purpose except to talk about whatever came to mind over a few drinks, and they always began at the same beer hall in the basement of a department store next to one of the main rapid transit terminals in the city. The first one to arrive waited for the other on the sidewalk at the top of the basement stairs, which, being also the entrance to an underground walkway, saw a constant flow of pedestrians.

They had met there once at the beginning of July and once toward the middle of August. Today was the first of September, so Shibahara's classes would start up again in about four or five days. They wanted to get together before that happened, to catch up on their talking one last time.

Yomogida had been the one who phoned.

"Right now my daughter's away," Shibahara said, "But she should be back in about two hours, and then I can go out."

"School?"

"No, school doesn't start until next week. She went to visit her cousins."

Since there was no one else to watch the house, Shibahara said he would call when his daughter got back, and they could decide on a time then. He hung up the phone. Almost exactly two hours later, he called to say his daughter had returned.

In the Shibahara household, it was the daughter—she looked and sounded just like her mother—who cooked the meals. She'd learned to cook by watching her mother, and her specialties were hamburger steaks and potstickers. But Yomogida wondered if she ever steamed *komatsuna* greens or sautéed burdock and carrots to make the garnishes that gave color to a meal. And did she make rolled sushi? Yomogida doubted she ever went to that kind of trouble.

If Yomogida were on his way to visit Shibahara at home, he could take some of these *nori* rolls along, but meeting in town made things awkward. It would probably be after midnight by the time Shibahara got home, so even if Yomogida took him some sushi to share with his daughter, it would be tomorrow before they had a chance to eat it. The fillings might still be just as good, but the *nori* and rice would not. It seemed a waste.

In that case, Yomogida went on pondering, how would it be if he took some along for the two of them to eat tonight, whenever they thought they'd had about enough to drink?

"Let's stop in for some rice balls," Shibahara often suggested when they were nearing the time to head home. Even when they ate something fairly substantial early in the evening, by midnight they were usually hungry again. Tonight they could eat this sushi instead of their usual rice balls.

The tricky part might be deciding just when and where, though. Most times when they went out, the evening had a kind of flow to it, and they could simply drift along with that flow knowing it would eventually tell them when it was time to go home. But if taking the sushi along put him on edge, wondering when was the right time, it could turn into a troublesome piece of baggage.

Yomogida was still turning all this over in his mind when it came time to leave the house.

"How many minutes fast is that clock?" he asked.

His wife glanced back at the clock under the dish cupboard. "Seven," she said. "So it should actually be about 4:30 right now."

"Good," he said, setting his watch by his wife's calculation. "I think maybe I'll be going."

"Yes, if you start now, you'll have plenty of time."

Rising from the table, Mrs. Yomogida went to the front foyer and took out Yomogida's shoes from the shoe cupboard.

"Last time," said Yomogida, stepping into his shoes, "the train pulled in just before I got to the station, and I missed it by seconds. It made me five minutes late. I wouldn't want to keep Shibahara waiting again."

"No, you wouldn't."

He now had his shoes on, and the only thing left was to open the door and leave, but he paused.

"I'll bet they never have homemade sushi at the Shibahara's," he said.

"No, I don't suppose they do. Will you take some along, then?"

"Maybe I should," he said, carried along by the strength of his wife's voice.

"Yes, why don't you? Wait just a second, I'll wrap some up."

They both went back to the kitchen.

"I have the perfect container." She opened the cupboard and took out a foil au gratin pan, then kneeled at the table again, selected the nicest looking roll, wiped her knife on the wet cloth, and started slicing.

"I've got plenty of time," Yomogida said as he stood watching.

"Yes, I know."

"Put those end pieces in, too."

"Okay. I'll do that."

2

Yomogida stood at the edge of the sidewalk near the rear corner of the department store, looking up and down the street and watching the people go by. Since his arrival a chill wind had begun to blow.

This time a train had pulled in exactly as he got to the station, and he'd decided to go ahead and take it even though he knew it would make him arrive too early. How could he pass up a train that seemed to have come just for him? Since he'd not only left the house earlier but also caught a train without having to wait, he wound up getting there a full thirty minutes ahead of time.

"I should have worn my jacket."

Yomogida had worn only a short-sleeved shirt and light pants, and brought with him only the package of sushi, like a take-out lunch. He'd been kicking himself for his mistake almost from the moment he'd arrived.

It wasn't that he thought he should have worn his jacket because August had turned to September today. He thought so because it actually was cold.

When he left the house, the sun still shone high in the sky. It had in fact been quite a hot day.

The sun was still shining, too, when his train crossed the big river where sailboats dotted the water. But by the time it had passed through the sparsely built outskirts of the city to where the houses gradually crowded closer together, the women he saw walking the nearby streets with their shopping baskets had taken on an evening glow. That was when he really began to worry about the bare arms extending from his short-sleeved shirt.

In fact, to tell the truth, it was only a short time after leaving the house that he had first started thinking he should have worn his jacket. But by then he had already descended the steep hill by the cliff, and he was reluctant to turn back. He'd left home early, all right, but if he went back to get his jacket now, it might make him late. Perhaps not oh-so-terribly late, but probably just-a-few-minutes late, like the last time.

Besides, this was no place for dashing home to get something he suddenly realized he should have brought. To run up that steep hill by the cliff was out of the question. Just running up, he could perhaps manage—if that were the end of it. But to run up the hill and get his jacket and then have to turn around and run the whole long way to the station would be a test beyond his endurance. At times like this, living on top of a hill had its disadvantages.

If it were something else, Yomogida thought—something like his train ticket or his wallet—then he'd have to go back no matter what. But he was only talking about a jacket, not something he simply couldn't do without. It was merely a precaution: he was going drinking and he'd be out late and it might get cold; if he wore his jacket, he wouldn't have to worry about the cold.

In the end Yomogida chose to walk on toward the station dressed as he was rather than risk being late by going back for his jacket.

"It's not as if I'll be spending time in a refrigerator," he mumbled to himself.

When his wife had put his shirt out for him, she had chosen one with a warmer fabric—a shirt suited to the period a little before summer, around June. She hadn't completely forgotten that it would cool off in the evening, but rather had made what she thought was the perfect choice for the circumstances.

As Yomogida stood at the edge of the sidewalk watching the passersby, he mainly observed the men. A lot of them still had on short-sleeved shirts. Now and then a man with thinning hair and quite evidently much older than Yomogida would walk by wearing an ordinary short-sleeved shirt.

"Now there's a man who's kept his vigor," Yomogida thought. "That's the way to be."

On the other hand, when he saw a young man who still looked like a student walk by sheathed head to toe in an obviously new and expensive suit, he felt somehow let down.

Those wearing suits were clearly in the minority, and most of the men coming from work were still in summer wear. But seeing so many short-sleeved shirts held no consolation for Yomogida. These people, after all, had finished their day's labors and were now headed straight homeward. They had dressed themselves correctly for working during the day at the office. Even if a nippy breeze came up after the sun went down, all they had to do was get on the train and go home. Short sleeves were fine.

But Yomogida had remained at home during the heat of the day and come into town about the time everything cooled off. And he'd dressed exactly the same as the people who'd worked in downtown offices during the day—even though he planned to be out until near midnight.

If you divided the passersby into two groups, the people headed home and the people staying in town, those staying in town were wearing suits. There was no way to know what kind of business they had or where they might be going, but the men who were on their way to evening appointments had all fortified themselves with suits. There were no bare arms among them, only bare faces. And they strode briskly by in front of Yomogida with the confident air of men who had taken full measure of what the evening held in store.

Behind the stairs leading down to the basement, set back a little from the sidewalk, was an elevator. The elevator provided direct service to a beer garden on the roof (Yomogida had never gone there), and four or five young men serving as touts hung about the stairway—standing, squatting, and sitting on the steps.

"Rooftop beer garden! Right this way!"

Their job, it appeared, was to call this out and point toward the elevator whenever they saw a potential customer, but in all the time Yomogida had been watching, the only ones to go in were a middle-aged man in an open-collared shirt and his date.

The young men seemed quite bored. One of them came out onto the sidewalk and stood beside Yomogida watching the cars and busses race by on the street. They all wore white, short-sleeved shirts, but none of them showed any sign of being cold.

They simply had nothing to do because they weren't getting any customers.

3

"I'm afraid I'm a little late," Shibahara said as they started down the stairs.

"Not at all," Yomogida said. "I got here way ahead of time. It was only 5:30."

"Sorry about that."

"No, no, not at all. I was late last time, so I wanted to make sure I'd be on time today, and I left the house a bit early. But then a train came as soon as I reached the station, and that made me get here even earlier than I'd planned."

Shibahara had worn a jacket, and under his jacket he had on a long-sleeved shirt.

I knew it, Yomogida thought. I, the one with a wife, came in short sleeves, while Shibahara, who lives alone with his daughter, came appropriately jacketed.

He doubted it was the daughter who'd thought of the evening chill and told Shibahara to wear his jacket. True, she was a girl and a high school senior, so she might well be attentive to her father's needs. But she probably wouldn't think of something like that. No. It had to be Shibahara himself.

"I suppose I'd better wear my jacket today," he'd no doubt said to himself. "It'll get pretty chilly after dark."

The last time, too, Shibahara had come in a long-sleeved shirt. That was in the middle of August, when one sun-scorched day followed another. Even at a time like that, because he knew they'd be out until late, he'd worn a long-sleeved shirt. Yomogida had come in a thin, short-sleeved shirt.

We're backward, Yomogida thought. You'd think I was the one living alone with my daughter, and Shibahara was the one with a wife.

Actually, Shibahara had always been careful this way, even before his wife died. In early winter, when office workers still went about in the daytime without their overcoats, Shibahara wore his overcoat any time he expected to be out after dark.

Maybe the illness that had kept him in bed once for nearly half a year had taught him to be more careful about his health. Or could it really have all been from his wife's attentiveness? Perhaps it wasn't either of them in particular, but both tried to be careful.

Reaching the bottom of the steps, Yomogida and Shibahara came to their usual beer hall. They could not find any empty tables, but when they turned back after surveying the room all the way to the rear, a waiter they knew showed them to a table already occupied by another man.

This was what they did here whenever the place got crowded. The man was older than Yomogida and Shibahara, and he had a tankard of beer on the table in front of him.

"Excuse us," they said with a bow and sat down.

"I wonder if I'll forget this if I put it under here," Yomogida said, peering under the table. "Seems a bit chancy."

"What is it?"

"A *nori* roll."

"A present for your wife?"

"No, no. She was making them when I was getting ready to leave. I thought it might be nice to have some while we drank."

"Oh, so you brought it from home?" Shibahara had seen the department store wrapping paper and jumped to conclusions. "I thought maybe you'd bought it. While you were waiting for me."

"No, it's homemade. She was rolling them right when I was about to leave, and they looked so good . . ."

"Well then, we can have some later."

A waiter brought a plate of skewered shrimp to the man sitting beside them. The man picked up his knife and fork and dug right in. It was the dish Yomogida and Shibahara always ordered first when they came here.

4

"The other day I stepped out to the bookstore, and on my way home I saw this great-looking French bread," Shibahara said.

The man beside them had long since finished his shrimp and departed, leaving the table to the two of them.

"So I bought a loaf and took it home and had some that evening with my whiskey. It's really good with a little bit of butter, because of the salt."

"I can imagine."

"Well, at first I was breaking off small pieces by hand and putting them in my mouth, but after a while that started to seem like too much trouble, so I picked up the whole loaf and tried to bite a piece straight off with my teeth. You know, I'd always told my daughter it was bad manners not to break the bread into small pieces first, but there I was sticking the whole loaf in my mouth. Then all of a sudden I heard this big noise."

"Where?"

"Right in my mouth. My daughter sat there staring at me, saying 'What'd you do, Dad?' You should have seen the startled look on her face."

"It must have been an awfully big noise."

"I guess. I didn't know what it was, but it seemed like I'd bitten into something hard in the bread."

"And?"

"I wondered, What could *that* have been? and then out comes my false tooth, broken clean in two right at the gum." Shibahara laughed. "What a surprise!"

"One tooth?"

"Uh-huh. Right here." He touched his cheek at the spot. "I've already had a new one put in, of course, but, I mean, I've never had anything like that happen to me before."

"I've never heard anything like it either."

"I got that tooth year before last in December, so it hasn't been quite two years yet. I remember feeling kind of disappointed when I had to have my own tooth pulled and replaced with a false one. Now I have to have this strange thing put into my mouth, I thought. Since it was only one tooth, they had to stabilize it with gold wires looped around the teeth on either side, you know, and I thought, what a bother, what a sad case. I forgot all about how sore it had been and started thinking, Oh, oh, oh, I wish I had my own tooth back, why was I so hasty, I've made a big mistake. But after a while I got used to it pretty well, and it didn't bother me anymore."

"Uh-huh."

"I got so I played with it with my tongue, pushing it half-way off and pushing it back in place. I guess even with something like a false tooth, once you get used to it you start to grow fond of it. But then I went and busted it to pieces by biting into that loaf of French bread."

This time Yomogida laughed.

"It's like I chewed up my own tooth with my own teeth. I can't blame anyone but myself."

"So you chomped down hard on it when it had slipped part-way off?"

"That's what I figure."

The waiter came by and lifted the lid on Shibahara's tankard. It was empty so he removed it from the table. Yomogida still had some left.

"Shall we order another?" Shibahara asked.

"Let's do." Yomogida reached for his wallet.

"I'll pay this time," Shibahara said. He took out a hundred yen bill and some change and handed it to the waiter.

"Two more of these."

"Yes sir."

The two men came here often enough that they knew quite a few of the waiters.

"So then," Shibahara continued his tale, "I wrapped the broken tooth in some tissue paper and took it to the dentist. I didn't think he'd be able to simply glue it back in place. It looked too far gone for that. Completely demolished. But I thought showing him the tooth would be the quickest way for him to see what had happened."

"And there were the gold wires, too."

"Uh-huh. I thought he might be able to reuse the wires. When I got there, I unwrapped the tissue paper to show the tooth and told him how there'd been this big noise when I was eating some French bread. Without batting an eye he said, 'Well, then, we'll just have to make a new one.' That was the last I saw of that false tooth."

"Uh-huh," Yomogida nodded. "I suppose it felt a bit like you'd lost a friend."

"A little bit. I thought, This is it? I don't need it anymore, so it just disappears? It all seemed so sudden."

"Yeah, even with something like a false tooth, if it's been a part of your body for almost two years, it'd feel like a real loss."

The waiter brought the two beers and wiped the wet spots on the table with a cloth.

"You've got good teeth, don't you?" Shibahara said.

"Well, I'm not so sure anymore. A tooth up here has been bothering me lately when I take a drink of water." Yomogida pressed a finger to his cheek. "I get this piercing pain."

"Oh, now that sounds bad. Once they get sensitive to liquids, you've got to be prepared for the worst."

"I can't gargle or rinse my mouth because the water goes straight to that tooth. You know we're on a well at our place, right? Well, when that icy well water hits—"

"It really smarts," Shibahara said, laughing. "And let me tell you, it doesn't take well water to do that."

"Yeah?"

"You've got an exposed nerve, and that's what it hits. It's gum disease."

"I know. They started warning me ten years ago. They said I had gum disease, and it'd get worse and worse."

"I'd say you've got troubles ahead."

"You think so?"

"It's not so bad so long as it's only cold liquids, but when hot liquids start to bother you, too, then you can't ignore it any more. Or when it suddenly starts aching in the middle of the night—now *that's* when it really gets bad. You won't be able to stand it."

"Don't scare me like that," Yomogida said.

"I'm not just scaring you. I'm telling you exactly how it was for me."

"I suppose I believe you," Yomogida said, and then added, "Actually, my wife says pretty much the same thing."

"Does she have bad teeth?"

"Uh-huh. Cavities *and* gum disease, both. Bad news all around. When I told her my tooth bothered me when I took a drink, she said hers were that way all the time. I said, 'You've got to be kidding,' and she said it hadn't been so bad since she got the two worst ones pulled, but until then it was constant. When I asked her if it was the same for hot liquids, she said hot or cold made no difference."

"And you didn't know about it?"

"She'd never said anything, so I had no idea. How was I to know she had trouble with both hot and cold? After twenty years, I finally find this out."

Shibahara laughed. "So I suppose your tooth is sensitive to beer, too," he said.

"Uh-huh. I have to drink like this," Yomogida pursed his lips for a moment, "blocking off one side of my mouth and letting the beer through the other side. I keep the beer away from the tooth that hurts."

"Sounds like you've worked it out."

"Of course! I don't particularly care if I have to go without gargling or rinsing my mouth, but I'm not about to give up drinking beer. So I figured out a way. I have to admit, though, drinking with pursed lips takes away some of the flavor."

"It does, huh?"

"Yeah, you can't beat drinking with an open mouth. To begin with, it's more efficient."

They both laughed.

"Anyway, that's why I've been slowing the pace today. You always finish your mug first, when I've still got a ways to go."

"Never mind that. I'm in no hurry. If you'd like we can switch to saké."

"That's okay. As I drink, I get so I can't tell any more whether the tooth bothers me or not."

Yomogida's package of sushi sat unopened on the table next to the plate of crisp-fried chicken they'd been eating since finishing their skewered shrimp. The package was small enough that it had not gotten in the way. At first, Yomogida had put it on the rack under the table, but later on Shibahara had suggested he move it to where they'd be sure to see it and not forget it.

5

"Overlooking the beach where we swim, at the top of some stone steps, there's a small shrine."

Yomogida was in the midst of a story. Gone from the table was the chicken plate, and gone, too, was the plate for the asparagus spears they had ordered next. Gourd-shaped saké servers and small saké cups had replaced the large beer tankards. A plate of pickled pepper leaves had come with the saké, but it was so salty that neither of them had touched it much.

"It sits on a bluff. The first time we go swimming on the day we get there, we always stop by this shrine on our way down to the beach. And on the day we come home, we stop by again. In the course of ten years, going back to that same village over and over, it somehow got to be our custom."

"Do the children go up to the shrine with you, too?"

"Uh-huh. The very first time we went I was thinking, if the village has a shrine we should visit it. Since we were going to be staying there for several days I thought we should pay our respects to the local divinities. So we went and told them we'd come to swim at their beach, and thanked them for their hospitality. We didn't know then that we'd keep going back year after year, so that first time we really didn't think of it as anything more than a simple greeting."

"You say it's been ten years?"

"Uh-huh. In fact, if we count the years since our first trip, this is already the twelfth year. But three of those years we couldn't make it, so we've only actually gone nine times."

"Still, altogether it's been more than ten years."

"That's right."

Shibahara lifted his saké server and poured into Yomogida's cup.

"This year we went to the shrine as usual on the day we arrived, in our swim suits, but as we came up to the front of the shrine, this old man was there and he kept repeating something to us. We couldn't understand him at first, but then we realized he was saying, 'The festival is over.' I said, 'Is that right?' and we all went on up to the shrine and prayed, but when we turned back he called out to us again and said 'The festival is over.'"

"What could he have meant?"

"That's what *we* wondered."

"I suppose he thought you needed to know."

"I suppose so. Maybe he was trying to say, 'You folks look like you've come from far away, but what a shame. The festival at this shrine was over just the other day. If you had only come a little sooner, you could have seen the festival. What a shame.'"

"'The festival is over,' huh?" Shibahara tried saying it himself. "It's a good phrase."

"Yeah, it is," Yomogida agreed. "In all those years, we never came across anyone else praying at that shrine. Not a one. I remember the very first year, they had an outdoor movie there to bring people out in the evening cool, and the children and the old grannies from the village were all spread out on straw mats they'd brought from home. But that's the only other time we've seen anyone else there."

"So then maybe the old man was happy because you came to pray there with your whole family, but he also felt sorry because you'd made the special trip when nothing was going on."

"And he was trying to let us know."

"Something like that, anyway."

A waiter came by.

"How's the saké? Shall we get one more?" Shibahara said. Both of their servers were empty.

"Yes, let's."

Turning toward the familiar waiter, Shibahara lifted his gourd-shaped saké server from the table and said, "Another of these, please."

"Yes sir."

When the waiter had gone, Yomogida glanced at the package he'd brought and said, "What do you say? Shall we break out the sushi now?"

"Not yet."

"Okay."

Yomogida still hadn't figured out when they should eat the sushi. They had been at the beer hall quite a long time, but they hadn't decided yet where they would go next. They never decided that until they were ready to leave. Fallen leaves, swirling and stopping in the wind, eventually make their way onward. The night would grow deep, and sooner or later the time would come to go home.

"I think I told you this before," Yomogida said, "but there's a view from the train on the way there that never changes. It's a really nice place, not far from the station where we get off. The tracks are set back a way from the ocean, and you gaze out the window at rice paddies stretching on and on with a small river flowing through them toward the sea."

Shibahara nodded as if to say, yes, maybe he had heard this before but he had no objection to hearing it again.

"Two or three boys stand on the bank of the river doing something or other. A boat drifts slowly by, carrying a lone fisherman. There are several houses scattered about—"

"A river village of eight or nine houses," Shibahara quoted from an old poem.

"—and every one of them is surrounded by trees. Oaks and black pines, I think. The sun beats down from above, and a gentle breeze stirs."

"Mmm."

"Every time I see that place, this feeling that I'm gazing at something truly marvelous comes over me. The scene hasn't changed the tiniest bit since the first time we went, yet it doesn't seem like that should be possible. You know how we normally go around thinking there's nothing in the world that doesn't change, there's nothing in the world that remains the way it was. That's how we see ourselves, as well as everything around us. It's a kind of resignation, you could say, and we're completely steeped in it, through and through. So when this scene that's still exactly the same as last year comes into view, all I can do is gaze at it in wonder."

"Hmm."

"Maybe it's also that we always go by that place when everything is at its best, at the very peak of the summer."

"That could be."

"You know how we sometimes say something's 'as beautiful as a dream'? I always think, 'That's what this is.' I suppose it's the bright sun that makes it that way."

The saké came. Shibahara lifted the server by its neck and poured some into Yomogida's cup. "It's a little hot," he said.

Yomogida took the server and poured for Shibahara. "Yes, a little," he said.

THE WORKSHOP

*t*he woman opened the door but found no one inside. The cutting table had been neatly cleared off, and a lid covered the sewing machine. A spool of basting thread hung from the ceiling.

"Hello," she called.

Separated from the rest of the house by a plywood divider, the tiny workshop had barely enough room for two people at a time.

Had the owner gone out somewhere? The whole house was still.

"Hello," the woman called again.

This time the door to the right opened and the dressmaker appeared wearing a sweater.

"Hello," she said with a bow. "I'm sorry to keep you waiting."

Perhaps she had been resting.

"Do come in, please."

The woman shuffled her feet into a pair of slippers as she stepped up into the room.

"It's gotten a bit colder again, hasn't it?" the dressmaker said.

"Yes, it certainly has," the woman agreed. She set the box she was carrying on the cutting table. "I wanted to place an order," she said, taking out the material she'd brought. "For a wedding dress."

The dressmaker caught her breath a moment. "Oh!" she said. "Your daughter's?"

"Yes."

"She's going to be married already?" Then after another brief pause she added, "I'd be honored."

The dressmaker owned and ran the little shop herself, with only her younger sister to help. Nearly all of her business came from women in the neighborhood—ordinary dresses and suits, for the most part. (The younger sister lived in an apartment nearby and came to the workshop just during the day.)

"It's a very nice fabric."

"I didn't know how to choose so I asked the clerk to choose for me."

They both remained standing by the cutting table.

There were two round stools in the room, one at the sewing machine and one at the cutting table. The shop owner was the one who ran the sewing machine, most of the time, while her sister did hems and such by hand.

One other chair, an old, worn armchair, sat to the right of the entrance, pushed back against the wall right next to the mirror. Only once had the woman seen another patron sitting in this chair—eating stir-fried noodles and exclaiming how delicious they were.

"How soon will it need to be done?" the dressmaker asked.

"The wedding isn't until the end of next month, so there's no hurry."

"The end of May, then. In that case, it'll be no problem at all," the dressmaker said, sounding relieved. "But I can hardly believe she's getting married so soon. It's not all that long since she went to work, is it?"

"Actually, it's already been two years."

"Has it really? It seems like it was practically just the other day."

When the bride-to-be had graduated from high school, she had had a skirt and jacket made here. A checked skirt. And she and her mother had been having things tailored here ever since. The dressmaker did good work, and she charged relatively little for her labor. When they thanked her for keeping her rates so reasonable, she responded self-deprecatingly that she was still learning.

"I suppose you'd like to have it ready early," she said, "so you can display it and have it to look at for a while before the wedding."

"No, it might get dirty, so I think we'd rather have it done just in time."

The dressmaker got out her notebook and a pencil. "Well, then," she said. "Tell me what you had in mind."

"I want it scooped out around the neck like this." The woman took out the sketch she'd drawn as she planned the design the night before. "With short sleeves, and a curved seam across the bust. I considered putting in several pleats, like on the light blue dress you made for me last year, but I think that would look too frilly afterward, when we raise the hem and make it into a dress for other occasions, so just put in a single curved seam." She pointed to her sketch as she explained.

As she listened, the dressmaker drew a sketch of her own in her notebook.

"So I only need to allow for the same fullness as with darts?"

"That's right."

"That's how I'll do it, then." After a moment, the dressmaker went on. "Won't it seem kind of plain with just ordinary sleeves? I don't think puffing the sleeves a little will make it too frilly."

Perhaps she was right.

"Please put all the rest of the fabric into the skirt, to give it more fullness. There's five yards here."

"That'll be plenty."

"I want to keep the top relatively simple and let the skirt liven things up."

"That sounds fine. But a little bit of puff in the sleeve won't particularly stand out, and I think it would actually look better."

"I suppose you're right. That much wouldn't make it too frilly."

"No, it wouldn't. Not at all."

And so the woman decided to accept the suggestion.

The dressmaker always worked this way. First she listened carefully to all of the customer's requests, then, after a pause, made her own suggestions.

"For the ceremony," the woman said, "I thought we could trim the sleeves with some flowers. And the waist, too. Of course, we'll take them off afterward."

"What kind of flowers?"

"White flowers, like marguerites, maybe."

"Something small?"

"Yes, small, like you might not even notice unless you came up close."

"Yes. Okay. Shall I pick something out? The store where I get my supplies has all kinds."

The woman knew the store. It was located in the main shopping

district, and she sometimes went there to buy lining cloth. They
sold the kind of flowers she wanted on the fourth floor, the dressmaker told her.

"In that case, I'll go have a look myself."

That took care of the flowers.

"What about a petticoat?"

"Well," the dressmaker examined the material. "Since your fabric
is quite heavy, I don't think it should be necessary. A gauze lining
around the waist should be all you need."

"Do you think so?"

"Yes, you can do without a petticoat."

"Could you buy the lining then?"

"Yes, of course," the dressmaker said as she moved her pencil back
to her sketch.

"Thank you."

Beneath the large, full skirt the dressmaker drew what looked like
two wooden shoes. She couldn't have actually intended wooden
shoes, of course, but that was the way they looked.

"Well, I guess I can leave the rest to you, then."

"I appreciate your patronage." The dressmaker returned the fabric to the box, then looked up at the calendar on the wall. "When
shall we schedule the first fitting?" she asked, contemplating the calendar. "Next month, on . . . " she started to say, but then stopped
to think some more.

"I'll have my daughter stop by on her way home from work. On
Saturday."

"Oh. All right."

A baby started crying in the back room. A few moments later a
second voice joined in.

"Well, well," said the dressmaker. "They've both woken up."

"Your sister had her new baby?"

"Yes. Going on three months already."

A grandmotherly voice could be heard trying to calm the baby.

"A boy or a girl?"

"A boy."

"So both of hers are boys."

It was perhaps three years ago that the dressmaker's younger sister had started helping in the shop. She had worked with her first
baby asleep on the floor beside her—in a basket like the ones you
put your clothes in at bathhouses.

That baby was now old enough to be pushing a tricycle around in the street out front. He must have been taking a nap beside his new brother while his mother went out on an errand.

Some time ago—it must have been toward the end of fall—the woman had run into this sister on the street. The sister already appeared very pregnant then, like she could have her baby any day.

As the woman stepped into her shoes to leave, she looked at the large black tropical fish swimming about the aquarium on top of the shoe cupboard.

"Your fish seems to be doing well," she said.

"Yes, he is."

There had been another one just like it, only smaller. Now it was gone.

"What happened to the small one?"

"This one ate him up."

"My goodness!"

"Their usual food is goldfish, as you know, and one time I forgot to feed them."

Some other half-eaten fish, which must originally have been about the size of a person's finger, now lay at the bottom of the tank. It was not a goldfish.

"I rushed out to buy some, but when I got back and came through that door," she pointed at the door she had emerged from earlier, "this big fellow already had the little one in his mouth."

She had come back into the workshop through the house, to feed the fish. But she hadn't quite made it in time.

"In *that* mouth," she added, following the fish's movements with her eyes. "I hit him on the head with the chopsticks, but he wouldn't let go for anything."

The disposable chopsticks she used for transferring the goldfish at feeding time lay on the screen covering the tank.

"He ate him all up, in the end."

The woman had once seen the dressmaker walking along the street with a bag of goldfish in her hand. In the hot season, she recalled.

"Such cute goldfish!" she had said. There were five or six in the bag. You could buy them this way at the flower shop in front of the station.

"They're tropical fish food," the dressmaker replied, but it hadn't really registered then.

When the woman visited the dressmaker's shop some time later, she saw the aquarium with two black fish swimming in it. Their stomachs were speckled red and black, and reminded her of newts.

A half-eaten cocktail wiener lay at the bottom of the tank.

When she asked what the fish were called, the dressmaker said a word that sounded something like "astronautus." The woman was sure of the "astro" part, but not so clear on the rest.

Though the dressmaker had said "tropical fish food," the woman still hadn't realized that these black fish were the tropical fish she meant. She still hadn't connected them with the goldfish.

The next time she went, the two black fish seemed to have grown a bit. This time, instead of a cocktail wiener, a half-eaten goldfish lay at the bottom of the tank. She finally made the connection.

"So the goldfish are for these?" she had asked.

"That's right. One gulp and they're finished," the dressmaker said. "When I bring the goldfish home and put them in the tank, they swim right off into the corner trembling in fear. Then this big fellow comes along and gulps them down."

"Oooh!"

"If he spits them back out only half-eaten, he'll never touch them again. The little one eats those."

Perhaps the pair were male and female.

"They're really quite vicious, aren't they?"

"Yes. I don't know why I ever bought them," the dressmaker had said.

The bottom of the tank was now green with moss.

"He seems to have grown some more since last year," the woman said.

"Do you think so?" The dressmaker seemed pleased.

The woman had her shoes on now, so she turned toward the dressmaker.

"Well, then," she said. "Thank you very much." She let out a rather tense-sounding sigh and bowed deeply. She stepped outside and started to close the door.

"Goodbye," she said.

"I wish your daughter every happiness," the dressmaker said.

The baby's cries and the grandmother's attempts to quiet him could still be heard in the back room.

PICTURE CARDS

*W*hen Ryoji hunched over his homework at the *kotatsu* and lifted his head to think, two crooked lines creased his brow.

Back in second grade (now he was in eighth) he had collided with a friend in the hallway at school one day. It had given him a huge bump on the forehead and loosened the other boy's front teeth.

Father wondered how they had managed to hit so hard, but Ryoji was matter-of-fact: "I was running one way, and Toyoda was coming the other, and kaboom!"

But couldn't he have swerved to one side or something? Father still wanted to know—though, given what had happened, perhaps the answer was obvious. Ryoji explained that it was at a narrow place in the hall.

And why was he running at such a reckless speed in a narrow hallway? He had to get to the bathroom. And Toyoda was coming back from the bathroom? Probably.

The bump was enormous. Cold packs gradually reduced the swelling, but still left behind a small knot that refused to flatten out.

So long as it didn't bother Ryoji, there was no harm in letting it be. But what if he got teased?

"Ryoji's got a ho-o-rn, Ryoji's got a ho-o-rn."

The doctor advised removing it before that happened, so they scheduled a "dehorning" operation.

Akio, in sixth grade at the time, went along to give moral support. He stood next to Ryoji and watched the procedure from beginning to end, playing the big brother.

"Speak right up if it hurts," he said.

And when Ryoji seemed about to cry, he comforted him.

"Don't cry now. You're almost done."

Only two months before this, "big brother" Akio had done something equally foolish. Hopping on one foot—starting some distance away, even, in order to gather speed—he had tried to leap up onto the speaker's platform in the schoolyard, but didn't quite make it. His leg bashed against the concrete edge, and he fell to the ground with a piece of flesh hanging loosely from a deep cut on his shin.

His teacher had carried him piggyback to this same hospital. After X-rays to check for fractures, the doctor had stitched the dangling flesh back in place. It took about twenty stitches.

So the one who had ripped a hole in his shin as carelessly as he might have ripped a hole in his shirt now stood by to reassure his younger brother.

Father stayed a little farther back, watching Akio's face rather than Ryoji or the doctor. The expressions on Akio's face gave him a good enough idea of how things were going.

Just once, Akio averted his eyes.

"What happened that time you looked away?" Father asked afterward. Akio described how blood suddenly welled up from where the doctor had made a cut, and Father could understand why he might have turned away.

The time with Akio, too, Father had avoided watching when the doctor injected the painkiller or when he stitched the wound shut. He found himself recalling the scene in "Ali Baba and the Forty Thieves" where the clever Morgiana finds a tailor and leads him blindfolded to her master's house to have him sew her dead master back together. With a shudder, he pushed the association from his mind as quickly as he could.

The doctor had said the scar from the "dehorning" should eventually fade and blend in with the other wrinkles on Ryoji's forehead.

Had he been right? Now two main creases flowed across Ryoji's forehead, taking an ever so slight detour around the place where the "horn" had been—like a wide spot in the river.

Such was the history of the two crooked lines on Ryoji's forehead—nothing to make all that big a deal about, really. But Father couldn't help wondering about how Akio's forehead remained smooth almost no matter how he screwed up his face, yet Ryoji had gotten those two deep furrows before he was even out of grade school. Had the doctor's words about the scar and wrinkles had the power of suggestion?

One evening in the middle of March, Ryoji of the crooked creases suddenly started singing "Santa Lucia" in the middle of his homework.

Father and Mother and his sister Kazuko (she had just finished dinner after getting home late from work) listened in amazement as he sang. He broke off halfway through.

"Don't stop, you're doing great," Kazuko said. She coaxed him to sing it again. "Is that from school? Did you learn Italian for the whole song?"

"The teacher sang it for us in music class," Ryoji said.

"So it's in your music book?"

"The book only has Japanese, but she sang it for us in Italian."

"And she taught you the Italian words?"

"Uh-huh."

"Sing it again."

By this time all the attention had made Ryoji self-conscious, and he wouldn't sing.

"Come on, sing it again."

The continued prodding only made him even more bashful, but Kazuko and Mother kept at him until he finally had to give in. He pulled an empty fruit basket over his head to hide his face and started singing again.

Through the woven bamboo came the changing voice of a young boy, dwelling just a little too long on each note. It did not seem quite right for a Neapolitan folk song; somehow it lacked the appropriate liveliness. His voice was better suited to Japanese nursery songs, Father thought. That was what he usually sang when he suddenly started in like this with a song from school.

Two months ago, something had reminded Ryoji of a song he'd learned in the fifth grade called "Shikenjo," and he had burst out singing it one day at home. It was a song from Kyushu, in dialect:

> *Ikkenjo, nikenjo,*
> *Sankenjo, shikenjo.*

So far, there was no telling what the song might be about.

Shiken ma Hotada no norikura no ue ni . . .

Father listened awhile, thinking it a rather sad-sounding song. Finally, he called Ryoji and asked him about it.

"What's that you're singing? What sort of a song is it?"

"I think it's called 'Shikenjo.'"

"'Shikenjo'? What does it mean?"

Ryoji went to get his music book and found the song. *Kenjo* meant "steep place," so *shikenjo* apparently meant "four steep places."

"It says it's a song about cowherds who're moving some cows from one spot to another through the mountains, and they come to these really steep places in the path," Ryoji said.

"I see."

"*Ameushi keushi* means there were several different kinds of cows."

All the cows had to be led along one treacherous mountain path after another. They became exhausted, and so did the men.

The song ended with:

Saruzaka tsue tsuite
Jitto yuute
Sorehike, sorehike.

When they got to Saruzaka the men had to dig their cowsticks into the ground and pull with all their strength to help the cows.

"*Jitto yuute*" was the best part, Father thought. You could really hear the cowherds grunting as they pulled and sweated right along with the cows.

The song now coming from beneath the bamboo basket was not one of Ryoji's usual nursery songs. He sounded a bit stiff compared to when he sang nursery songs. Apparently he didn't feel as comfortable with "Santa Lucia"—especially in Italian.

"Bravo! Bravo!" Kazuko applauded when Ryoji had finished, and she immediately wanted to learn the words herself.

What could he do? Ryoji hid under the basket again and started over from the beginning.

"*Sulmare luccica—*"

Mother and Kazuko repeated the line after him, and then he sang the second line.

"*L'astro d'argento—*"

He went through line by line, but it was hard to remember them at first. When they got through to the end, Ryoji quickly gathered up his books and papers and went to put them away, making it quite clear he'd had enough of such nonsense.

Kazuko pulled the basket over her head and repeated the first part of the song several times. Even after she quit singing, she kept the basket over her head and looked around the room, raising and lowering the basket a little as she turned her head.

"This makes the room look nice," she said. "It's like looking at pretty scenery through a bamboo blind."

"I gaze at the snow on Xiang-lu Peak. . . ." Mother said, quoting from an old classic.

"That's right. That's what this is," Kazuko said. Affecting a more mannered voice, she repeated, "I gaze at the snow on Xiang-lu Peak,"—she lifted the basket and looked around the room—"From beneath a half-raised blind."

"Except that with a blind the bamboo strips would all go across the same way," Mother noted. "That thing has crosspieces, too, so it's more like the baskets they carry chickens in."

"You're terrible. So much for my fantasy of Lady Sei Shonagon."

But her disappointment lasted only a moment. She pulled the basket back down over her head and crowed:

"Ock-a-oodle-oo."

Did she think a normal "cock-a-doodle-doo" was too ordinary? Father wondered. Did she want the cry to sound muffled because of the basket?

Or was it perhaps a carryover from pretending to be a noble-woman of the tenth century?

"Bravo! Bravo!" Father said. "It's the rooster of Kibizaka."

Kazuko was to get married in a little over two months, and she and her new husband would move to a house they had rented in Kibizaka. The landlord lived right next door, and, in fact, had a chicken coop in his yard. It was a quiet area: a whole day could go by without hearing anything but the clucking of chickens. In back of the house, rice paddies spread out to the foot of a small, bamboo-covered hill.

"I gaze at the snow on Xiang-lu Peak," Kazuko said again in her noblewoman's voice, "From beneath a half-raised blind." She looked around for a moment with the basket raised to her forehead, then slowly lowered it.

"The rooster of Kibizaka crows," she said.

"From beneath a bamboo basket," Father quickly added, turning it into a couplet.

Just as he finished saying the line, Kazuko let out another shrill cry:

"Ock-a-oodle-oo!"

The door behind her slid open to reveal Akio. He cast a dubious look at Kazuko as he came in.

Akio had graduated from high school a month ago but unfortunately failed to pass any of the entrance exams he had taken for college. Only that morning he had finally put an end to the uncertainty about his future by going to register at a cram school—so he could try again next year.

"That was the rooster of Kibizaka you just heard," Mother explained.

"So it was Kazuko." He extracted a pack of picture cards from his back pocket as he joined them at the *kotatsu*. "I wondered what could be shrieking like that in the house. It sounded like a dolphin."

Kazuko burst out laughing. "That's mean," she said.

2

The family had played the picture-card game together for more than forty days now.

Every night around 9:30 or 10:00, after Kazuko had finished her late dinner and the dishes were done and the rest of the family were relaxing around the *kotatsu*, Akio would appear with the pack of cards tucked in his hip pocket.

The nice thing about this game was that it never dragged on too long. It lasted only about as long as it took to have a cup of tea.

The origins of this nightly contest went all the way back to New Year's. On one of her days off, Kazuko had bought a book for Ryoji at the little bookstore in front of the station—a thick novel called *The Bird of Dawning*, written by a British poet.

The story told of a race among British sailing ships to see who could go from London to China, load up with tea, and get back to England in the shortest amount of time. Apparently, such races actually took place during the nineteenth century.

The drawing on the cover showed several clipper ships coursing the high seas with their sails stretched full before the wind. This, no doubt, was what had drawn Kazuko's attention. She had always loved the sea. That was the very reason she'd chosen to work for a steamship company.

The book was actually supposed to be a Christmas present, but things had gotten so busy at the office that she couldn't find the time to go to the store. Akio's present had been easier: since he was captain of the soccer team, she'd simply given him the money for a new pair of soccer shoes. Both the shoes and the book were a bit on the expensive side, but Kazuko wanted to thank her brothers for taking turns meeting her part way from the bus stop every night.

In any case, when Kazuko bought the book, the lady at the store had given her the picture-card game as a bonus gift. The object of the game was to collect sets of three cards that fit together to make a picture. Each completed picture had a different value, and the player with the highest score won the game.

Ryoji put the cards on his desk and promptly forgot about them. No matter how many times Mother made him clean it up, this desk quickly became Ryoji's private junkyard again, piled high with all kinds of clutter. So Akio didn't notice the cards right away either, even though his desk was back-to-back with Ryoji's.

One day about a month later, Akio noticed the cards. In fact, they weren't actually cards yet, since they were printed on one big sheet of folded cardboard. With characteristic dispatch, Akio got out some scissors and set to work cutting the cards apart one by one. Then he brought the deck to the family room.

"Can we try this once?" he said, almost apologetically. He knew he ought to be studying for his entrance exams, which were scheduled every third day (or even every other day) from the end of February into the first part of March. The first was only two weeks away, and after that he would hardly have time to recover from one before the next came along. He didn't exactly have the time to get involved in some new game.

Barely a month before they had all been caught up in the game of the hundred poets.

"All right now, this is the last time for this year," their mother had finally told them one day as they laid out the poem tiles. Akio had won that final game with forty-one tiles.

"You just wait," Kazuko had gritted her teeth. "Next year I'll start memorizing the poems in October, and by New Year's you won't know what hit you."

That was supposed to be the end of play for Akio. He was supposed to ignore all other distractions and study, study, study.

But since Akio himself was the one to suggest the game, Father decided to go along—though it was bound to be something pretty silly, meant only for little kids. He picked up his cards.

"The busiest men find the most time," he and Mother teased Akio as the game got under way.

They all laughed every time another outlandish, unfamiliar name came up. Some of the cards had scenes from children's stories they all knew, like "The Starling's Dream" or "The Swan Prince"; or from famous novels, like *Little Women* or *The Count of Monte Cristo*. No one thought these were particularly funny. But others showed characters from samurai films with long, convoluted names, or scenes of rockets and spaceships in an intergalactic war. One of the sets pictured a bank of strange-looking machines lined up all in a row.

After the way everyone had laughed at the cards the first night, Akio wasn't sure whether anyone would want to play again, but even so, he appeared in the family room the next night and produced the cards from somewhere in his clothes with the motions of a magician's sleight of hand.

"Seriously, Akio, that's enough," he expected Father to cut him short. But to his surprise Father had approved, and he happily began dealing out the cards.

Almost before they knew it, the game had become a regular event for which the entire family gathered religiously every evening, and it had continued without interruption through all of Akio's exams, as well as through all the days he went to see the results posted and came home without finding his name.

As the one who had gotten them started in the first place, Akio was also the best player. He always came out way ahead of the others.

"It's from being all charged up for the exams," Father said.

"Must be," his wife agreed.

But when the results came in, and he had failed to make the cut anywhere, Akio broke his winning streak and went into a prolonged slump. Apparently he had been charged up only when he emerged from his room to play the picture-card game.

Ryoji had found the rental house in Kibizaka.

During winter break, on the final day of their holiday training (the second-to-last day of the year), the track team decided to go on a long-distance run.

Seven or eight miles from Ryoji's school was an area of wooded hills that had been set aside as a large nature park. The track team would run to the park, fool around there for a while, and then run back to school.

One of Ryoji's friends on the team, Osawa, lived along the route, and as they ran past his house Ryoji noticed three new houses, all exactly the same, going up on the adjacent land. They looked like they must be almost finished.

"For rent, I bet," thought Ryoji.

With Kazuko soon to be married, Mother had asked Ryoji to be on the lookout for a place she and her new husband could rent.

Since he was in the middle of track practice at the time, he couldn't very well stop to inquire right then. But he mentioned the three new houses to Mother when he got home.

One day shortly after school had started again, when Ryoji was walking home with Osawa, he asked him if he knew who the landlord was for the new rental houses going up next to his place.

"They're ours," Osawa said.

On Kazuko's first day off in February, she and Father and Mother took a walk out that way to see the houses for themselves. Following Ryoji's directions, they came to an old farmhouse they thought must be the place, and, sure enough, when Kazuko stepped into the front yard to inquire, she immediately caught sight of Osawa and a younger boy building something on top of the tool-shed. Osawa greeted her with a cheerful bow.

(When Father asked Ryoji afterward, he learned that Osawa was building a pigeon coop.)

As they sat on the veranda sipping tea served by Osawa's grandmother, the boy's mother told them that the first of the three units had already been promised to a greengrocer relative of theirs, whose second son would be getting married in March. The other two were still open, but would probably find renters as soon as the weather turned a little warmer.

Back at home, Kazuko telephoned her fiancé's mother, who wanted to leap into action as soon as she heard what the rent was. She said they'd better hurry and make a deposit or both houses would get snapped up by someone else.

So the next Sunday, Kazuko's fiancé came to look at the houses with her, and they decided to take the one in the middle.

What had started like a dream, too good to be true, had quickly become reality.

"Ryoji's a real hero."

"Really. I'm so happy. It's such a nice house."

Mother and Kazuko exclaimed back and forth, rejoicing over their good fortune. And of course Father thought Ryoji was a hero, too, for having noticed the houses while running that day, before the carpenters had even finished them. Seeing the houses could have ended as no more than a fleeting glimpse of a mayfly by the roadside. If Ryoji hadn't paid attention to what Mother had asked, things would not have come to this happy conclusion.

Even if it turned out that Kazuko and her husband didn't stay there long, even if they decided to move elsewhere after only a short time (no one could tell what the future might hold), Ryoji was indeed a hero for finding this house. The families had agreed in general terms to hold the wedding sometime in the spring, but until Ryoji's discovery, no one had had the slightest clue what the newlyweds would do about a place to live.

3

"He said South America has lots of poisonous snakes."

Kazuko was talking to Mother as she ate her late dinner.

That afternoon, she had listened in while her boss and one of her co-workers chatted with a travel agent they knew who'd dropped in at the office. The agency he worked for specialized in arrangements for people emigrating to South America, and he visited Kazuko's office quite often.

(Kazuko's office handled reservations not only for the South American routes but also for passenger cruises that called at Hong Kong and Taiwan. Until a year ago she had been at headquarters, but then the three men and two women in her section had moved to their present location, which was conveniently near several other steamship companies and travel agencies.)

"So everyone carries tins of kerosene around with them."

"Why kerosene?" Mother asked.

"Because they never know when they might get bitten by a poisonous snake. They carry kerosene around just in case."

"But what do they do with it? Rub it on the bite?"

"No, it's not for rubbing, it's for drinking."

"And you're safe from the poison if you drink kerosene?"

"It's not that you're completely safe, but evidently if you drink the kerosene right away the bite doesn't swell up. Though it still hurts."

"But you don't die?"

"I think some people die even then, but it's supposed to lessen the poison's effect."

"So you can still die."

"To make sure you're safe you have to get the antiserum. But when you can't get an injection right away, you use the kerosene as a kind of stopgap."

Father lay on the tatami with his legs under the *kotatsu*, listening but not joining in. The details weren't very clear, but he thought he got the general idea.

Tins of kerosene, she had said. It sounded like it would be a lot of trouble, carrying a big tin around all the time. Especially if it was full. But if you got bitten, and you wanted to save your life, maybe even drinking the whole tinful of kerosene would seem a small price to pay.

"Because they have so many poisonous snakes, the government asks people to capture them alive and bring them in so they can make the antiserum. And the people *do* catch a lot of them."

"That's good."

"They do catch a lot, but the problem is, they catch them and eat them. So they still can't make the antiserum."

"They eat them?"

"That's what the man said. They go snaking just like we might go fishing. He said he'd done it, too."

"How do they do it?"

"Well, they have this special kind of pole with a wire loop on the end that closes when you pull. Snakes always raise up their head when they get angry, so all you have to do is slip the loop around their head and pull. He said he'd never gone fishing, but he'd gone snaking lots of times."

The visitor had come to talk with the two men, but Kazuko and the other secretary both paused in their work to listen.

"Once he saw a really long snake stretched across the road," Kazuko continued. "The first thing he saw was its tail, so he turned to look at the other end, but that end was a tail, too."

Mother let out a sound of surprise.

"He couldn't figure it out so he looked to the right again, and then to the left, but it was still the same."

"Both ends were tails?"

"Uh-huh. Both ends."

"Oh, I know," said Mother. "It was one snake eating another snake, right?"

"That's right. One snake was right in the middle of swallowing up another. But snakes that eat other snakes don't have any venom, and they only eat poisonous snakes, so if you see one snake eating another, you know it's not poisonous and you're safe."

"It's a strange world we live in," Mother said. Father was thinking much the same as he lay listening.

"He told us about snakes on coffee plantations, too. They have these snakes that are completely green."

"Green?"

"Uh-huh. And they're always hanging down from the trees, which makes them even more creepy. Though these ones aren't poisonous."

"Do they drop down on you from the trees, I wonder?"

"I don't know. He didn't say anything about that. There's also a snake that tunnels under the ground like a mole. Especially after it rains, you can watch the ground and see where they're going."

"Really?"

"They're called 'mole snakes,' and they always stay underground. Their venom is so strong, if you ever get bitten you don't have a chance. There's no antiserum. They're the most poisonous of all."

"Sounds scary."

"But I guess they're fairly gentle and quiet and don't bite very often."

"Then you're okay so long as you don't run into them when they're tunneling."

It was quite a collection of snake stories to hear all at once: non-poisonous snakes eating poisonous snakes; green snakes hanging from the trees; mole snakes burrowing along just under the ground.

A colorful lot, and even beautiful—though you wouldn't want to have them appear in your dreams.

4

"What do you think Brazilian women say," Kazuko began when her mouth was free.

Until then she had been chewing pieces of rice cracker to feed to her white Java sparrow, which was now roaming the tabletop on its own. A friend had given her the bird as a baby when she was still in high school, and she had raised it as her pet.

". . . when they're especially happy or especially sad?"

"Is it something we're likely to know?"

"Yes."

"Something we've said, too?"

"Well, you've never used it the way they use it, but I think you've probably said it sometime or other. Maybe not, though."

"That's not much help. Which is it?"

"No. None of us says it."

"Is it Spanish?"

Kazuko seemed caught off guard. "I think so," she said. "But wait a minute. I guess she could've been speaking either English or Spanish."

That day a Brazilian couple had come into Kazuko's office. They had come to Japan to sightsee but were now getting ready to go home, and they needed help with some freight they'd arranged to have loaded onto the ship in Kobe. The sailing date was approaching rapidly, and they were worried that their freight might not get through customs in time. Miss Taniguchi at the desk next to Kazuko's usually handled such matters.

She started making phone calls. It didn't look good at first, but after a while the picture seemed to change. There was hope: things might work out after all—just maybe.

Then other difficulties arose. Still, Miss Taniguchi didn't give up. With everyone in the office cheering her on, she kept trying, insisting over the phone that there must be some way to expedite things, and in the end she succeeded in finding a way around the impasse.

Each time she learned something new, she explained it to the lady in English, so the lady was probably speaking English, too (it was the wife who did all the talking).

On the other hand, every advance and setback showed instantly on Miss Taniguchi's face as she talked on the phone, which meant the lady didn't have to wait for her explanation to know what direction things were taking. Her exclamations of joy or distress at those times seemed more likely to be in her native tongue, which was Spanish.

"I think," said Kazuko, "it's the same in both English and Spanish."

"You don't sound very sure."

Kazuko had been with the steamship company for two years, but she still got nervous when she answered the phone and heard English coming at her from the other end. "My heart starts pounding, and the blood rushes to my head," she said. No wonder she didn't sound very sure of herself.

The whole family had been listening to her account, and now they all tried to think what a Brazilian woman might say in those circumstances. But no one really had any idea. They all gave up.

"So, what did she say?"

Starting with both hands at her breast, Kazuko swept her arms wide open and exclaimed:

"Sa-a-nta Mari-i-a!"

The startled Java sparrow took off for the top of the parakeet's cage.

"Whoops. Sorry, sorry."

"So that's what it was."

"She also said 'Ave Mari-i-ia!'"

"Hmm."

"And you really should have seen her," Kazuko went on. "She sat there right in front of Miss Taniguchi, chewing on the corner of her handkerchief and clasping and unclasping her hands while she listened."

Kazuko pulled at her own handkerchief with her teeth.

"When the prospects looked good, she'd lean forward excitedly on the edge of her chair, but the tiniest sign of doubt and she'd go all to pieces."

"Really?"

"She'd put her face down on the desk and cry in big, loud sobs. She never waited to find out what was really going to happen. The first hint of trouble, and already—"

"She's too quick."

"—she'd burst into tears. But then as soon as things started looking favorable again, she'd grab Miss Taniguchi's hand and pat it."

Kazuko and the others in the office were so caught up in the suspense that no one could concentrate on work. They all listened with the Brazilian lady as Miss Taniguchi made her calls.

Finally Miss Taniguchi hung up and said, "Everything's set."

"Ohhh, Sa-a-nta Mari-i-a!" the lady burst out.

She patted Miss Taniguchi on the head and shook hands with everyone in the room as she was leaving.

"You're the most wonderful people I've ever met," she said extravagantly as she went out the door.

"And what was her husband doing all this time?" Father asked.

"He just sat there without saying a thing," said Kazuko. "Way across the room."

"Not a word?"

"And a completely blank face. You'd have thought he had nothing to do with what was going on. Except, of course, he got up and left with his wife when it was all over."

5

A shallow basin originally intended for flower arrangements now served as a birdbath in the yard. In the winter, the water would often freeze overnight. Mother changed it each morning with fresh water from the well, and scattered bread crumbs all around for the sparrows to eat.

But a brown-eared bulbul always came and chased the sparrows away — even though he never actually ate many of the bread crumbs himself. It happened every morning right in front of the study window where Father worked at his desk.

Beneath the wild maple was a small, unidentified shrub the children had transplanted from the nearby woods. The bulbul would perch on one of its branches to watch over the area. When a sparrow came for the bread crumbs, the bulbul would swoop down on it and chase after it as it fled from tree to tree. Sometimes in midair, just when the bulbul seemed to have closed the gap, there'd be a sharp click like the shutter on a camera. It was apparently the sound of the bulbul's beak snapping shut.

The sound carried clearly all the way to where Father sat inside the house, so it must have been sheer terror for the sparrow to have it explode practically right next to his ear. Especially when it came in the midst of such desperate flight.

One evening when Father told the others about this daily drama, Ryoji had a similar story.

"I once saw a shrike chasing a sparrow," he said, "and you should have seen the fierce look on his face."

He had seen the chase about a year ago.

"It was down at the water plant. At first they were going back and forth in the pine trees, but then the sparrow came flying out toward the road."

When the bulbul attacked the sparrows, it was to scare them away from the bread so he could have it all for himself, but the shrike apparently had different motives.

The fleeing sparrow came to the chain-link fence and flew right through one of the links near Ryoji. The shrike came over the top in hot pursuit. Ryoji had gotten a clear view of his face.

"He looked like this," Ryoji said, pushing up the corners of his eyes. "Really vicious."

Ryoji's long and narrow face became the face of a shrike attacking a sparrow.

"Of course for the sparrow," he said, "it's a matter of life or death." Then he added, "But it's a matter of life and death for the shrike, too. He can't let his prey get away."

"Or else he'll starve to death himself," Father said as if finishing Ryoji's thought.

Ryoji smiled and nodded. "Sometimes I find dead frogs impaled on tree branches."

"That's from shrikes, too?"

"They're all shriveled and dried out. I suppose the shrikes leave them there intending to eat them later and then forget about them."

Ever since grade school, Ryoji had liked to play in the woods on the nearby hills. He'd seen a lot.

"I find grasshoppers the same way."

"Where?"

"Stuck on nettles."

6

April advanced toward its end. In the yard, the aronia buds had opened their petals into bright round flowers. Next to them, the blossoms of the redbud tree had deepened in color.

On a Saturday evening, after their usual game of picture cards,

Mother went back to the kitchen. Standing on a chair, she began scrubbing the wall between the stove and the overhead vent.

"You don't have anything I could use for a rag, do you?" she asked Kazuko after a while.

"A rag?" Kazuko stopped to think. "I have some remnants, but . . ."

"No rags? I just thought I'd ask because it seems like you never throw anything away."

"Sorry. I don't have anything you can make into a rag."

"That's okay, then. I'll manage with this."

A few minutes later, Kazuko went into her brothers' room. Perhaps she thought Akio might have something since he was always shining up his soccer ball.

From the room came the muffled voices of Kazuko and Akio. Ryoji had been out of school with the measles and had already gone to bed.

Most evenings Ryoji's track practice ran late and kept him at school until just before dinner, but five days ago Father had returned from his afternoon walk to find Ryoji home early. When Father asked him what he was doing home so early, he said he'd caught a cold and decided to skip practice.

For Ryoji to voluntarily skip practice had to mean he was feeling pretty bad.

A fit of coughing had awakened him the night before, and in the morning he had looked a bit feverish. Kazuko felt his forehead as he sat in the kitchen eating toast with his brother, and when she said he felt hotter than Akio, Mother urged him to take his temperature.

"I'm all right," he brushed her off, and left for school.

After coming home early, Ryoji confessed he had been feeling too worn out to practice the day before as well. He had stayed around, but only to watch the others practice. The day before that, which was Sunday, he had entered the 1500-meter race in the annual city track meet. Packing a lunch of four big *nori* rolls, two apples, and a summer orange, he'd left home boasting he would bring back a prize. But far from winning anything, he'd placed fifth in his first race and got eliminated right away.

He ran a high fever from the night he skipped practice, staying home from school the next day and then again the following day. Everyone assumed he had the flu. But on the third day he broke out in a rash all over his face, and they realized it was the measles. He had never had them before, so there was no reason he shouldn't get them now, but both Mother and Father had long since forgotten about measles. Who would have imagined he'd come down with them in ninth grade?

"Thank goodness you got them now," Mother said to the red-faced Ryoji as he lay in bed. "A month later and we would have been right up against Kazuko's wedding. I hate to think what that might have meant."

This was now the fifth day since he'd skipped practice, and for the first time his temperature had stayed normal again all day long. Since the incubation period is about ten days, Ryoji must already have had the measles when he raced in the city track meet. What a crazy thing he'd done!

The voices in the other room became more hushed, as if conspiring in some secret. Mother went to investigate. Suppressed laughs were followed by voices:

"You look great."

"That's even better."

A moment later, Kazuko came down the hall. She had dressed up in a pair of jeans and an oversized jacket that belonged to Akio, and she wore Ryoji's school cap on her head. Dangling her arms loosely in front of her and pointing her knees out to the side, she walked in short, waddling steps.

She took a bow, and the hat fell off.

Mother and Akio watched from the hallway, joined by Ryoji in his pajamas. Most of the redness had faded from the rash on his face, but many of the bumps still remained.

"Where'd you pick that up?" Father asked.

"It's like in those acts from overseas, you know, when the clowns come out front."

"But when did *you* learn to be a clown?"

"I've always liked this kind of thing." Kazuko walked back and forth across the room. She took another bow, and the hat fell off again.

"When the hat falls off," said Akio from behind, "you're supposed to pass it around for money."

"Oh, right!"

"Like Gelsomina," said Father

"That's right, that's right. It's just like Gelsomina," Mother agreed.

When Kazuko was in high school, she and Mother had gone to

see an Italian movie. The movie had already had its first run, several years before, and Mother had seen it then with Father.

The story was about a man who could break a chain wrapped around his bare chest merely by flexing his muscles, and who eked out a living from such feats of strength by going from town to town in a traveling show. And it was about the man's unfortunate wife.

Both Mother and Kazuko cried so hard they were embarrassed to show their faces when the lights went up.

The wife (she was the one called Gelsomina) is from a poor family in a seaside town. She's still practically a child when the traveling showman pays her family some money and takes her away. The man makes her his assistant, teaching her a clown act to draw a crowd, and training her to beat the drum for his own act as well. They live out of a trailer pulled behind his motorcycle.

With Gelsomina beating the drum, the man would snap the chain.

"Bravo! Bravo!"

"You look much better that way than in a wedding dress."

"It's true."

"You should do this at the wedding."

The whole family cheered Kazuko's performance. She bowed once more, replaced the fallen hat on her head, and retreated up the hall.

The jacket was a new one that Mother had bought Akio only a month ago. When all the results of the exams had been posted, one after the other, and the last of them made it clear that Akio would not be going to college this year, Mother had taken him to the department store the very next day. He wouldn't be using his high school uniform anymore, so he needed something else to wear.

"With his build, he'll set off anything to advantage," the saleswoman said to Mother as Akio tried on several different jackets.

They settled on a conservative gray jacket and bought a pair of pants to go with it. Akio had worn them once before starting cram school, but the rest of the time they had stayed on a hanger in the corner of his room.

After Kazuko's exit, another round of laughter came from the boys' room. Then Akio appeared wearing Kazuko's apron over a muscle shirt, with her neckerchief tied over his head and her purse looped around his arm. His bulging shoulders and arms stuck out incongruously as he walked forward on tiptoes. Kazuko and Ryoji followed from behind.

"Hey, hey! It's Zampano!"

Zampano was the name of Gelsomina's husband, who one snowy day abandons her by the roadside and runs away. Later, on the night he learns of Gelsomina's death, he wanders out to the seaside and sinks down upon the beach in throes of unbearable grief.

"*Arriva Zampano!*"

"It's the Matchless Muscleman, Zampano!"

Kazuko pulled the neckerchief off from behind, exposing Akio's short, athletic haircut.

7

"In the train on my way home," Kazuko said, "the man sitting in front of me was snoozing."

Kazuko was standing at the time, holding onto a strap. When she looked down, the sleeping man had a big happy smile on his face. He appeared to be in his upper twenties.

"And he just smiled on and on. I figured he must be having a nice dream. Then I turned away for a while."

It took several minutes for the express to get to its next stop, where Kazuko had to transfer to another train. As she headed for the door, she looked at the man again.

"But this time he looked really sad, ready to burst into tears. Still sound asleep." After getting off Kazuko had smiled to herself.

"I wonder what he was dreaming," Mother said.

"I wonder."

"I suppose something terrible must have happened."

"Though he seemed so happy at first."

"We got another one of those cables today," Kazuko said as she gently cradled the Java sparrow in her hand.

The cables she spoke of came from immigrants to South America who had run into difficulties and couldn't go on any more.

"If they do well, they make lots of money and live in luxury. But some of them aren't so lucky. They can't make ends meet."

Finally they would reach the point where they had no choice but to return to Japan, but they wouldn't have the fare. That was when a cable would arrive at Kazuko's office from one of the branches in South America. Kazuko's office would contact relatives in Japan and arrange to have the ticket paid for at this end so that the unfortunate family could come home.

"The cable's always in English. First it gives the name of the ship, 'S. S. *So-and-so-maru*, Santos to Yokohama,' and next it says something like 'Tanaka family of five,' to indicate how many tickets they need." After a slight pause she added, "It's usually quite a few. Even more than five. Then it says 'Please collect fare,' followed by the amount—in dollars—always a really high figure."

The adult fare from Santos to Yokohama was about ¥210,000, so just for husband and wife the total would be ¥420,000. Children only cost half, and small children only a quarter, but they came in greater numbers and easily pushed the final figure beyond ¥500,000.

"After that it says 'from his brother Tanaka Taro,' and gives the address. I don't know why, but the address is always somewhere way off in the country, like Tohoku or Kyushu."

Once Kazuko's office had the name and address, they could call information to see if the brother had a telephone and find out his number. When they got through and explained about the cable, no one ever seemed surprised.

"Oh yes, yes" the brother would answer, as if he had been expecting the call all along. "Yes, I understand. I'll transfer the money right away, from Such-and-such Bank, so please proceed with the arrangements."

They agreed just like that. It was the kind of money you wondered that anyone could afford, but they agreed to pay it just like that. And sure enough, it was never more than a day or two before the transfer actually came through.

"The person who answers always speaks in dialect, and lots of times we have trouble understanding. Today's call was to Fukuoka, and we always get a little nervous when it's places like that."

Kazuko had had to make dozens of such calls in her two years on the job, and only once had the person said he simply couldn't get the money together. All the others had sent it without the least delay, and said they would come to meet the ship as well.

"When will the boat arrive?" they wanted to know. They inquired what day and which port the ship would come in, and they were always there to meet it when it did.

8

"I went to visit Miss Hamashima yesterday," said Kazuko.

Kazuko's friend since school days was an international telephone operator and lived in a company dormitory. She had offered to make the veil and headband Kazuko would wear for her wedding, and on Saturday afternoon Kazuko had gone to see her so she could take the measurements.

Miss Hamashima's sister had recently gotten married, and she showed Kazuko the wedding pictures. The family lived in San'in, in western Japan, but Kazuko knew them from having visited once when still in school. Miss Hamashima was the youngest of three sisters.

"She's pretty," Kazuko said, looking at the pictures.

After a few moments she spoke again. "You said she lives in Awabi now, right?"

"There you go again," said her friend.

Kazuko had meant to say Warabi. The name of the city came from a kind of edible fern that grew in the mountains, but she had confused it with the name of a shellfish that sounded almost the same.

They both laughed.

"That's quite a slip," Kazuko finally said. "All the way from mountain to sea."

If one of her closest friends had said, "There you go again," Kazuko must have made this kind of slip lots of times before, Father mused. Apparently, it wasn't only at home that she said funny things.

9

"When I looked up from my desk," Kazuko said as she ate her late dinner, "I saw this tiny little bagworm descending from the ceiling. I wondered how a bagworm could have wound up in a place like that, without any trees or plants."

Today had been her third-to-last day at work.

It was a small office of just five employees, but the bagworm dangled from a spot directly above Kazuko. Everybody ignored it at first, but it kept on coming, until it almost touched Kazuko's shoulder. She took it by its thread and put it on the paper punch she had sitting on her desk. After that it stopped moving, and hung there in the same spot all the rest of the day.

"You should take it home, Miss Imura," the others said, worrying that without any trees or plants around it wouldn't have anything to eat.

Kazuko emptied a box of matches to carry the bagworm home in her pocket. When the train got crowded, she held it in her hand to keep it from getting crushed.

As usual she called from the station so that Akio could meet her at the park (Akio had come for her every night since Ryoji had come down with the measles; when one of the boys got sick, the other got double duty). She found him practicing his heading technique for soccer. Walking side by side, they started home.

"Look, I brought home a bagworm," Kazuko said, opening the matchbox. "The poor thing was crawling around at the office. I'm going to let it go here." She climbed the small embankment at the edge of the park and placed it at the foot of a cherry tree already in full leaf.

Suddenly Akio burst out, "That's bad!"

"What do you mean?"

"That's really bad."

"But if I'd left it at the office it wouldn't have had anything to eat."

Akio wouldn't listen. "I can't believe you'd do such a thing. That's called misguided charity!"

"What do you mean?"

"Don't you know it'll grow up and devour all the trees in the park?"

Kazuko denied it, but Akio wouldn't yield. "It's our ruination! It's our doom! It's the end of the world!" he cried exaggeratedly, and sprinted up the road.

"Wait!" Kazuko called, running after him. . . .

"And the empty matchbox," Kazuko said to finish her story, "I threw in the garbage can out back when I got home."

10

In the yard the wild maple and several varieties of camellias were putting on new spring leaves, and off in one corner the broom tree was bursting with yellow flowers. But the old parakeet that had been with the family for ten years was not doing so well.

What could be wrong?

He'd hardly eaten anything for quite a few days now, and he had obviously lost some weight. And that wasn't all. Every so often he would let out a strange, husky gasp as if suddenly short of breath. Or they would see him waver and almost lose his balance on his perch. Or he would sit there panting with his mouth wide open, as though he just couldn't get enough air.

It had all begun on the day Ryoji finally started back to school after staying home for two weeks with the measles. Having grown used to sleeping in, he now had to get up at the regular time again, and he went off to school grumbling about still being tired. That evening had brought the first episode of the parakeet's strange behavior.

He'd never acted this way before, so it raised quite an alarm, but after a short time he returned to normal.

He had always been a healthy bird, and, especially since they always kept him indoors, everyone had assumed he would go on being healthy. Apparently this was no longer the case.

Two days later, Father returned from his daily walk to find Mother by the bird cages, peering in at the parakeet.

"A while ago he made the same sound he did day before yesterday," she said. "Twice. Then he cried on and on in this really faint voice, so I came over and called 'Bogie, Bogie,' when suddenly he starts tottering back and forth and can't hold on anymore and falls off his perch."

"He actually fell?"

"I thought, my goodness, and started to reach inside, but as soon as I did that, he climbed back up onto the perch."

"He got up by himself?"

"In a big hurry. Up the side."

Three cages stood one beside the other on the enclosed veranda, each occupied by a single bird. First came the Java sparrow, next was a younger parakeet, and last came the ailing, old parakeet. All three were male.

The old parakeet had originally had a mate. The family's first pair of parakeets had had to go back to the pet store because they didn't get along, and the male kept pulling out the female's tail feathers. The new pair, Bogie and his mate, turned out to be real love birds.

Provided with a nesting box, they started producing an endless succession of young. When there got to be too many, the family gave away all but one to friends or to the pet store.

The bird in the middle cage was the lucky one who'd gotten to stay behind with his parents. His name was Frosty. He had hatched on the day the family moved to this new house, in the car on the way, as Kazuko (an eighth grader then) held the cage on her lap. Frosty's older brothers and sisters had all turned out fine, but Frosty, for some reason, had always seemed a bit abnormal, a bit feebleminded. That was why they had decided he should stay with his parents.

Not long after his siblings had gone, his mother died, and ever since then it had been just his father and him in their adjoining cages. Because the family had actually watched him hatch that day in the car, he had somehow remained forever a baby in their minds, but he, too, was already nine years old—not young anymore.

So, side by side in their cages lived the father who had lost his mate and the son who would go through life without ever taking a bride. Everyone hoped they could stay together yet for a long time to come.

11

Sunday evening, most of the family was listening to a record in the darkened study.

"It's just like last year, isn't it?" Mother said. "The four of us here, listening to music, and Akio alone in his room, studying."

"You're right," Kazuko agreed.

"Nothing's changed," Father said.

"I guess it's his destiny never to hear the music."

Even as they spoke, the door gently opened and Akio came in. Slander is quicker than summons, they say, and here was living proof.

Akio stood for a moment in the dark, then quietly lay down on the floor. He had listened to records with them on occasion—though not very often. When he did, he always lay on the floor with his head next to the great antique crock that stood near the door. He brought along something to cover up with, and sometimes he actually fell asleep. He wouldn't even know the music had ended until everyone got up to leave.

"Don't you want a blanket?" Mother said.

Akio rose and went to the door, but then paused. "I can't find the cards," he said weakly.

"The cards?" Mother said. "They're on top of the TV, from last night."

Akio crumpled to the floor as if going limp with relief, but then he got right up and went out. A moment later they heard a squeal that could have been either laughing or crying—it was hard to tell which.

The music ended. Kazuko turned on the light and was flipping the record over when Akio came back with the cards.

"I hunted everywhere," he said. "I looked through all my drawers and under the beds and in the closet and turned everything upside down, but I couldn't find them anywhere. I knew they couldn't have just disappeared, but I was really starting to sweat."

"You forgot them last night," Kazuko said. "You left them on the table. Mom and I decided we'd just put them on the TV."

"You hid them from me?"

"We didn't *hide* them. They were right out in the open. We figured you probably wouldn't even realize they were missing until today, and then you'd push the panic button."

"And little did I know, all this time," said Akio. He looked at the clock on the shelf. "I spent forty-five minutes searching for them."

How could they have known he had been tearing his room apart looking for the picture cards? He was supposed to be hard at study.

Akio dropped down on the couch and looked at the cards in his hands.

"What a relief!" he said, sounding very relieved indeed.

Normally, Akio might have really launched into Kazuko for hiding the cards, but today he seemed happy just to have found them.

"Here goes side two," Kazuko said. The lights went out and the music resumed.

In the darkness Akio spoke again, as if to himself. "I thought they might actually be gone—for good."

12

"He makes us do exercises," Ryoji said, speaking of his homeroom teacher. "Right in the middle of class."

"What kind of exercises?" Kazuko asked.

"We do our shoulders like this." With his arms dangling limply at his side, Ryoji raised and lowered his shoulders.

"He wants to loosen you up, I guess."

Ryoji nodded.

"But it's funny because he gets us going hup, two, hup, two, and then he starts singing."

"Singing what?" Kazuko always wanted to know all the details.

"That's the thing," Ryoji said, almost as if telling a secret. "He sings 'The Coal Miners' Song.'"

"You're kidding!"

"Uh-uh."

Kazuko started to laugh. "Your *teacher* sings it?"

"Uh-huh."

"As he counts?"

When Kazuko was in high school, she had gone to Ryoji's junior high (it had also been her own) for two weeks of practice teaching. Her main assignment was seventh grade English, but she had also been placed in a homeroom—as it happened, the class of the teacher Ryoji had now.

"Show us how he does it," Kazuko said.

"Hup, two, hup, two." Ryoji started moving his shoulders in time with the count, and Kazuko followed suit.

"Hup, two, hup, two, 'The moon, came u . . . u . . . up.'"

"It works," Kazuko said. "It really does."

They continued all the way to the "Hey, hey" at the end, and then stopped.

"Everyone does it together? The exercise, I mean."

"Uh-huh," said Ryoji.

"In time with your teacher's singing?"

"Uh-huh."

"Doesn't anyone laugh?"

"No, no one laughs."

"Why not?"

"We don't have any cutups in our class."

"Oh, that's right, he's the famous taskmaster."

This teacher was also known for the stories he told. He had run away from home when he was young, and had worked as a shoeshine boy as well as a ditch digger. He liked his saké, and he liked to drink it in the old-fashioned kind of taverns, with the rope curtains or red lanterns out front. He wouldn't go anywhere else, he said.

He had taught them "Red River Valley" in English the other day, Ryoji remarked a little later. That reminded Kazuko that she had been asked to prepare a handout of the song when she'd gone for practice teaching.

"Do you still have the handout?" Ryoji asked Kazuko.

"Uh-huh. Do you?"

"I had one, but I lost it."

"Then I'll give you mine."

Kazuko went to her room to fetch the paper with the lyrics to "Red River Valley." At times like this, it helped to have a pack rat in the family.

Ryoji and his sister sang the song together, holding the song sheet between them.

Hup, two, hup, two wouldn't work with this song. You had to sing this song in a way that made it feel like the tall hills and the deep valley and the river flowing through it were all right there before your eyes.

A young man is going on a long journey, and he's just about to leave. His sweetheart is asking him not to be in so much of a hurry to say goodbye—the valley will be so lonely after he is gone.

Mother came in. "I was enjoying your song in the bath," she said. "It's really pretty."

Mother had learned the song from Kazuko before and now joined in. Late at night when everyone ought to have been getting to bed (except for Akio), the three went on singing their song of the American West.

13

Mother and Kazuko set out in the rain for Kazuko's fitting.

Kazuko no longer had to leave for work every morning; she no longer had to be the first one at the office so she could get the key from the night watchman and open up before the others arrived. Instead, she could start taking care of all those things she hadn't had time to do before. She especially needed to start packing for her move to Kibizaka.

Kazuko had wanted to quit work a little sooner, to avoid such a

last minute rush, but they'd asked her to stay until the boat scheduled to leave for South America at the beginning of May had safely
set sail.

Father thought back to the day when Kazuko learned she'd been
accepted for the job. He and Kazuko and Ryoji had visited two
nearby shrines together that evening.

It was hotter then, he remembered. It was around the time of the
Weaver Festival in July.

Kazuko had been asked to return a second time for an X-ray and
a one-on-one interview. Afterward, she came home and told her
parents all about it, and then only a short while later a telegram
arrived offering her the job. The whole family cheered.

Ryoji said he was going back to give thanks at the shrine where
he'd prayed for rain several days before, and Kazuko said in that
case she would go along, too.

In the previous weeks, a long dry spell had been causing serious
water shortages. Ryoji (he was a sixth-grader then) had gone to the
shrine all on his own to pray for rain, and as if in answer to his
prayers the skies had finally given forth—quite heavily, in fact. But
he had not yet had a chance to go back and offer a prayer of thanks.

He had another reason for going as well. The swimming pool at
school would open for the season the next day, but the rains that
had continued for three days showed no signs of letting up. His
prayers had worked too well. Now he had to pray for good weather.

Near the house was a shrine to the tutelary deity of the area. In
the summer the neighbors all gathered there for Bon dances around
a specially built drum tower. But Ryoji had bypassed this shrine in
favor of a smaller shrine deep in the woods.

Father recalled wondering why in the world Ryoji had chosen the
shrine in the woods. They'd had to go through quite an ordeal getting to it. Trees and undergrowth heavy with rain pressed in on both
sides of the path. It was hardly the sort of place you wanted to go
on a rainy day. To make matters worse, the path angled so steeply up
the side of the hill you practically had to crawl—at the same time as
you were trying to hold an umbrella overhead. It had no doubt
been an easy climb the first time Ryoji came because everything was
parched dry, but on a rainy day it was ridiculous.

The three of them stood side by side before the shrine in silent
prayer. On the way home they decided to visit the second shrine,
and turned down a road that went by some rice paddies.

I remember how pretty the hills were, all misty with rain, Father thought as he reflected on the events of three years before.

Kazuko had been so happy that day. At the second shrine, too, she had stood with bowed head for a long time, in earnest prayer. But now her life as a working woman had come to an end.

Mother and Kazuko returned from the fitting with their raincoats drenched. Instead of coming in at the front door, they went around to the yard.

"We brought you some of those daylilies," Kazuko said, opening the sliding glass door to the study.

Not long before, Mother had come back from a trip to the station saying she had discovered some daylilies growing off to one side of the road along the river, almost completely hidden among the other grasses and plants on the river bank. Father had said it'd be nice to have some for the yard, so Mother and Kazuko decided to dig some up on their way back from the dressmaker's near the station.

A tall, sharp cliff rose up just in front of the spot, and when you got right down to where they grew, it felt as though you had entered a deep mountain recess.

From a large bag Mother and Kazuko took out two garden trowels and several plants wrapped in wet newspaper.

"Where shall we put them?"

"Maybe over there," Father said, pointing toward the foot of the wild maple. On this side of the maple, against a bamboo brace, was the climbing bittersweet Ryoji had planted, and next to it grew some spring orchids. On the other side was the shrub, already full with new leaves, from which the bulbul descended on the sparrows.

"Here?"

"Yeah, that looks good."

They were already wet anyway, so they ignored the rain (now reduced to a drizzle) and began digging. Softened by the moisture, the earth turned easily. After planting the three daylilies, they went around to the back door with their muddied hands.

The fitting had gone well, and both women heaved sighs of relief as they came in. The dressmaker ran the little shop all by herself and had sewn a number of things for them before. They knew she understood their tastes, and they knew how much care she took with her work, so they had decided to have her do Kazuko's wedding dress as well.

"It took forty-five minutes," Mother said. Apparently the fitting had included something else besides the wedding dress.

"Were the daylilies hard to dig up?"

"No. We each had a trowel, so we could go at them together."

"On the riverbank, under our bamboo umbrellas."

14

A bamboo pole tied across the posts of the wisteria arbor served as a sunning rod for their bedding. Father was taking in the futon around two o'clock when Akio came home.

"I'm home," he called out in a loud voice.

"Hi, Akio," Father called back from the yard.

"Is that you, Ryoji?" came his voice again. "Is everyone else gone?"

What was he saying?

He poked his face out from the entrance to the hallway and repeated, "I'm home."

"Hi, Akio," said father as he carried the futon from the veranda into the room.

Akio looked surprised and said, "Huh? You're here, too?" As soon as he'd said it, he realized his mistake. "Oh, I thought you were Ryoji. Your voice sounded just like his."

That explained it, thought Father.

"But I should have known. Ryoji's never home this early." Akio went off to his room with a quizzical look on his face, as though still trying to figure out how he could have made such a mistake.

15

"I've cleared some shelf space," Kazuko came to the study to tell Father. She had been in her room, sorting through her things and packing. "Would you like to move some books?"

"I sure would."

"If you'll just get them out, I can do the moving."

"No, that's okay."

Father never had enough space for his books. The overflow from his study had already taken over most of Kazuko's shelves, leaving room for only a few of Kazuko's own books (though she did have a separate, smaller bookcase for her textbooks from school).

At any rate, he was grateful for every bit of new shelf space he could get. He sorted through the books he'd crammed into the shelves on top of other books, as well as the ones sitting out in several stacks around the room, and he took those he didn't need close at hand to Kazuko's room. Mother came to help arrange them on the open shelves.

Yesterday morning, Kazuko had gathered up as much baggage as she could carry in her two hands and taken it to the house in Kibizaka by bus. She copied down the bus schedule—during the day it ran only once an hour—and went again in the afternoon.

"Kibizaka shuttle, now departing," she called out as she left on her second run.

The wedding was only a little over two weeks away. In that time, she would need to make good use of the "Kibizaka shuttle."

Father soon filled up Kazuko's shelves again.

"From now on," he said, "this room will be our library."

"And when someone comes to spend the night," Mother added, "it can be the guest bedroom."

"Then we won't have to shove things around in my study to make room for a bed on the floor anymore."

"It'll be so much more convenient."

"Except if you forget about this cupboard and get up too quickly, you bump your head. We'll have to be sure to warn people."

"That's true," Mother said. "It seems a bit cramped at first, but the little window makes you feel like you're bunking in the cabin of a ship, and it's actually kind of nice."

At this point, Kazuko broke in. "It has fleas, you know."

"Fleas?" Mother said. "So that's it. That's why I always get so itchy when I sleep here."

"That's right. I've been keeping a pet flea. I've had it a long time."

I still belong here, she seemed to want to say. I still eat with you, I still do the dishes, and I still help with the housecleaning. At night I still sleep peacefully in this bed, which has been my bed for more than nine years. Please don't be so hasty with your plans for my room. This seemed to be the real meaning behind her joke about a pet flea.

"My goodness!" Mother said in sudden surprise. "You're not actually planning to take these with you, are you?"

Two worn-out stuffed toys, a tiger and a rabbit, sat on top of the boxes and bags Kazuko had packed for moving. The rabbit's threadbare pants had torn through in one spot, revealing the stuffing inside. As for the tiger, it had managed just barely to keep all its parts together in one piece, but it hardly looked like a tiger anymore.

"Don't take these along," Mother said. "Please don't."

"Why not?"

"Imagine what he'll think."

To put it bluntly, they were little more than rags. Considering the condition they were in, it was amazing they were even still around. In a house full of new things, they would stand out as real eyesores.

"He might start wondering about you," Father said.

"He might. You really should leave them behind."

Father turned to Mother. "When was it that we got these?"

"I think Kazuko was in fifth grade."

"That's right. Fifth grade," Kazuko nodded.

"So it's not as if they're all that old."

"No. But we really played with them a lot."

Father remembered it well. Part of getting ready for bed every night had been figuring out who got to sleep with the stuffed tiger. To keep Akio and Kazuko from always fighting over the tiger (Ryoji had sole claim to the rabbit), Mother had set up a system for taking turns every other night. But even so, someone would forget one night, and the next night they'd wind up fighting over whose turn it was.

In the quiet of the night, Father would listen from the next room as brother and sister squabbled. . . .

"Oh, what's the harm?" Father said. "Let her take them. They're keepsakes from when she was little."

Mother changed her mind, too. "I suppose you're right," she said. "You're right."

"She can give them to her own children."

"Kids can surprise you. Sometimes they really take to these old, raggedy things."

"That's right." Father took the rabbit and chomped on the tip of its ear. "They sink their teeth in, and won't let go."

Mother and Kazuko laughed.

So the tiger and the rabbit would be going along after all—on that afternoon's "Kibizaka shuttle."

16

The nightly games of picture cards were heating up.

Five was just the right number for this game. Add one more player, and it became much harder to guess who had the cards you wanted. One fewer made it too easy, and the game would end too soon.

Having an extra player was still all right, but with only four the game lost all its fun.

"Even if we don't miss a single night from now on, we can only play so many more times," Akio had been the first to note some time ago.

He was assuming their games would end when Kazuko got married, but the others said it wasn't so. Even after that they could still play whenever all five got together.

Besides, Father had thought at the time, the wedding was still a long way off. If they really played as often as Akio had counted, they would probably have had their fill by then no matter how much they enjoyed the game. And considering everything else that had to be done as the special day approached, they might well start missing nights even before the wedding.

But from around the time Kazuko quit work to get her things in order at home, the energy level seemed to go up a notch or two. Wiping the slate clean of all their past scores (Akio had won so much he'd gotten too far ahead of the next player), they had begun an entirely new round, and perhaps that had made the difference.

Akio started doing various stunts during the games, some of them almost acrobatic. Apparently he did them reflexively, without thinking, just from being so caught up in the game.

For example, he fell on his back on the tatami and "applauded" with the bottoms of his bare feet. They made a louder, crisper sound than his hands, which he clapped in front of his face at the same time. That is to say, he "applauded" with all fours. He had been running neck and neck with Kazuko, and she had just made a major error.

"We have a monkey in our midst," she sniffed, but then burst out laughing.

This took place the night Akio had spent forty-five minutes looking for the cards in his room, and it was the very first of his game-time stunts.

Another time he leapt up to clap simultaneously with his hands over his head and his feet in the air. He jumped and clapped, jumped and clapped, over and over, each time clapping his hands so many times and his feet not quite so many. He kept doing it again and again without pausing between leaps. Perhaps all his soccer practices had made him more coordinated than most people when it came to jumping and using his feet. This turned out to be a one-night-only performance, though.

In other stunts, he clapped his feet while standing on his head; or he stiffened his arms against the tatami like a gymnast on a pommel horse and thrust his legs out to the side; or he crouched in the "get set" position like a runner ready to burst from the starting block; or, when somebody else won a card, he stood up and bent slowly over backward until his head touched the tatami.

"Just sit down and play, will you? We can't concentrate," Father would scold in the end.

Akio had recently taken up another new habit as well. While all the others held their cards in the normal way, fanned out in their hands, Akio spread his cards on the floor beneath the table and was always peering down there when his turn came. It seemed like a lot of extra trouble, but that was what he did. Sometimes he studied his cards at length this way—hunched over, with his forehead pressed against the edge of the table.

Three days ago, Father had inadvertently looked under the table and seen that Akio had two cards left. He hadn't intended to peek, but accidentally saw the cards when he shifted in his seat.

Normally, everyone's hand grew smaller near the end of the game, but Akio somehow managed to keep a full hand. Even when he completed more matches than the others, it didn't seem to make his hand grow smaller. But that day, Akio was down to his last two cards.

"No fair! You peeked!" Akio clamored in dismay, but Father had not seen which cards they were.

That night everyone came out about even in the end, with Ryoji winning by just a few points.

Perhaps about a week ago, as the game was winding down, Father made the right guess and got the card he needed, but when he set it down with the two matching cards from his hand, there was a chorus of "Hey!"s followed by laughter.

He had put down the wrong card by mistake—the one he should have held back as his last card. He quickly switched it, but now everyone knew he had "The Lion in Glasses."

Akio's turn came next. Father expected him immediately to ask for "The Lion in Glasses," but Akio asked Mother for an entirely different card instead. Mother didn't have it. Then Ryoji, too, passed over Father's card and asked for a different one from Kazuko. Another wrong guess.

Kazuko followed Ryoji without a moment's pause. "Dad, do you have 'The Lion in Glasses'?" she said.

Father gave her the card and the game ended.

"Have a heart, Kazu," said Akio.

"Huh?" Kazuko said, obviously puzzled by the remark.

"After I stood by samurai's honor and let him go."

"Oh, I get it now."

"Ryoji let him go, too."

"I'm sorry," Kazuko said. "I wondered why neither of you asked for it."

17

The old parakeet began acting strange again. Mornings were always bad for him now; afternoons and evenings were better. According to Kazuko, when he fell off his perch and struggled to get back on his feet, his claws turned completely white.

Did it mean his circulation was failing?

Compared to Frosty in the next cage, his plumage was dull and lusterless, and he had grown noticeably skinnier.

An episode during breakfast one morning passed as usual. But after Father had been in his study awhile he heard Kazuko calling the bird's name. There was obvious alarm in her voice as she called his name over and over.

Father went to see and found Kazuko trying to prop up the fallen bird with her hand. The bird lay on his stomach on the bottom of the cage without moving.

Mother came in. "It's better if you take your hand away," she said. "He doesn't like to be held."

Kazuko gently withdrew her hand.

Bogie's eyes remained open, but he lay with his head flat on the floor.

Was this going to be the end for Bogie? It was certainly beginning to look that way.

On the other hand, Father thought to himself, he might lie like that for a while until his suffering eased and then come back to life. He had looked like he was on the brink before, but had in the end picked himself back up. Perhaps that would happen again.

The three were still watching the prostrate, motionless bird, taking turns calling his name, when all of a sudden he hopped up onto the lower perch. From there he climbed the side of the cage to the upper perch, where he sat quiet and still.

Beyond a certain point was a world of no return. By all appearances, Bogie had just now gone up to that point and started to step beyond. Where, then, had he found such reserves of strength—that he could suddenly bring himself back to this side with all the agility of a vigorous young bird?

How long ago could it have been? Half a month?

When Kazuko went to change the birds' food and water and clean their cages, as she did every morning before going to work, Bogie was missing. As she stood wondering what could have happened, he came crawling out of the nesting box.

Never once had Bogie gone into the nesting box before. That was where his mate, dead now eight years, went to lay and hatch her eggs. He seemed to know that it wasn't for him.

He *had* gone up to the round opening of the box and peered inside before. But when they stopped to think about it, that, too, had been a recent development—something he had started doing just in the last year or so.

"Maybe he thinks Bess is still in there?" Father suggested.

"Maybe," Mother nodded.

Did Bogie's going into the box he'd never gone into before mean he was now actually getting senile? There had been several other changes, too, in recent months. His droppings had always been neatly piled up in one place before, but now he messed the whole cage. He had started scattering the millet seed from his feed bin all over the floor. And he acted more and more like Frosty, who had always seemed a bit feebleminded.

Kazuko and Mother said he had gradually become this way over the last six months.

18

As they prepared dinner, Mother and Kazuko talked about the new record they'd bought that day.

"Let's hurry through the dishes so we'll have time to listen to it tonight," they said.

The whole family minus Akio gathered in the study a little after nine. Living as they did high on a hill, their house grew quite chilly after dark, even in the middle of May. Father put on a padded vest and draped a woolen shawl over his lap, and for good measure picked up a floor cushion to hug against his stomach. Mother also had a shawl for her lap, but Kazuko had nothing. Ryoji came in in his shirt sleeves, and mother suggested he get a blanket or something, but he said he'd be all right. He sat next to Kazuko on the couch.

Part way through the record, Ryoji's head dropped against the back of the couch as if he were dozing off.

"If you're going to fall asleep," Father said, "you'd better get something to cover up with."

His school's field day was coming up, and the preparations for it had tired him out. Belonging to the track team meant he had had to pitch in even more than most students. This morning, too, he'd come running home almost as soon as he'd gone, to get a knife for something or other.

Ryoji went to the next room and came back with three floor cushions in his arms. This time he sat at the end of the couch and lined the cushions up to cover his body. A while later he twisted his body sideways and laid his head against the armrest.

Near the end of the music, Akio came in. Mother and Kazuko and Ryoji were all listening with their eyes closed—or perhaps sleeping. Akio looked at them absently for a few moments, puffing his cheeks in and out.

Not saying a word, he went to the record player, opened the lid and peered inside—probably checking to see how much longer it would be. He then turned back toward the door, but instead of going out lay down at his usual spot beside the large antique crock.

Before long the music came to its lively finale and the record ended. Akio leaped to his feet.

"All right. Let's get started," he said.

In no time at all he was at the table in the next room dealing out the cards. As the others came in and took their seats he declared ambitiously, "Today I'm going to win for sure."

He was really fired up. He had supposedly been studying, but it seemed more likely that he'd been watching the clock and calculating the time when the others would be finished with their record.

And who could blame him? Kazuko had won twice in the new round, and Mother and Father and Ryoji had each won once, but Akio had yet to come out on top.

"That's five straight losses," he had said when the game ended the night before. "But you just wait. Tomorrow I'll score ten thousand."

But that was asking too much. By Akio's own calculations, even if a single player won all the cards (this couldn't actually happen, of course), his total would still be only a little over ten thousand points.

The night of Akio's fifth loss, Father had been out late at a party, and didn't get home until eleven. Mother later told Father that Akio had started getting restless a little before ten.

"I bet he's on the bus now," he had remarked.

When Father rang the doorbell, Akio was in the bath, but less than five minutes later he was at the table with everyone else, dealing out cards. If Father hadn't gotten home until after midnight, they couldn't have played. With so few days remaining, to miss even a single day loomed large. That was how Akio felt.

But in spite of the zeal with which he had emerged from his bath, Akio managed to complete only a single picture, and the others split the rest of the points so that Father came out on top for the first time in quite a while. Such had been the previous day's results.

On this, the sixth day of the new round, Akio managed only three thousand points—far from the ten thousand he was shooting for. But it was good enough to tie for the win with Mother.

"It's not much fun if you have to share the prize," he grumbled.

"Don't be so greedy," the others said.

They had all become much better players, and it was no easy feat to win anymore.

Akio's penchant for hoarding cards didn't change. He had a way of quietly gathering up cards without the others catching on, and when everyone else was down to two or three cards he would still have five or six.

Near the end of the game someone would go around asking how many cards each of the others had left.

"Let's say you can't do that," Akio would protest.

But he was always alone.

"No, no," the others would say, and the majority would prevail.

19

When Father awoke, the house was quiet. Then he heard a sniffling sound from the kitchen. He couldn't tell who it was—it could be either Mother or Kazuko. Then came a low voice.

"The poor thing."

This, he could tell, was Mother. Kazuko was apparently there, too, but she didn't say anything, and he couldn't hear her crying either. But Father guessed that either Mother or Kazuko had woken up that morning and found the old parakeet dead at the bottom of his cage.

So Bogie had died, Father pondered inwardly. After all those times of defying death with spurts of renewed vigor, this time his strength had run out. The bird that had been part of their family for ten years had died in the month Kazuko would be married.

Father had intended to speak to Kazuko so that she'd be prepared when it happened. He had searched for the right words:

"Over and over he falls off his perch like that and lies there as if he's stopped breathing. The day may come when he won't be able to pick himself back up again."

"I suppose so."

"He's lived a long life and he's old, so that's what could happen in the end. You shouldn't cry."

"Okay."

"In human terms, he'd be almost a hundred. You can't ask for much more than that."

This was what he had wanted to say to Kazuko, but now it was too late.

"I hope she doesn't let it get her down," he thought. "I hope she doesn't connect it up with her wedding and think of it as a bad omen."

Was the old parakeet still lying on the bottom of his cage? Or had they already wrapped him in a shroud of some kind. Who had found him first—Mother or Kazuko? Father had been asleep, so he had not heard the first shocked cry.

He had thought both Mother and Kazuko were in the kitchen, but now just one of them came to the cages on the veranda. She seemed to be changing the other birds' food. What was going on?

If that was Mother, then had Kazuko perhaps taken the old parakeet outside to bury it, leaving no one in the kitchen anymore?

Akio came down the hall. Father could hear the usual sounds of breakfast getting started.

"How far did you run?" Mother asked.

"I just did sprints today."

"Oh."

The night before, Akio had announced he would get up at six and go jogging one day a week from now on. To stay in shape, he already went to the park every evening and kicked his ball around, and he had a long routine of exercises he did in his room. But apparently he didn't think that was enough.

Why wasn't Mother telling him about the bird? Father wondered. Had she already told him earlier?

Ryoji came in next.

"Morning, Mom."

"Good morning."

Mother still didn't say anything about the bird. What could be the matter? Was she deliberately holding back? Bogie had been with them a long time. Did she think it would be too much of a shock to greet them with such sad news the first thing after they got up? Perhaps that was it.

"Is there any more tea?" Akio said.

"Sure."

Ryoji began eating, too.

Akio was finished. "Thanks, Mom," he said.

From where Father lay in bed, it sounded no different from any other morning.

He heard Kazuko's door open, and she came down the hall.

"Good morning."

"Good morning."

"Morning."

They all exchanged morning greetings. Wait a minute. Kazuko

just now got up. In that case, maybe . . . Father had a sudden urge to slide open the door to the next room, so he could see the cages.

"No. Never mind," he decided.

Soon, Akio said goodbye and left. Ryoji followed close behind. Father dozed off again, and the next time he awoke the clock said 8:00.

He washed the sleep from his eyes and went to check the cages. He found Bogie sitting on his usual perch.

20

The junior high field day scheduled for Sunday had to be postponed until Tuesday because of rain. Sunday then became the make-up day for Tuesday's classes. Ryoji got up early by himself and went to school.

The rain gradually let up in the afternoon. In the yard, the azaleas were in bloom, and soft new leaves had appeared on the tips of the camellia branches. The camellias had grown a little taller again this year. The beautyberry bush Ryoji had dug from the side of a nearby cliff and planted next to the camellias was also sending out new branches from its center.

Kazuko knocked lightly on the door to the study and came in.

"Do you have any seven-yen stamps?" she asked.

"Sure."

Mother had apparently heard her, too, in the other room. "Did you say seven-yen stamps?" she called. "I've got lots here."

Father had lots, too. He had won them in the post office's New Year's card lottery.

"I've got plenty here," Father called back.

He took the lid off the box he kept his stamps in. It practically overflowed with orange stamps bearing the picture of a stuffed dog. There were even quite a few stamps left over from last year's lottery, with the picture of a rooster.

"Just look at this," Father said, "The place is teeming with seven-yen stamps."

The box was so full of seven-yen stamps, he often had trouble finding any others.

He took out a block of four stamps, and Kazuko tore off one.

"Thank you," she said, and went out.

Earlier that day when Father had gone to ask Mother to run an errand for him, she and Kazuko were in the other room with all the sliding doors pulled shut.

"Can I come in?" he said.

"Go ahead, it's okay."

They were fitting a dress for mother. Against the wall was a mirror they'd borrowed from Akio and Ryoji's closet, and Mother stood examining herself in it, her back straight as a rod. Kazuko's hands were busy at the shoulders, tugging and smoothing, over and over.

"You're making a dress for your mother?" Father said to Kazuko.

"Uh-huh."

"And this is the first fitting?"

"That's right."

He recalled Mother mentioning that Kazuko wanted to make her a dress, as a thank-you. Had Kazuko picked out the fabric, too? he wondered.

After Kazuko left his study with the stamp, Father noticed two one-yen coins stacked neatly atop a five-yen coin at the edge of his desk.

He laughed. "She paid me," he said aloud, to no one but himself.

In the other room, he heard Mother set her iron down on the ironing board. The sky had turned brighter, and the rain seemed just about over.

PART THREE

still together

THE ROOSTER

"*i* went to buy some eggs from our landlady, but all I found was the rooster strutting around the front yard. No one else was home."

So began Kazuko's story. '

She had come in from Kibizaka bringing a gift of *wakame* for her parents in an old candy bag. Someone had given her more than she could use. She left the baby strapped to her back, saying she wanted to return by the next bus and could only stay a minute.

But even that was long enough for the older boy, four months short of his second birthday, to gobble down his usual quota of snacks and drinks: some cookies he had brought along as well as some his grandma gave him; some black tea; a piece of bread and butter; a rice cracker broken in two and dipped in green tea; a solution made of powdered kelp dissolved in hot water, dubbed "Masao's tonic" (it baffled them all how a child of less than two could develop a taste for such a drink, but he had demanded a taste once when his grandpa was having a cup, and kept coming back for another spoonful until it was all gone—as if it had been his favorite drink since before he was born); an apple; and, finally, some Calpis in a baby bottle. By then, it seemed, he had had enough. He started shaking the bottle upside down and got a quick rap on the head from his mother for trickling several drops on the sofa.

His hands had been red and stiff from the cold when they first arrived (though the spring equinox was only a few days away, the wind still had a sharp bite to it), but they quickly warmed and he was soon grabbing at everything in sight.

"What time of day was it?"

"A little after noon, when Takeo here was taking a nap," Kazuko said, turning her head toward the baby who had been quietly surveying the room from his perch on his mother's back. "Koki had come over to play with Masao, so the three of us went together."

Kazuko and her family lived in the middle house of three rental units that stood together in a row. Koki was the four-year-old boy of their neighbors to the right. His father worked at home, putting together parts for electrical appliances with the help of a young man who commuted there from somewhere else.

It must not have been Kazuko's day—going to buy eggs but finding the landlady out, and only the rooster roving the front yard. The landlady was the one who gathered the eggs from the chicken coop, so without her, Kazuko could not get what she had come for. And it certainly didn't do any good to find in the landlady's place a rooster, who couldn't lay eggs if he tried.

Kazuko had told her parents about this rooster before.

"Guess what," she had said one day. "There's a rooster at the Osawas' now."

As the story went, some friends of the Osawas' had bought a baby chick to raise as a pet. But what started out as an endearing little "cheep-cheep" soon became an unrestrained crow, and since they lived in a crowded area where every house was built practically on top of the next, they were worried that the neighbors would start complaining about the noise if they kept their pet any longer. So they brought him to the Osawas'.

The Osawas already had a whole coop full of chickens, but they were all hens. They let the new rooster run loose in the yard all day.

"He's really a fine looking bird," Kazuko said. "All white, with a big, thick tail and a wobbly red comb on his head."

Masao had just learned to walk, and was bent on having a closer look for himself. No amount of warning could keep him away. But as soon as he got very near, the rooster would start toward him, and he would take to his heels.

"Ay, ay, ay!" he cried as he fled.

Kazuko demonstrated how he ran with his stomach leading the

way. In his excitement, it seemed, his legs couldn't quite keep up with the rest of him.

One day toward the end of November, Kazuko went with Masao to buy some eggs and found several dozen peck-holes in the freshly papered shoji doors facing onto the veranda. They stretched from one end to the other in a neat row, at exactly the same height along the bottom grid of each panel.

"I tell you, he's a real good-for-nothing," the landlady said. "I think I'll get rid of him the next time the butcher comes."

Apparently though, the rooster had been spared that fate. He had been allowed to stay on.

"Look! The rooster!" Kazuko said to the boys. "Cock-a-doodle-doo." She squatted down and put out her hand as she called to him. He stopped moving and stared back at her.

"Cock-a-doodle-doo. Cock-a-doodle-doo."

Suddenly the rooster ruffled the feathers on his chest and charged straight at her.

"Where were the boys?" Kazuko's father wanted to know.

"Koki was off to the side, but Masao was right behind me," Kazuko said. "And you should have heard him scream. I've never heard him scream like that before."

"What happened then?" her mother asked.

"I got a couple of nasty little pecks on my knee—I didn't even have time to blink. Thank goodness I was wearing slacks."

"He's gone after Masao before, hasn't he?" her father asked.

"Yes, but that's always been more like he was tagging along behind. This time he really attacked."

"What got into him I wonder?"

"Who knows? I shooed him a couple of times, but then I decided we'd better leave. I didn't want to get him stirred up again, and the landlady wasn't home at any rate, so . . . we went to play at the shrine across the way."

Several branches of the Osawa family lived in the area, and together they had established an Inari shrine just across the road, on top of a small hill. In the grounds was a small play area for children, with swings and a sandbox.

"While we were up at the shrine, a young salesman came along and went in the gate next door."

"Which next door?"

"Koki's house. He came back out almost right away—probably

Koki's mother had turned him down—and went in our gate. Lucky me, I thought, for being out. So then, since there was no one at our place, he moved on to our other neighbor's. But he must have gotten refused there, too, because he came right out again and went into the Osawas'."

"Do salesmen come around often?" her mother asked.

"Yeah, quite a bit. You'd hardly expect it in such an out-of-the-way place, but we get quite a few. Anyway, when he gets into the Osawas' yard, he suddenly starts running around all over the place, from one end of the yard to the other."

Kazuko moved her hand back and forth in front of her face.

"Except, all I could see was his head, so I couldn't really tell what was going on until later. Anyway, after that, even his head disappears for a while—two or three minutes, maybe—and then the next thing I know he comes racing full tilt out of the gate with the rooster hot on his tail."

The salesman cut diagonally across the road in the direction of the shrine. The rooster followed him right out into the middle of the roadway, and he didn't quit the chase until he saw that his quarry had reached the other side.

Perhaps the salesman thought he would be safer at a higher elevation—he climbed the stone steps leading up to the shrine and came to where Kazuko had been watching.

"Wow! What a scare!" he said when he saw Kazuko. "I've had my share of dogs, but I've never had a rooster come after me before."

He was panting for breath.

"Just now, at that farm there," he explained. "No one answers the door, but there's this rooster in the yard, and, can you believe it, he goes and attacks me! Starts pecking at my leg!"

He stooped to rub the place the rooster had pecked on his shin.

"Damn, it hurts. It still hurts!"

Kazuko tried not to laugh. "That *would* be a scare," she said.

"Right out of the blue, for no reason at all!" the man exclaimed. "I gave him a piece of my shoe across his neck—the dumb bird. Never should have done it, though. He just puffed out his feathers and started in all over, coming after me and coming after me no matter which way I ran."

The beleaguered salesman had finally found refuge at another tenant's house, which had a small yard connected to the landlord's. The rooster did not pursue him there. But when he came back, the rooster quickly resumed his offensive. By this time he was even more riled up than before and soon chased the salesman right out the gate.

"I figured I'd better not get too rough with him 'cause I was on private property. But if it had been anywhere else, I'd have given him a good one right in the belly." He kicked the air with his tormented leg. "With chickens, that's all it takes. One good whop in the belly and they're finished."

How did he know that? Kazuko's father wondered.

After a while the man took a brochure from his briefcase and started making a pitch about the educational books he was selling. You were supposed to be able to start your child on the first book at only three months; then you would pay so much per month as the rest of the books in the series came, and seven months later you would have the complete set.

He opened his briefcase again and got out an oversized, foreign-looking book with an English title on the cover. Kazuko could tell only that it said, "Something-or-other Book."

"You really can't wait until they're two or three. By then it's too late," he pressed.

"I see," Kazuko said. "But we don't have any money, so we can't afford it."

"Oh."

He looked over toward Koki and Masao playing in the sandbox. They were loading sand into a plastic dump truck some other child had left behind.

"Well, if you don't have the money, I guess you can't," he shrugged.

He put the brochure and book back into his briefcase and started down the stone steps.

THE MOUSE

"When I let the water out of the bath, it takes a little while before it comes out the drain pipe in the gutter by the back gate."

Having finished changing the sheets, his wife had come to the study to tell him about a desperate sewer rat she'd seen a couple of weeks ago.

The dreary rainy season had finally ended, but a string of sweltering days had immediately brought them another installment of suffering. It was still before noon, and the thermometer on his desk already approached ninety.

Over by the shrubs in the corner of the yard, the summer's first goldbanded lilies had opened their buds this morning.

"If I pull the plug and run to the shed for the broom, and hurry past the well out to the street and get set at the end of the pipe, it's just about then that the water starts coming."

At first he imagined the water gushing out all at once, but she told him it didn't. It began with a small trickle, like an advance team scouting the way, and then a moment later the main force arrived in full strength.

With the help of the bath water, she swept the gutter clean. It was one of her regular routines.

"That day, as I was watching the end of the pipe, this rat comes scurrying out even before the water."

The bath water had followed almost immediately, in hot pursuit.

The rat had only to get up out of the U-shaped gutter to escape to safety, and the gutter was shallow enough that it should have been a single easy leap. Instead, he went charging off down the gutter as fast as he could go. Perhaps he was in too much of a panic to think of anything else.

The water picked up speed from the slope of the street and quickly overtook the rat. The rat splashed on as best he could, with his tail held high.

"As he ran, he looked over his shoulder, but the water just kept on coming, so he kept on running—even though he was already surrounded by water. And then after going a little further he looked back again. So he looked back twice."

"I wonder what he was thinking?"

"Yes, I wonder. He kept on running until he came to the drainage grate, which made him hesitate a moment, but he managed to leap across to the other side without falling in, luckily. Then he went scrambling off toward the Satake's below."

A veritable sewer rat, indeed—since he'd come out of the drain pipe. But what could he have been up to in that pipe? Not to cavil, but shouldn't he have been perfectly well aware that the place was a passage for drain water?

You can't expect to find a nice, cool, quiet, comfortable place where no disturbance will come sweeping by. If that's what the rat thought he'd found, he was being much too naive.

And just because a flood of bath water came rushing after him, why should he have gotten himself worked up into such a blithering panic? The water might have been from the bath, but it had already sat over night, so it couldn't have been all that hot anymore. If it had been boiling water chasing him down the drain, he'd have had good reason for alarm, but that wasn't the case.

"A little before that, there was something else," his wife said as if to change the subject. "In the kitchen, in the drawer where I keep my dishcloths, I also keep the dried kelp I use for soup stock, wrapped in rice paper. Or sometimes tissue paper. I got tired of having to cut pieces off every time I needed some, so now I cut it up all at once, and wrap it in bunches of seven or eight squares so I can easily get out however much I need."

The cabinet under the stainless steel drainboard in the kitchen had two drawers.

"I keep my kitchen shears in the same drawer. I use them to cut up the kelp and *wakame,* or to open bags of sesame, or to cut the straw they tie bunches of popbeans with, and other things like that. Also, I keep the brush I use for basting when I make teriyaki."

"What sort of a brush is it?"

"It's actually a watercolor brush, but I trimmed the tip to make it flat. I use it to brush egg yolk on cakes, too."

She had started out talking about a rat, so all this detail about the things she kept in the kitchen drawer made him tighten with anticipation. He was all ears.

"That's everything in the drawer," his wife said. "Dishcloths and scissors and a brush and kelp wrapped in rice paper. I always open this drawer every morning because I need the scissors to cut *wakame* for the *miso* soup. Then one morning I found the rice paper from the kelp torn up in little bits and scattered all around the drawer.

"What about the kelp?"

"One edge had been bitten off, just a tiny bit."

At the time, she had thought only of cockroaches. She'd forgotten all about mice and rats because she hadn't seen any in the last year or two. Or at least they hadn't caused any damage. Her recent concern had been with cockroaches.

Back before Akio got accepted to the university, when he was studying for his second try at the entrance exams (that would make it three years ago), he often came across cockroaches when he got hungry late at night and went to the kitchen for a snack.

To open a can of fruit cocktail, he needed to get the can opener; to peel an apple or cut an orange, he needed the paring knife. These utensils shared a drawer next to the dishcloth drawer with such things as the butcher knife, the bottle opener, and the grater.

Whatever Akio needed, it was usually in that drawer, and when he went to get it he often found two or three young cockroaches, still relatively light-colored, crawling around among the utensils.

"It's dirty, Mom," he said.

His mother hadn't come across them herself, so she never showed much concern.

"Well, kill them when you see them," she said lightly.

The following year, though, she found about thirty small cockroaches drowned in a can of honey in the cupboard. They had apparently chewed their way through the plastic bag she'd used to cover the can.

It seemed a waste, but what could she do? She had to throw out what remained of the honey—about a quarter of the can. She couldn't go on ignoring the problem after that, and started saying she had to do something about it.

Finally, last year before the rainy season, she took everything out of the cupboards and sprayed them top to bottom with a strong cockroach killer.

The man at the drugstore had told her that all the cockroaches had to do was walk over a spot where this solution had been sprayed, and their legs would start rotting away right under them. Whether it had really worked that way, no one could say, but it did get rid of the cockroaches.

One thing and another delayed her plans to repeat the treatment again this year, and the rainy season was already under way when she finally got around to it. Still, even if it was later than she'd intended, she felt safe once the important task was done.

Then, two or three days before she found the paper and the kelp chewed up in the dishcloth drawer, Akio had opened the knife drawer late at night and found a large cockroach inside.

"I found a cockroach again. A big one," he later told his mother. "Of course, I killed it, but . . ."

Such discouraging news, just when she had been so sure she'd seen the last of them.

All this explained why discovering the tiny bites in the kelp had made her think of cockroaches, and why mice never occurred to her.

That day she wrapped the kelp in foil instead of rice paper, then she cut up plastic bags into squares and wrapped these over the little foil packets, fastening them with rubber bands. She put them back in the drawer, confident that they would be safe.

The next day when she opened the drawer, not only had the plastic been chewed open but the foil as well, and once again several tiny bites had been taken out of the kelp inside.

It was then that she began to suspect a mouse.

"I'm sure you remember," she said at this point in her story, "how I showed you the damage and asked if you thought it might be a mouse. You said a cockroach could never chew through so much, so it probably *was* a mouse."

He did remember. The bite marks were such that they could well be mistaken for the work of cockroaches. They were all so tiny. But even if cockroaches could somehow have managed the plastic, he couldn't imagine them being able to cut through the foil no matter how strong their jaws might be.

They agreed the culprit must be a mouse.

"There was one other thing, actually," his wife said, "that made me think it was cockroaches. The dishcloths are folded at the back of the drawer, and I always have to stack them in really tight to make them fit. I even have trouble getting the drawer open sometimes. The kelp wrapped in paper and the kitchen shears and the brush are all in the front of the drawer. When I thought of how a mouse would have had to come in over this mountain of dishcloths, I just didn't think it was possible."

Now she had said too much. Now, whether he liked it or not, he had to contend with the image of a soft little mouse squeezing its way between the layers of dishcloths on its belly and poking its head out the other side. He made a sour face.

"Oh, I forgot," his wife hurried to add. "A bag of sugar also had some bite marks. Just a few. It must be a baby mouse."

They decided to put some mouse pellets in the drawer. His wife went and found a box of faded red pellets left over from before. The picture on the box showed a mouse with a halo and wings flying through the air.

"It's supposed to mean he's dead. He's turned into an angel," she said.

"I get it."

"It says inside that they're good for any kind of rat or mouse."

She placed five pellets in the drawer around the kelp, and when she looked the next morning they were gone. Hooray! she thought.

But it was too soon to be cheering. When she pulled out the dishcloths to check, she found the five pellets at the back of the drawer, all still intact. Her doubts returned. Perhaps they were wrong that it was a mouse, and it was cockroaches after all.

Or perhaps these faded red pellets had simply gotten too old and lost their strength. Looking at the picture of the dead mouse's radiant spirit flying off into the sky, she decided she would buy a fresh box of pellets.

ON THE ROOF

*t*he elevator light hadn't moved from Reserved for quite some time.

What did it mean, the patient wondered. That the elevator was out of service for everyone else?

A sign saying For Patients Only had been posted to one side of the doors.

When the doctor had told her to go up to the roof to get some sunshine, she had asked:

"Are there some stairs?"

What she was really asking was how to get to the roof, but she had chosen a strange way to do it. No matter how small and modest a hospital it was, a building of four stories could hardly get by without stairs.

Perhaps she'd been thrown by the unexpectedness of the doctor's suggestion.

The door to the nurse's station diagonally across the hall from the elevator stood ajar. A nurse and another woman in white stood just inside, chatting casually.

She decided to ask. "Excuse me, but the elevator won't seem to come."

The woman in white, apparently from the pharmacy, came through the door.

"I'm supposed to go up to the roof to get some sun," the patient explained.

"Oh, it's on Reserved, I see," the woman said.

They stood side by side watching the elevator light for several more moments. Finally it began to move.

"There. There it comes."

"Thank you."

The woman in white went back to the nurse's station.

The patient had only needed to wait a little longer, but since this was her first time she hadn't known what to expect. The elderly nurse from the surgery clinic who had brought her to the elevator in the first place had shown no concern about the red light.

"Oh, it's on Reserved," she'd said, as though it was entirely normal. "It'll be right here." She had turned immediately to go back to her office.

But it had remained stuck on the fourth floor with the Reserved light on for so long, the patient had begun to wonder. And besides, she was anxious to do as the doctor had told her—to go up to the roof and get five minutes of sunshine.

When the doors opened a young nurse wheeled out an elderly man on a stretcher.

"May I use this now?" the patient asked. "I need to go up to the roof."

"Just push R."

Entering the elevator, she saw that instead of the usual square shape, it was long and narrow from front to back. It did not give her a pleasant feeling to be alone in such a space. She pressed the R button.

The doors opened onto a small, dim hallway that had the feel of a storeroom. Had she not reached the roof after all?

Over the glass door straight ahead was a plaque saying Hospital Director. Next to the director's office seemed to be an equipment room of some kind, and across the hall from that was a row of six lockers, each with a doctor's name on it.

So this must be where the doctors come to change, she thought. Here, in front of these lockers.

A door at the end of the hall said Exit. Since there seemed to be no other way out, she tried the steel door and emerged onto the roof.

The sun was shining brightly, and there was a brisk breeze.

This had to be the place the doctor meant. There were some poles for hanging out laundry. There was a water tank. There was a high-voltage room. And she couldn't imagine what purpose they served, but a row of low, concrete-pillar stumps stuck up out of the roof.

It was not a large roof to begin with, and the structure she had just come through filled one entire end—a considerable area, really. All these other things cluttering up the rest of the roof inevitably made it feel rather crowded.

Without taking off her coat, she sat down on one of the concrete stumps.

On the laundry poles hung some sheets and underwear, a pair of socks, and a well-worn pair of men's pajamas with a flower pattern.

In the distance, she could see the bamboo grove on the hill behind the station. She could see the new elementary school building.

Next to the high-voltage room the top of some steel stairs was visible. Soon she heard someone coming up the stairs.

She had been sitting with her gauze bandage off and her bare legs stretched out in front of her. So long as she was alone on the roof this was fine, but not if others were going to come.

An elderly lady carrying a futon appeared at the top of the stairs. She was quite tall and wore a sweater and slacks.

After throwing her thin futon over one of the laundry poles, the lady came toward the patient. The patient couldn't very well cover her legs now, so she remained as she was.

"What have we here?" the lady asked.

"I burned myself, with water from a tea pot."

"Oh, my goodness. That must have been terrible. How many days has it been?"

"Today's the ninth day."

The older lady looked surprised. "For only nine days, it's healed very well," she said.

"The doctor told me to give it some sun. Today, for the first time."

"I see. Sunshine must be good for healing. I often see patients sunning themselves up here with their casts off."

Apparently there were casts that could be taken on and off.

"People who come in with injuries are lucky," the older woman said. "Every day is like medicine."

"I'm sorry. Are you here looking after someone?"

"Yes, Grandpa had a stroke, and he's still in a coma."

The tall lady remained standing diagonally in front of the patient sunning her leg.

"He won't get better, but there's no telling how long he might go on the way he is now."

"Is he completely unconscious?"

"Sometimes it seems like he must have some sense of what's going on around him, but . . ."

"Is he able to take meals?"

"He's on a liquid diet. With tubes, you know. It's hardly the sort of thing I could ask anyone else to do. And besides, I'm the only one who knows what Grandpa wants. I tried having my son take my place, and his wife, too, but it just didn't work."

"It must be a real hardship for you."

The patient had meant the hardship of nursing Grandpa single-handedly, but the lady seemed to think she was talking about expenses.

"But you know, we have his pension, and that takes care of the hospital costs, so I can go on this way by myself without having to depend on my son."

"And how old is Grandpa?"

"Sixty-eight. Actually, just the other day he turned sixty-nine without knowing it."

The corners of the lady's eyes moistened a tiny bit.

"Has it been long?"

"Two and a half months, now."

"Oh dear."

"But that's still on the short side. The man in the next bed has been here five months. There're a lot of people like that here."

"Did he have high blood pressure?"

"Not at all. He'd never even had it measured. Never had to go to a doctor before."

"A model of health?"

The lady nodded. "Yes. He was always so full of energy, and never knew a day of sickness. Even after he retired, he started serving on several different boards that kept him dashing from one place to another. 'I'm so lucky,' he used to say. 'Until now, I got paid for what I did, but I didn't have free time. Now I don't get paid any more, but I can help people with things that need to be done. I'm really so lucky. Now, if I had just a little more money, there'd be nothing left to desire,' he'd say, and I'd say, 'We don't need any more money, Grandpa, we're doing quite well enough as we are.'"

The steel door opened and a student wearing a black turtleneck came out. A gauze bandage covered his wrist. Walking past the two women, he went to the concrete pillar farthest away and sat down with his back toward them. Another "sunbather" had joined them.

"He was always in perfect health, so he'd go to visit his friends who weren't. Friends from when he was younger, you know. Everyone else seemed to have problems of one kind or another. They were at that age, after all. Grandpa felt sorry for them and went to visit them to try to cheer them up."

"I see."

"I suppose with people who don't drink, everything gets all pent up in here," the lady said pressing her hand to her breast. "They've got nothing at all wrong with them, and yet suddenly one morning they're found dead."

"Did your husband drink?"

"That's just it—he couldn't drink at all. His older brother was a different story. He really liked his drink. He used to say how grateful he was to his parents for giving him a body that let him really enjoy saké. He drank all day and still he was the picture of health. He'd tell Grandpa he should have a little, too."

"But Grandpa wouldn't?"

"That's right. It's kind of strange, isn't it? They're brothers in the same family, but they're so different. His next brother was the same as the other. He really liked his saké, too."

So Grandpa had two older brothers, it seemed. Would this one be the oldest?

"*He'd* drink all day long, too. Once he knocked his cup over, and he wanted to say 'Wipe up the spill,' but I guess he was already too far gone. He couldn't get the words out, so he motioned with his hand to wipe it up, like this."

The lady gently moved her hand in front of her.

"So someone wiped it up, and he smiled happily and lay down, and that was the end. What a blessed way to go!"

The patient had long since exceeded the five minutes ordered by the doctor. She needed to go back to her room.

"But there's one thing that still seems so uncanny," the lady continued. "Only the day before, he was having a few in the morning, and his grandson came up to him and said, 'It's bad for your health to drink so much, Grandpa.' Grandpa said, 'Okay, then, I'll tell you what. I'll stop drinking tomorrow. I'll just quit.' Everyone laughed and said, 'Grandpa quit drinking? Fat chance.' But then, exactly as he said, the very next day he got so he couldn't drink anymore."

The patient rewrapped her bandage and stood up.

"It's nice that you have Grandpa."

She had abruptly changed the subject from the grandpa the lady had been talking about, who had died in his cups, to the grandpa who continued his long slumber but still remained with her, just the two of them, here in this small hospital.

The older lady smiled cheerfully. "Take good care of your leg," she said.

"Thank you."

The lady went off toward the steel stairs.

As the patient opened the door to go inside, she glanced over toward the student sitting on the far concrete stump. Hunched over a paperback, he had his injured hand stretched out in the sunshine.